A teenage girl goes mis
in Pennsylvania, a North Korean missile with a nuclear
warhead plunges into the Pacific Ocean, and a team of
professional remote viewers is charged with finding them.
That's just the premise. Stephan Schwartz, for decades a
leading scientist doing consciousness research has turned
himself into an award-winning novelist, and once again
delivers the kind of taut well-crafted drama that might first
appear to be science fiction, but is today the stuff of real life.
Sidney D. Kirkpatrick,
Best-selling author of: *Edgar Cayce, An American Prophet*

The Amish Girl is the second in a series of thrillers grounded in
research into remote viewing. Any reader who likes
psychological thrillers with a paranormal twist will enjoy this
one. Since I couldn't put it down, I'd say it's truly a page-
turner.
Rob Swigart
Author of: *The Lisa Emmer Novel Series*

The Amish Girl is a captivating tale providing readers with
an understanding of nonlocal consciousness, why it is
important, and how it can, and has, been used by Schwartz
and others to solve real-world problems.
Colonel John B. Alexander, USA (Ret.) Ph.D.
Author of: *Reality Denied*

In this wonderful and fascinating book Stephan Schwartz
presents a thrilling story about events that could
only be resolved by scientific remote viewing. It is an
intriguing tale that I could not stop reading it. Highly
recommended.
Pim van Lommel, MD
Author of: *Consciousness beyond Life*

Professor Michael Gillespie and his diverse team of remote viewers track the abductor and murderer of a 14-year-old Amish innocent, while seeking to locate and recover a North Korean multi-nuke warhead. It is a wild ride showing Schwartz' approach to making remote viewing work.
Damien Broderick, PhD
Author of: *Consciousness and Science Fiction*

The Amish Girl

A Novel of Death and Consciousness

Volume II
The Michael Gillespie Mysteries

STEPHAN A. SCHWARTZ

Greenwood Press
Langley, Washington

Other Books by Stephan A. Schwartz

Non-fiction
The Secret Vaults of Time
The Alexandria Project
Mind Rover
Opening to the Infinite
The 8 Laws of Change

Fiction
Awakening
The Vision

In memory of all those
who helped me along the way

CHAPTER ONE

Noah Ebersole was bitter and angry. It had been made clear to him that morning in the first week of April at a meeting of his Amish community that he would not be fully accepted back into the Amish life he had grown up in, abandoned, and now wished to rejoin.

At seventeen, a year into his Rumspringa time, in contrast to most of his friends who stayed with their families and within the community, Noah had chosen to leave. He had a fascination with seeing what the English world was like, as the Amish called those who were not members of their sect. It was not unheard of. Rumspringa, literally "running around," was the period in adolescence where Amish teenagers were given the freedom to do whatever they wanted. Being Amish was a conscious spiritual commitment. Each man, each woman, committed to a theology and life style of simplicity in many ways unchanged from the late seventeenth century when Jakob Ammann and his followers withdrew from the larger Protestant world. It was from his name that the word Amish derived.

You did Rumspringa, and if you found a girl, courted her, and she returned the affection, you ended Rumspringa, stopped using unsanctioned technologies like cellphones and tablets, returned to houses without electricity, and went back to horse and buggy transportation. You accepted the Ordnung, the oral traditions, the cultural rules that ran Amish daily life. You married, and at that point were formally accepted as adult members.

As Noah trimmed the hedge that ran down one side of the old fashioned one-room school, his mind was flooded with images of the meeting. In Old Order Amish congregations like Noah's, leaders were chosen by lot: a deacon, a preacher, and a bishop from the men of the community. His father was the deacon.

He could see them all sitting in the simple room with its wooden wainscoting, dark wooden floor, and large pane curtainless windows. The only light had been the morning sun streaming in. He understood, although it was never said outright, that the reason his situation was getting special consideration was the affection the congregation had for his parents. Normally a community vote would have ended with his ostracism by shunning.

Instead, he had been told, he could continue working as a janitor at the school; the humiliation the offer represented and the fact that he had no other immediate option and had to take it, grated on him still. It was the community's way of offering the eldest son of one of its most respected families a modest income and a place to live while keeping him at arm's length. The community saw what they were doing as a mercy, but Noah had left the meeting bitter and resentful; he was not going to be accepted.

As he replayed the meeting over and over in his mind, he realized the tipping point that had decided his fate was his enlistment into the military and that, as a soldier, he had killed people. It had all come out when his friend, Leroy, whom he had known all his life, was brought into the room. The Amish took no oaths, but when asked to testify were expected to speak only the truth they knew. At the end of the meeting one of the elders had asked Leroy, "Did Noah tell you anything about his military service?"

Leroy was the only person to whom Noah had said anything about Afghanistan. One afternoon, a few weeks after he had returned when it was just the two of them working in the barn, he had confessed what he had done.

It had started when Leroy asked him, "What did you do after you left? You were gone for three years."

Noah felt he owed his best friend the truth, so he told him.

"I went to Philadelphia. You know I'm good with mechanical things. But I didn't have a high school degree or even a GED. I was turned down over and over again until I got a job in a motorcycle repair shop."

As they moved bales of hay Noah explained how he had come to know a club of men with motorcycles.

"They called themselves the Highway Men. They were mostly vets, most older than me, and they were the first people to accept me," Noah said, setting his hay hooks in a bale. "But they made it clear if I wanted to ride with them as a full member I needed to serve. After I had repaired some of their bikes they invited me to ride with them down to Shepherdstown, West Virginia. The owner loaned me a bike I had rebuilt that had been abandoned for nonpayment," Noah said, wiping sweat from his face. "I was lonely, Leroy. The English world is lonely, and I was excited to go. I missed being part of a group, a community, so when we got back I went down to the Army recruiter and signed up."

"But you didn't tell anyone?" Leroy asked, in a hurt tone.

"I couldn't tell my family… I mean the army… we don't serve in the military, you know that. You know what my father would have said… so I just went. The Army sent me to Ft. Jackson in Columbia, South Carolina. I wasn't scared to go," Noah said proudly.

It was a myth the Amish never travelled away from their communities. The Amish liked vacations as much as anybody, and Noah's family had once gone to the beach in South Carolina. The Amish could not own a car but were permitted to ride on trains and buses because they were driven by others.

"What was it like?" Leroy asked, swinging a bale into place on the pile they were building in the barn's loft.

"At first I liked the military. I was in much better shape than most of the men in my platoon. I thought 'this is going to be easy.'"

"Was it?" Leroy asked.

"It was kind of like living here, only with electricity and things," Noah answered. "It's English but the same in some ways. There are strict rules, and like us they put great store by personal honor. Those first weeks for the first time I imagined a life outside of our world, the Amish world. I thought I would do my tour, learn a skill, and come back and be a Highway Man. I thought about coming back and starting my own repair shop to service my friends' bikes."

"What happened?"

"I was sent to Afghanistan. On my first patrol I was caught in an explosion in a house where we thought the Taliban were hiding. I woke up in the hospital; I had been out for five days. In the afternoon on the fourth day back with my platoon, near a village south of Kandahar, I was in a convoy and the vehicle in front of us ran over an IED. A piece of shrapnel hit my helmet; it made me dizzy, and the explosion left me deaf. Then when we stopped, we were attacked. I was on machine gun," Noah said, putting down the bale he was holding.

"Oh, Leroy… you get caught up. It's all adrenalin; you just slip into a different place in your mind. Those Muslims were trying to kill us. It's you or them. I fired and killed what I thought were two men."

Noah looked at Leroy and realized that his friend was looking back at him as if he belonged to some other species. "When it was all over, Leroy, we went over to the bodies, and it turned out to be two boys way younger than me."

"You killed people, Noah," Leroy said in horror.

"Yes, and when I saw those boys… I had shot them in the chest, and one of them was still alive. I watched him die…" Even as Noah spoke he could feel Leroy withdraw even further from him.

"Noah, how could you do something like that?" The question was worse than open condemnation.

"I don't know, something just snapped. I had a terrible headache. I knew I had to get out of there. I tried to be a conscientious objector, but it was too late. Instead they told me they were going to give me a medal. It was horrible. I didn't think I could continue, but sometimes I was swept away by anger." The words came pouring out of him; they had been bottled up so long.

"A week later we were on patrol when we were attacked again. My best friend in the platoon was Zacharias Weston. He was from one of those mountain hollers in West Virginia. His father had been a coal miner, and his grandfather, and his father before that. But the mines shut down and the family just hunkered down. In some ways his life was as simple as we are here, except they were very poor. Zacharias had joined because there was no other work, and it meant one less mouth for his mother to feed. Anyway, when we were attacked Zacharias was shot in the face. I saw it happen. It made me crazy, and something changed in me. I threw a grenade so hard in my rage over Zacharias' murder it made it across the cut in the mountain where we were fighting and killed two more of the Taliban, and I was glad I had done it. They were the ones who had killed him. An eye for an eye."

Noah and Leroy had both stopped working as this story unfolded, and it ended with the two of them just standing in the loft, the air filled with little particles of hay, looking at each other.

"When we got back to our compound after that second attack," Noah continued, "I thought about what I had done, and I began to pray. There was a chaplain, but he was an evangelical. They actually try to convert people; I couldn't talk to him. I asked Jesus for help. I realized I had to leave, I was becoming a monster. It was awful, Leroy. Over the next several weeks I had spells when I would either burst into tears or go into rages I couldn't control. I couldn't sleep. I knew I wasn't right, and the other guys didn't want to go out with me. My lieutenant finally sent me up to the hospital in Kabul. They told me I had PTSD." It came pouring out of Noah, things he had told no one. He started to tell Leroy about going to the brothel in Kabul, after they had begun to let him go out. He could see once again the young girl with whom he had lost his virginity. She said she was fourteen and her body confirmed that. But as he began to speak, he realized Leroy would not understand.

"It ended a week later when I blew up and hit one of the doctors. I was shipped home and given a general discharge. All I could think to do was to come back here. Please don't tell anyone about this, Leroy," Noah said, picking up another bale.

"I don't know what to say." Leroy turned away, then looked back at Noah. "I will pray for you," he said, then went over to the ladder and began to climb down out of the loft. As his head was about to sink beneath the loft floor he stopped and looked again at Noah, who looked back defiantly. Both knew their friendship, as they had known it, had ended. Six weeks later, that was confirmed. When pressed to say what he knew, Leroy told the truth. It wasn't acceptable to lie to the community, and his words left Noah filled with the sudden rage that swept over him now.

When Noah had first arrived back in Lancaster, he thought he was being realistic; he expected a mixed reaction and that's what he got. His childhood friends and their families were initially wary, but slowly they had begun to accept him again. That was all ended now. He thought about what that meant as he finished trimming the hedge and went back to get the push mower. As he was standing in front of the toolshed he heard the bell; school was over, and the students came streaming out. As they flowed past him, he saw Rachel Swayze, and she looked over at him. She was almost fifteen, in the eighth grade, the last year of Amish school, and even in her old-fashioned Amish dress he could see her young breasts and imagined cupping them in his hands.

They had known each other all her life until she was twelve and he had gone away, and there had always been something between them. Rachel had a sensuous quality unusual in Amish girls, and it had strongly attracted him. Unlike most of the young people, Rachel had sought him out and welcomed him back. He was no longer a virgin, and from his first day back he wanted her. As he stared at her going down the walk she looked over, smiled, and started toward him. Someone shouted her name, and she turned and went back to the crowd of students.

A buggy came up the road pulled by a beautiful bay. Noah could tell the driver was on Rumspringa because he could hear the buggy's stereo, something an adult would never have. The driver was Amos Lapp, seventeen and clearly courting Rachel.

She got into Amos' buggy, and Noah became furiously jealous. The emotion was made all the worse because he knew now that Rachel would never marry him. No girl in the community could. He wasn't quite English, but he wasn't Amish either. Thinking about that he felt the anger and stress the doctors had warned him about. To keep himself under control he did as another soldier in the treatment program had taught him. Long slow breaths until he felt he was back in control. Then he started mowing again, the physical effort helping to calm him.

As he worked he began to think about finding a way to connect with Rachel. Her Rumspringa would start soon. Could he get her to leave with him, he wondered as he worked? He needed some way to interact with her regularly, he thought, as he finished and pushed the mower back to the shed where it was stored.

As the days went on, he became more and more aware that he was a known person but no longer a real part of the community. Two weeks later he lay in bed in the room built into a barn that was allotted by the community to the school janitor. The only light was the kerosene lantern burning next to his bed. His mind drifted back to good times he had had with Zacharias and the others; feelings and images flooded into his mind. Going into Columbia to a bar favored by soldiers. Or into a village near Kandahar where he could buy grilled skewers of spiced meat. As he pictured the skewer in his hand he could recall the meat's spicy tang. He remembered the Highway Men and abandoned himself to his memories.

The next morning, he got up and shaved off the biblically sanctioned beard he had been growing, but still dressed in the simple clothes that marked the Amish. In his community men could wear something other than black as long as it was dark. He had chosen a dark blue-gray gabardine suit cut in the traditional mutza style with no collar lapels or pockets. It reminded him of a jacket an Indian merchant in Kandahar wore. He had decided he would continue to wear Amish clothes as long as he worked at the school, otherwise he would stand out too much. Once dressed he got the pickle jar he had hidden between his mattress and box spring. He had saved almost all his pay and put it in the jar.

As he counted the bills and change, he decided what he needed was something with a motor, not a horse and buggy. He had three thousand four hundred and thirty-two dollars. As he put the money back in the jar he went back and forth about whether it should be a motorcycle or a car, and decided a car would be more practical.

When he went outside he saw the driver of a delivery truck drop off something at the school. As he turned to go back to his van Noah went over to him.

"Are you going back into Lancaster?"

"Yeah."

"Could I catch a ride with you?' Noah asked.

The driver was about his age, a local boy from another world.

"It's not really allowed, but I guess so. Hop in."

Noah went around to the passenger side and got in. He could tell the young driver assumed he was an Amish man, and that they had very little in common. They rode in silence until the driver asked, "Where do you need to go?"

"Take me to that strip where the car dealers are."

"Car dealers. You're Amish, dude; what do you need with a car dealer?"

To his own surprise, Noah answered, "I may be leaving the community."

"On that Rump thing you people do?" the young man asked, looking closely at Noah for the first time.

"Something like that," Noah responded.

They rode in silence again until they turned onto Manhelm Pike which was lined with a series of car dealerships.

The driver asked, "Any particular dealer?"

"No… you can let me out here," Noah said, and the driver pulled over. It was only when he got out of the van and it drove away that he realized he was the only pedestrian on the street.

As he walked he thought seriously about what kind of car he needed and was glad for his work at the motorcycle shop and in the service. He had not only learned to drive, something very few Amish men knew how to do, but had been exposed to different kinds of cars and trucks as well as motorcycles, and he understood how they worked.

There were colored triangular flags flapping to his left, and one of those colored inflated tubular figures that wave in the air. He was used to walking and relaxed into it. Memories began to come one after another: his tactical vehicle in Afghanistan, his first time driving a motorcycle. Going out with the Highway Men. They had stopped for a barbeque, and he recalled one of the men's girlfriends had followed in a pickup with a camper shell, and while everyone else was sleeping on the ground, they slept in their truck. In the middle of the night an unexpected rain had started, something the weather report hadn't mentioned. Those who didn't have tents, which included him, had gotten soaked. The more he thought about it, a pickup with a camper shell seemed a better idea than a car.

His emotions were in turmoil; the daily reminders telling him he was an outlier had hardened into anger. He would reject them. They would pay him as he planned, and when he left, if he planned it right, he wouldn't be alone. He had already decided that.

A week earlier as he had lain in bed masturbating to images of Rachel, he imagined her naked, sucking him, as a woman who hung out with the Highway Men had. After he had come, he decided that he would get Rachel to leave with him under the guise of Rumspringa. It had focused his mind; he had a plan.

As he walked by the third dealer, a little shabbier than the others, he saw a black Toyota with a camper shell. It was far from new, but Noah felt he could handle anything mechanically wrong if the engine was fundamentally sound. The price in red letters on the windshield was $2,495.

He walked over to the truck and was getting ready to raise the hood, when an overweight man his age in a polyester shirt and tie but no jacket walked over.

"Can I help you?" he asked in a calculating way, clearly confused seeing an Amish man looking at a truck.

"Can I open the hood?"

"Do you know how?"

"Yes," Noah answered, and taking that as permission, opened the truck door, reached down for the hood release, and pulled it.

"Can you start it up? I'd like to hear the engine."

"I don't understand," the man said, and Noah knew the man saw him as Amish and could not make the connection. He felt trapped in an image that didn't want him. It irritated him and he spoke more harshly than he really meant to. "Do you want to sell me this truck or not?"

The other man recoiled, but his desire to sell the truck which hadn't attracted a single look all week was stronger.

"Of course, let me go get the key," he answered, and went back into the manufactured structure like a single wide that served as an office. He came back out, handed it to Noah, and stepped back, curious as to what he would do.

Noah started the engine and looked into the engine compartment, watching and listening.

"Can we drive it around the block?"

"Do you have a driver's license?" the salesman asked, knowing full well that as a member of the Amish community, Noah would not have one.

"No," Noah responded, reaching into his pocket and pulling out his money. The Amish were not stupid nor were they suckers; they had a reputation for being hard bargainers.

The salesman looked down at the money in Noah's hand, then put on a smile that did not reach his eyes.

"Well, I suppose just around the block would be okay," he said, getting into the truck. Noah climbed into the driver's seat and expertly backed the truck out of its slot, turned it, and headed out the driveway.

"Where did you learn to drive? The Amish don't drive cars," the man said, looking at Noah's clothes.

"In the army."

"In the army. The Amish don't go into the army, everyone knows they are COs," the salesman said. "What's the deal? You dress Amish but you're not. I'm not a fool."

"Did you grow up here?"

"Yes, I went to J.P. McCaskey," the salesman said.

"I went to Nickel Mines," Noah responded, and as he said it, he was confronted again by the county's two worlds.

"Are you leaving?" the salesman asked, as Noah drove across the lot and turned right.

"Not quite yet. There's something I need to do," Noah answered.

They rode on for a while in silence. When Noah turned back onto the lot, he said, "The timing's off, the wheels are out of alignment, and the brakes need to be replaced. The rubber's okay." His tone was completely neutral but very firm, and it registered with the salesman, who knew all those things to be true. Noah parked the truck back in its slot, got out and did another walkaround. There was no body rust or significant dents, but the black paint was weathered, and the camper aluminum trim was dull. But he knew it to be a solid truck, just like the Toyota pickups he had known in Afghanistan. It wasn't flashy in any way; it wouldn't draw attention.

"The price is $2495," the salesman said when they were settled, "but I am prepared to make an accommodation for the things you noted. So, I am prepared to go to $2195," he said, making it a question, but not quite.

"I'll give you $1995," Noah said, and started to count out the bills, placing them one by one on the desk.

"I don't know that I can go that low."

"Last offer, $2000," Noah said, finishing the count. Both men looked at the pile of money. The salesman knew he had bought the truck at the auction for $1375. It had been a mistake, and this worked. "You have a deal," he said, extending his hand.

They spent thirty minutes doing the paperwork with no more mention about not having a driver's license, and Noah drove the truck off the lot as the salesman stood in the office doorway watching him go.

As he drove down the road that afternoon, he saw the school. Amish schools were all pretty much alike. Wooden one room buildings painted white. Very simple, no trim. They all had a little cupola with a bell worked into the roof. Amish children put down their hoes and rakes and picked up their pencils and books, in conformance to its ringing tones. In the back there were two white wooden outhouses. A white fence outlined the property. He stopped at the school and sat in his truck, looking at it as an outsider yet still connected.

He determined that he would stay until the school year was over. Then he would talk Rachel into coming with him. He just needed some way to regularly interact with her without making anybody in the community aware of his interest.

Two weeks later Noah saw his chance. A group of Amish girls had gone into Lancaster, and a car load of teenage boys had come into the town and walked around until they saw the girls, then gone over and hit on them. Local boys knew to leave Amish girls alone. But these were city boys charged up on meth; the girls were a challenge. Their tactics were crude and their wit lacking. The girls tried to ignore them but two of the boys had stepped onto the porch and one of them cupped a girl's bottom. A shopkeeper saw it and came out and said he would call the police if the boys didn't move on, and they had. But it had shaken the girls.

A few days later Rachel, with her friend Susan, had come up to him.

"Noah, when you were in the army did you learn something we could do if English boys came up like that again?" Rachel had blushed as she said it. He watched her mouth as she spoke; it was beautiful, with full lips. He imagined kissing her and was overcome by his sexual attraction to her.

"You're the only person we know who would... you know... know something like that," Susan said, breaking the mood, looking at him, speaking in a tone of need and judgment.

The three of them stood silently for a moment as Noah considered what to do, then recognized this was his opportunity.

"Yes, okay Susan. As it happens I was very good at that," and saying it made him feel proud because he had been. He was six feet and a hundred and ninety-five pounds of muscle; from the beginning he had stood out amongst the men with whom he trained. They were either inner city boys or Southerners, many overweight, few in very good physical condition. He was almost unique in not having grown up in a world of television, tablets, video games, and fast food, and he found the Army's early hours and disciplined work quite easy. Like all Amish boys he had labored in the fields, barnyard, and workshops of his family's farm or helped other families in the community when there was some kind of collective project like a barn raising. It was all very physical, and it had made him not only strong but physically agile in a way most of his sedentary fellow soldiers found hard to match. He enjoyed and excelled at the mix of jujitsu and kung fu martial arts he was taught.

"Today's Monday. How about after school on Wednesday?" he finally responded. "But you have to get your parents to agree. I don't want any more problems, Rachel."

"Of course, Noah. I wouldn't make trouble for you," she said, pouting.

"I know you wouldn't," Noah answered.

And so the classes started. Wednesday afternoons for an hour.

CHAPTER TWO

Michael Gillespie sat at his desk at the Lynn Hill Human Capacities Institute scrolling through his emails. The once torrential flow was now, almost two years later, down to two hundred and fifty a day. He no longer had media calls half a dozen times a week and was glad of it.

The lives of everyone associated with the Hill Institute had changed forever when the news, particularly the video from the news helicopter of Michael's struggle to stop the explosion, had gotten out. People learned how Michael and the remote viewers, through his nonlocal consciousness research, had stopped a five-kiloton nuclear explosion from destroying Washington, D.C.

None of them had sought or even wanted the attention that came with using a part of the mind many people didn't even believe existed to do something as dramatic as what had happened. How the terrorists had been killed and the bomb stopped at literally almost the last second. It was like something out of a movie, but he and the others had actually lived it.

His team had talked about it several times; it had bound them together. They were a disparate group, but they all now shared something that transcended any of the usual borders. Their closeness got them through the experience. First they were heroes and then, as time went by, they had become stereotypes. It had taken the media a while to get past the psychic woo-woo phase and to accept the reality of nonlocal consciousness and the science of working with it. The journalists and commentators had finally settled on the image of science fiction explorers. It had been a strange but fascinating trip, but things were calmer now and he was happy about that. There were fewer interruptions.

His schedule alarm chimed, and a little window came up telling him he was scheduled to do a session with Constance Walters, who like all teachers whose lives are ordered by bells, was always promptly on time.

He got up, stretched, and went down to the floor below and waited in the entry hall for Constance. She arrived almost to the second, a middle-aged Black woman who had received national recognition for her work with blind and deaf children at Gallaudet University, the only college in the world whose entire student body was deaf or hard-of-hearing. A number of students were also blind.

Constance had used the fame that came to her from the Vision Probe, as it had come to be known, to make people more aware of the needs of disabled children. She had turned almost every interview at some point into an "ask" and had raised nine million dollars for Gallaudet. Like everyone else at the Hill Institute, she had tried not to let the spotlight of publicity overly affect her marriage or her day-to-day work. For all of them there had been many temptations to change course, to cash in, but like the others at Hill Institute, Constance did not give way and still worked with her students. She was changed, though, Michael realized as he looked at her coming in. He could see it in her body language. She moved with more presence and confidence than when he had first met her.

"Constance, good to see you," Michael said, and embraced her. "How's Herbert?"

"You too, Michael. This is the first session we've done in almost two months. Herbert's fine, and sends you his best. I understand from Coyote that Tracy is in Brazil."

"She is," Michael answered as they started down the hall. "Her Richardson grant money finally gave her the chance to work with that tribe she had read about several years back. I think she told you about them."

"She did. I don't know if I would care for the living conditions, though. But I'll bet she is happy about the privacy. How do you connect with her?"

"The Richardson gave her enough money to get a satellite phone and a portable solar panel, so she has her computer and we can talk," he said. "But not for long; it's like six dollars a minute," he added with a laugh.

"How's it been for her?"

"Now that she's been a remote viewer and has experienced nonlocal consciousness herself and can talk with the shamans in a way that shows them she both intellectually and experientially comprehends their world view, they treat her as a White shaman," Michael responded, and Constance smiled at that.

They got to what had once been the dining room. Hill Institute was based in a large gray brick mansion in Georgetown, once a colonial port town, now a district in Northwest Washington, D.C.. Michael had preserved the nineteenth century architectural detail of the room. It had white wainscoting around the ivory walls, crown molding, a beautiful fireplace, and a mahogany floor.

Where the dining table had once been there now stood a smooth nine-foot high by twelve-foot wide ivory colored egg-shaped object, known to all in the lab as "the egg."

Beneath its simple smooth exterior, the egg was a very sophisticated custom-designed piece of technology—a combination Faraday cage and mild sensory deprivation chamber with complex biometric monitors that captured everything from facial expressions to blood pressure and brain activity. Those inside it were shielded from all electro-magnetic radiation except extreme low frequency, known as ELF, (3-300 Hertz). It was also soundproofed and temperature and humidity controlled. Inside there were no right angles to catch the eye; the walls and ceiling were covered in a soft gray pleated fabric. Being in the egg was rather like moving into a cloud.

There were two soft leather chairs in matching gray, with gray rounded tambours next to them, like short columns. Lying in the chairs were two gray cloth helmets with little pods distributed over the cloth's surface, rather like the old-fashioned leather pilot helmet with the ear flaps that Snoopy wore as a World War I pilot.

"After you," Michael said, gesturing for Constance to enter.

"I was at the briefing Gilbert gave, so I have some sense of what this is about," Constance said as she seated herself.

"Entropy," Michael answered as he sat down. "I am trying to better calibrate the effect of entropy on nonlocal task performance."

"And you think it is not just physical but information entropy, is that right?" Constance asked.

"Exactly. Once you get that consciousness is the fundamental, and is causal, it's not hard to see reality is a construct of intentioned conscious awareness manipulating information."

"Well, I'm not so sure it's as clear as all that," Constance said, smiling at Michael and then continuing. "So tell me again what we are doing."

"I will be asking you to describe a target which at the time you are giving me the description does not exist as a designated target. It's our standard session. It's not the protocol, but the targets, as informational structures, that are the focus in this series," Michael explained.

"Okay I get that. But what are you measuring?"

"The targets have been categorized by how much entropy is present and whether it is physical or informational entropy. In both cases there is some kind of movement towards disorder. I want to see if I can distinguish a difference between physical and informational entropy, and measure how robust the effect is," Michael said as he pulled on his helmet, and gestured for Constance to do the same.

When they were both settled, he pressed a button on the chair which brought out a monitor hidden in the chair's arm. On one side of a split screen was Constance's biometric data, on the other side his read-outs appeared. Blood pressure, heart beat, breathing rate, body temperature, and brain function were all charted. He clicked, and those images were replaced by a screen with a rectangular form in which Constance could make drawings or notes. All of it would be analyzed to extract the accurate information she provided in the session from what amounted to "noise." It was this monitoring, plus the lab's consensus protocol, that gave Hill Institute its high degree of accuracy.

"Okay, Constance, get comfortable," Michael said.

Constance nodded and adjusted her chair back a bit.

"This is series eight twenty-three, session twenty-one. Session begins following standard meditation period. Viewer is Constance Walters. Monitor Michael Gillespie. Time and date code now," he said, and tapped on the screen again.

"Close your eyes, take a deep breath, let it out; let's meditate for twenty minutes, then I will give you the task instruction."

The two of them sat quietly, eyes closed, and slowly their breathing, heartbeat, and brain patterns synchronized. When that happened, a soft chime went off and Michael said, "Constance, I want you to go forward in time to twenty minutes from now. You are life-sized. You are fully aware of the target location, all your senses report. I have no idea what the target will be; you can get nothing from me. What do you perceive?"

"It is a huge metal island. People live inside this thing. There is a kind of constant low level of noise...."

"Can you tell me about the people?"

"Everyone dresses the same. It's both men and women."

"Tell me about the place."

"It's a great big island, but it moves, although right now it is still."

"Does anything stand out about it?"

"There's something like a star inside this island… except it's not really an island… I don't understand."

"A star?"

"Yes. It is very hot. It's contained though… under control."

"Can you make me a drawing of what you perceive?"

Constance sketched something on her tablet, which was duplicated on his, saying as she did this, "It's a kind of long metal rectangle, with a raised place on one side in the middle," Constance said. "It's in the water. It's very technical. It carries other things, also very technical. They come and go." She put the tablet down "That's pretty much what I get, Michael.

"Okay, session end." They sat quietly, in an intimate kind of peace, then another chime and the interior dimmed. The holographic image of an aircraft carrier appeared in front of them.

Michael looked down at his screen as the AI judging result came out. "You have a hit, ninety percent concept accuracy, Constance," Michael said, smiling broadly at her.

Constance looked at the hologram of the carrier. "I don't understand about the star. I really got a strong impression of this very hot process."

"You wouldn't know it to look at the ship that she's nuclear powered," Michael answered. "Nimitz is her name… I think you were describing the nuclear reactor. A high level of physical entropy is taking place in the atomic process. You saw it."

They both stood up and Michael gave Constance a hug. "That was really good work," he said.

She smiled over her shoulder as she preceded him out of the egg. As they went to the library, which doubled as the living room for anyone waiting or just sitting and talking, they saw Istaqa Chester, a 28-year old Hopi warrior shaman known universally as Coyote. He was the most popular DJ in Georgetown, a tightly muscled man with high cheekbones and strongly red skin. Michael always thought he looked dangerous in an ancient way. He was sitting with Gilbert Exposito, an electronic neuroscientist and Michael's research associate. Exposito was completely bald, plump but not fat, and wore glasses with dark green frames.

Both of them stood up as Michael and Constance came into the room. They all took turns hugging and catching up with each other.

"Okay, you two are up for your session," Michael said to Gilbert, who nodded his head.

"Could you come up afterwards?" Michel asked.

"Sure," Gilbert answered. He and Coyote walked back to the egg as Michael and Constance said goodbye.

When Constance had left, Michael went back up to his office, stopping at Karen's desk to check in with her.

"You have a bunch of calls, but one I think... I think that one should be first. I logged them all in."

"Who's it from?" Michael asked.

"Sam Kassimir."

"Now what could the CIA want with us this time," Michael said, turning to walk back to his office. When he got there he dialed the number, and Denise Mailman, the Deputy Director's Executive Secretary, answered.

"Professor Gillespie, Dr. Kassimir had to leave suddenly but he wondered if you would give a talk."

"To whom and when?"

"The Army War College in Carlisle, Pennsylvania."

"Sam thinks it's important?"

"Yes, he does," she replied.

"Then I'll do it," Michael responded.

"Thank you. I know he will appreciate that. A colonel from the office of the commandant of the Army War College will contact you. I will call him as soon as we hang up."

"Okay, thanks," Michael said. Ten minutes later, just as he was hanging up from another call, Karen paged him. "Colonel Randall Bishop on the line," she said when he picked up.

"How I can I help you, Colonel?"

"Professor Gillespie, Dr. Kassimir's office called to say you might be willing to do a talk for us," Colonel Bishop said. "We'd like to invite you to present your research to the senior officers' seminar here at the War College. Dr. Kassimir has also asked that Jake Garth brief you in person before you come up."

As soon as Michael heard Jake Garth's name, he knew he was back in the secret mirror world where nothing is quite what it seems, and that there was some serious purpose behind the invitation. They agreed on a date a month ahead, and the arrangements all seemed very clear. But when Michael hung up he still wondered what had just happened.

He got up and walked out on the iron balcony that hung off the side of his office overlooking the Immaculate Heart Catholic Girls school playground. School was out now, but in his mind's eye he could see the girls playing. He was overwhelmed for a moment with memories.

The Vision Probe, as it came to be known, had started with Tracy Walsh, a cultural anthropologist who had wanted to become a remote viewer. He was doing some initial tests with her, standard triple-blind precognitive protocol, and she was having trouble staying focused because of events in her personal life; her marriage was coming apart. They had taken a break and come up to his office, and it was such a pretty day they had come out on the balcony. While they were standing there looking down at the girls at play, one of whom was her daughter, Sarah, Tracy had asked him to let her try again in that informal setting. It was just a test, he had thought, and he gave her the suggestion to go forward in time three weeks. She had had a very emotional response and reported an explosion.

It was so dramatic that he had asked others to view the same time and date, and that had started the search for what they eventually determined was a nuclear bomb. The events that flowed from Tracy's vision had changed the Hill Institute and all their personal lives forever. Not least, Tracy and he had become lovers and partners.

Michael went back through the French doors into his office, sat down at his desk, and began to go through the entropy study data. An hour later he was interrupted as Gilbert came into his office.

"Yo Great Leader, what's up?"

"I think we have proved it, Gilbert."

"Yes, I agree," Gilbert said, as he sat down in one of Michael's Brancaster leather club chairs with aluminum airplane metal sides. "I ran the numbers last night."

"I just did, too," Michael answered, "that's why I wanted to get together."

"Entropic process, whether physical or informational, makes targets more numinous."

"Yes. That's it exactly. Planck is correct. Consciousness is causal and fundamental. What we're looking at is how that fundamental works."

"So, what do you want to do?"

"I want to refine our understanding of the process further and run a second study, only this time with numinosity as the variable. I think entropy and numinosity are interdependent."

"In what way?" Gilbert asked.

"Acts of intentioned observation add information, that's what the data suggests. Like turning the voltage up on a neon sign. It glows more strongly."

"Then Jung is right," Gilbert said.

"I think so. He called the information 'numina' and described them as 'psychic entities.' I can't improve on that," Michael replied.

"Okay, so we're going to need targets that have themselves been the target of varying degrees of focused intention over time. I don't think that will be too hard to do. I'll put together a profile and get a couple of our grad students to work on it."

"How long?"

"I don't know exactly, but let's say two weeks."

Gilbert got up to leave, and Michael said, "I've been asked to go up to the Army War College to brief some kind of senior officer group."

"Are you going to do it?" Gilbert asked.

"Yes, Sam Kassimir asked me to."

"Well then, I'll bet there's more to it than a simple invitation," Gilbert said, standing in the doorway of Michael's office.

"You're probably right."

CHAPTER THREE

Noah sat quietly in his room in the barn near the school. He looked around the wooden room with its wooden bedstead, a wooden dresser, the chair upon which he sat, and a table upon which a kerosene lamp burned. Outside the curtainless window the night was dark. He had been under constant stress for the past two weeks and was glad that he was semi-shunned by the community because it meant nobody paid much attention to him, which made everything easier.

His plan had worked. The Wednesday classes teaching Rachel and the other girls the basics of self-defense had given him the opportunity to begin grooming her. And it felt righteous because he taught them real things. Thanks to his teaching they could make men let go of them; they could run away, and the man would be disabled enough to give them a head start. To teach them that he had to show them how to position their bodies. That was the first time he had been able to put his hands on Rachel. He had brushed against her young breasts, felt the firmness of her thighs. Breathed in the soft intimate smell at her temples as he helped her get into a posture.

Little by little she came to trust him, and the rest was easy. Amish schools do not cover sex education, and Amish girls are taught to defer to men older then themselves. By supporting her young imagination of adventure and recalling things they had done or talked about before he had gone into the Army, he got her to confide in him that she was waiting for her Rumspringa to begin, and that she wanted to see life outside of the Amish world. One day he brought up the idea that he could go with her. They began to talk about it in the short minutes they were together. He was careful not to draw any attention to their connection and was glad Amos Lapp was so obviously courting her, because it camouflaged his own interest. In a final meeting they chose the day, a week in the future. That night as he lay in bed he knew he had to tell his family he was leaving.

The next morning as he was working on the grounds of the school, he saw his family's buggy coming and went out into the road. It was his brother Samuel, two years younger. As Samuel brought the rig to a halt, Noah thought how different their personalities were; they had never been close.

"You're headed down to Father at the Hostetler place?"

"Yes," Samuel answered, looking down at his older brother.

"Would you ask him to stop by my room on his way home?"

"Sure. What for? What problems are you going to cause now, Noah?"

"Just tell him it's important."

Samuel did not reply, just flicked the reins, and the horse began again.

Later that day, after he had cleaned up from getting everything around the school in good shape, Noah sat thinking about what was about to happen, and was so lost in these thoughts that it took three knocks on his door to get his attention. He got up, walked across his small room, and opened the door to his father, Levi. They had not seen each other for several weeks, because even immediate family did not interact often with someone of Noah's status.

"Father," Noah said, then stepped aside to let his father enter. Noah was the oldest son, his father only eighteen years older. There was a twelve-year spread over all his brothers and sisters.

The older man took off his black hat and sat in the only chair. Like all Amish men he had a beard but no moustache, no facial hair around his mouth at all.

"You asked me to stop," his father said, not as a question but a statement.

Noah could feel his anger rising at the snub his father's tone implied. "I'm not in the community; you have made that very clear to me."

"You are still my son, and because of that you are still the caretaker of the school," Levi said, then sat in silence for a moment looking at his hands. Looking up at his son standing by the bed, he said, "I don't know where I failed you Noah. You have strayed from God in ways I don't even understand."

Without thinking, Noah answered, "You're right. I have strayed from your idea of God, I have, and I am going to be leaving."

"Where will you go?"

"Where there are a lot of motorcycles, I think. I am very good at fixing them. So, California maybe."

"When will you leave?"

"In a few days. You better hire another caretaker."

"Will you come by the house and say goodbye to your mother?" Levi said, standing and turning to the door.

"Yes, of course."

"I will ask God to be with you every day, my son," he said, and went out and closed the door.

As it closed Noah was filled with a sense of the finality of his rejection. But as he cleaned up his room and thought about how he would pack up, he felt he had handled things correctly. He would leave days before Rachel disappeared. No one would connect him with Rachel, not in the community and not the police. Although he hadn't thought it through, he felt what he had said was right. It was time to leave.

The next day, deliberately at dinner time, he drove to his family's farm, the farm that should have become his. He parked his truck, got out, and walked up to the door. Samuel opened it.

"Mother told me to tell you that she loves you and will pray for you, but does not want to see you, and neither does anyone else. Father told us what you are going to do. I wish you well," he said, and closed the door. Noah walked back to his truck, consumed in the moment by anger and humiliation. It was definitely time to go, and the next morning he got up and left.

He drove to Philadelphia with the idea of getting a job and an apartment where he could take Rachel. There was also another reason. He was leaving three days before he would pick her up so that no one would connect her disappearance with him.

He got to the section of the city where the Highway Men Repair Shop was located, parked, and went in.

"Hey, Sarge," he said as he went into the garage, and saw Daryl Stoddard standing there wiping a tool with a rag.

"Noah," Stoddard answered, smiling. He came over and they embraced. "You back for good?"

"Yeah."

"Where were you?"

"Southern Provinces, Hilmand, Kandahar, around Spin Buldak."

"Been there. Nasty," Stoddard said, leading the way into the Highway Men clubhouse in the back of the garage. "Why do you think you were there?" he asked Noah when they were seated, both drinking a beer.

"I don't know," Noah said. "What I do know is none of the stuff that oh-five told us when we first got there meant anything."

"Then why did you fight?" Stoddard asked, and Noah could tell his answer was important.

"Stick with your buddies, fight with your buddies, get everyone through, leave no one behind. That's what it was about for me."

"Then you learned the right lesson," Stoddard said. "So why are you here?" he asked, and Noah knew he would try to help.

"You got any work?"

"Oh... I'm sorry Noah. I just took on a new guy; there's not enough work."

That wasn't the answer Noah had expected. The motorcycle repair world was a small one. "Do you know anyone who might have a job?" he asked.

"You might try Keilor's. I heard one of their guys got banged up in an accident. You want to stay in our bunk room tonight?"

"That would be great."

"I'll take you out for some ribs," Stoddard said, and got up. "Come on."

They went out for dinner, and as they sat swapping stories of their service in Afghanistan and news of shared friends, Noah felt a sense of connection for the first time since he had come back from the service. Something he had not felt in the community in a long time.

He got up the next morning and drove further into the city to Keilor's, and said he had been sent by Stoddard. They were friendly but it came to nothing, and that meant he would not be able to get an apartment. As he was driving back from Philadelphia, he realized he would have to change his plans. He stopped that night and to save money slept on the foam mattress in his truck bed. As he lay there in the dark, he decided that maybe this was all for the best. If he was ever connected with Rachel and they checked, Leroy, who had already betrayed him once, would tell about his having gone to Philadelphia and the Highway Men. The more he thought about it, the more it seemed a good idea to get out of the area altogether, taking Rachel with him. Like most Amish he didn't have a very clear map of the United States in his head, but travelling South, where it was warmer, seemed like a good choice. Rachel had told him she found Pennsylvania winters hard and remembered a family trip by bus her family had once taken to Virginia Beach, Virginia.

The next morning, he cleaned his truck, getting everything ready, then stopped to fill his tank and check his oil. On impulse he bought a cheap digital watch. As he was doing all this, he could feel the tension in his body rising, much as it had when they had gone into villages or up gullies in Afghanistan.

He stopped at a Wendy's and ate lunch, and checking the time, realized he had to hurry to be at the pick-up point.

Rachel was working with friends when she saw her friend Ruth's watch. Not all Amish wore watches; Rachel didn't, but some did as long as they were simple mechanical watches, nothing digital, quartz, or solar. It was almost three o'clock.

"Oh my," Rachel said, "I was supposed to run an errand for mother. I have to hurry," she added, and left the field where they were working, walking away and down the road before Ruth or the others could ask any questions. She was soon at the crossroads and out of sight and turned right, walking half a mile on the road to where it curved to the left in a clump of trees. Halfway through them, invisible now to anyone looking, she stopped. She had been there no more than two minutes when Noah drove around the bend.

"Care for a lift?" he asked through his open window. She went around to the other side, got in, and Noah turned around and drove back the way he had come, unseen by anyone at the community farms further on.

Rachel had never been in a truck before and was fascinated by the experience. They laughed together, and she teased him the way young girls do, trying to flirt.

His plan was to get them out of the Lancaster area, and they started going west on Highway 741 headed to Columbia. As they drove along, he looked at her and realized they had to get out of Amish clothes. Their age difference would also have to be explained. Since he no longer had an Amish beard he thought if he took his jacket off, rolled his sleeves up and took off his Amish hat, he would pass for English. But Rachel's outfit would give her away.

The tension of pulling off Rachel's abduction, plus his sense of urgency that she might be missed and a police alert sent out, weighed heavily on him. He stopped at six p.m. at a takeout pizza place. Leaving her in the car, he went in and ordered a pizza and a salad, waiting until they were boxed. He paid for them in cash and returned to the truck. An hour later he stopped at a small inexpensive non-chain motel. Pulling into the parking area he could see only two other cars. Once again he left Rachel in the car and went in to reception where a middle-aged Indian woman sat behind a counter. She smiled as he went up to her.

"I'm driving to Cincinnati, could I get a room for the night?"

"You by yourself?" she asked, and Noah replied. "Yeah, just me." He reached into his pocket, pulled out his money, and looked at what he had while the Indian woman took all this in.

"I'm going to see my grandmother; they think she's dying, and I'm not sure what all this is going to cost," he said with a rueful smile. As he said it, he realized it was the first time in his life he had ever lied like that.

The woman was sympathetic. "Tell you what. Are you a vet, do you belong to AAA?"

"I just got out of the service."

"Afghanistan?"

"Yeah. I got wounded," Noah answered, trying to further invoke her sympathy.

"I'll give you the vet's discount," she said, handing him the registration invoice.

"Oh... I really appreciate that," Noah replied, giving her his best smile and counting out the money. "I'm sorry, I don't have any credit cards yet."

"Well, thank you for your service," the woman answered as she programmed the room key and handed it to him. "It's a quiet room in the back on the second floor."

He thanked her again and drove around to the back where he noted no one could see them.

They got out of the truck and went up to the room. It was shabby, mostly Formica, and smelled of cleaning chemicals. He brought in his army duffel bag, their only luggage, and set it down.

They both looked at the room's two beds, and to his great pleasure, Rachel volunteered, "I think we should bundle. I know the community doesn't approve. But the Ephrata community allows it."

Noah looked at her and realized she was making a very bold gesture of intimacy. As she set up the room's little table for their dinner, he watched her move, and his attraction to her increased. He took the blanket off the other bed and rolled it into tube which he laid in the middle of the bed they would use. Then he sat down across from her, and after saying grace they ate the pizza and shared the salad. They had few recent common memories, so they talked about the past, becoming more comfortable in one another's company.

They took off their shoes, and one at a time they went into the bathroom. When they came out, still with their clothes on, they climbed into bed together and pulled up the covers with the tube of blanket between them.   This was Amish bundling. As they lay there they talked, Noah had trouble keeping his hands off Rachel. But he knew he couldn't even kiss her, could only push her so far, so he just lay there and turned out the light.

"We need to change how we look so we don't stand out," he said as they lay there. "You understand?"

"Yes," Rachel told him, and he thought she seemed excited by the idea. As the tension drained out of both of them, they fell asleep.

In the morning, he opened his duffle and took out the clothes he had bought at the thrift store. He showed them to her and then gave her a pair of white cotton panties, a pair of jeans, white cotton socks, a blue cotton boy's shirt, a hoodie, and slip-on shoes. His first act in setting his plan in motion had been to measure her footprint after she stepped in some mud when he was teaching her and her friends self-defense. As he handed her the clothes, she seemed excited about the transformation, the first time in her life she had dressed English.

"Why don't you use the bathroom first," he said, and was surprised by her hesitation.

"What's wrong?"

"I went in last night; I don't know how to use all that. My family has a bathtub and we heat our water with wood."

"My family too. You've never taken a shower. Neither had I until I went to Philadelphia. I understand" he said, and led her into the bathroom to show her how to use the shower, then left her.

As he sat on the bed and listened to the shower through the bathroom door, in his mind he imagined her naked body. Finally, it was too much, and he got up and crossed the room and opened the door. Rachel was just stepping out of the shower. She stood naked, facing him, a towel in her hand for what seemed to him a timeless moment.

The water running down her body made it shine in the bright light of the bathroom. He was mesmerized by her shoulders, her young breasts, her nipples erect from stepping from the shower stall into the cooler air of the bathroom. He felt himself becoming aroused as he looked down to the light soft fledging of hair that covered her sex, whose cleft was still prominent.

What had been a fantasy, in that moment became reality, and he had to have her. She was more embarrassed than outraged, and he said something stupid by way of explanation, something about getting a towel. He knew it was nonsense even as he said it, but he had grabbed a hand towel and retreated, closing the door, his penis growing erect in his jeans. It was all he could do not to go back into the bathroom, grab her, and put her on the bed. But then he thought she might scream and decided to wait.

With her towel wrapped around her, she came quickly out of the bathroom grabbed her clothes as an English teenager and went back into the bathroom. Whatever she felt she kept to herself, only glancing at him. She came out and sat on the bed looking at him. He didn't know what to say and so just went in and showered. When he came out Rachel sat on the bed watching television.

He went over and sat with her. After a minute he told her, "I'm sorry. I didn't mean to walk in on you."

She was not mad as he had thought she might be. "You certainly got an eyeful," she said, blushing.

"And what I saw looked wonderful," he told her, and put his hand on her thigh.

It started with kissing, and Rachel was responsive. He felt her body over her clothes and then under them. She resisted when his hand came up between her legs but relaxed a little as he stroked her sex. He could feel her hymen with his finger but did not press. He got all their clothes off as he continued to gently massage her clitoris with his finger. She was close to orgasm as he moved between her legs and pressed himself into her. The pain of her hymen tearing brought her back, and she began to resist and cry out. He would not be stopped and reached down to the floor, picked up her sock, and shoved it into her mouth to keep her quiet. This frightened her, and she fought Noah. He grabbed her arms and pulled them over her head and pressed her into the mattress as he plunged into her body again and again.

He climaxed and pulled out of her. Using the skills for which he had trained her, she kicked his naked balls as hard as she could. The pain was excruciating, and in an eruption of anger he grabbed the phone on the table by the bed and struck the right side of her face. It knocked her unconscious and her body went limp. He couldn't tell if she was alive, but then she began to struggle in a frenzied way, unable to draw a breath. Before he quite understood what was happening, she quit breathing.

Noah looked down at her naked body lying lifeless on the bed, and panicked. For minutes he just stayed that way, gradually calming himself. He told himself that if she hadn't behaved the way she had and kicked him, he wouldn't have killed her. He would have been nice to her. He liked fucking her. It was her fault she was dead. He had watched as life drained out of her. Looking at her, he became aroused again and masturbated looking down on her body.

When he calmed down, he looked around the room and at Rachel, and began to think of what he needed to do. No one from the community or the police knew he was here. No one had ever seen him with Rachel. He got dressed, packed Rachel's clothes in his duffle, and went down to his truck. He opened up the camper shell and pulled out her sleeping bag, went back to the room, and stuffed her body in it. He carried her out as if she were still asleep in the sleeping bag and put her on the foam pad lying in the truck bed. If anyone looked, if they noticed her at all, it would seem she was asleep.

He went back to the room, got his duffle, carefully wiped the phone down with soap and water, and looked around the room making sure there was nothing to find. There was no blood, and he straightened the bed. They had already paid. It was just a guy getting off to an early start.

As he pulled out onto the road, panic began to overwhelm him again. What if a policeman stopped him and found her body? He drove carefully with his lights on and his speed a mile or two under the limit. For about an hour he just randomly drove around. He could not think what to do with the body that wouldn't leave evidence that might betray him. When he had been in the service, he had watched crime shows on television; they were popular with his unit. He had seen how meticulous the police were. Just as dawn was breaking he realized that he was hungry. A mile further down the road he saw a White Castle and pulled into the parking lot.

After he turned off the engine, he sat for a time telling himself that there was no reason anyone should suspect him of anything. He told himself he had to be careful not to act paranoid or freaked out. It was like going into combat. When he felt his breath become stable, he got out and went into the restaurant.

Inside the building, all hard white and black surfaces, it was quiet. There was only one other customer, a trucker. Noah sat at the counter and the server came over.

"What would you like?" the man asked. Noah noticed he had large red birthmark across the left side of his face. He had to make himself stop staring,

"Let me have three hamburgers and a coffee."

As he ate the small square hamburgers with onions and cheese, an idea of what to do finally began to take shape in his mind. He would take her body up into the forest and bury her.

He wiped his mouth, took a final sip from his coffee mug, wadded up his paper napkin, and went up to the counter and paid his bill. He drove down State Route 30, stopping at a Shell station where he filled his tank. As he was paying his bill he saw a trucker's book of maps and bought a copy. When he got back to his truck, he pulled over to one side away from the pumps, took the map book out. Pennsylvania State Game Lands 159 looked to be the densest forest he could easily get to, and he drove out of the station down US-30 until he connected with the interstate system, following the map. He left the interstate and began moving down smaller and smaller roads. The trip took almost three hours, through territory he had never seen; just the drive away from Lancaster on the empty roads made him relax. He listened to music and realized what an un-Amish thing that was to do. When he entered the forest the map didn't matter anymore, and he drove by random choice, moving northwest into the forest.

Another half hour and he was on an unmarked road, when he saw a low wood and brick building off to the left. As he drew closer he could see that it was abandoned. The windows were covered with sheets of plywood, some of them splattered with spray-painted graffiti. When he got to the building he pulled in behind it and saw that because of the structure's shape there was a pocket that could not be seen from the road. He pulled into it carefully. It was probably overkill. He hadn't seen another car in more than an hour, but it made him feel safer. Once parked, he opened the back of the cab and looked at Rachel and considered whether to carry her in the bag or just her naked body. He turned to look out the back of the truck, and in the corner of the parking area noticed a rusty fifty gallon drum and decided to burn the bag. If anyone came he would just be a guy who pulled over to camp and built a fire. There would be no evidence she had ever been in the truck, or with him. He pulled the mummy bag down Rachel's body by its foot, then packed it into its little sack and tossed it back into the truck's cab.

He picked up Rachel's body and looked at her naked form one last time and began to get an erection but stopped himself and slung her over his shoulder face down; her body was beginning to stiffen. He reached in and got the entrenching tool he kept in the back, closed up the cab, locked everything, and started walking into the woods. About an hour in, her bowels and bladder released, to his enormous irritation. Some of it went down his shirt and down vest and onto his pants.

The smell was awful, but he had no choice except to continue. He stayed on a slender little used trail until it crossed what he thought might be a deer path, and he took it. There was very little underbrush, so walking was not difficult. After about an hour he stopped at a little stream, put Rachel's body down, and tried to wash himself off with only partial success.

By now her body had stiffened into a permanent U. He picked it up and continued deeper into the forest, leaving even the small trail behind. After another forty minutes it started to rain, and he had to stop and put on a light pullover. He picked her up again, but this time went only another few minutes before he decided to stop. He didn't see any point in going further and couldn't imagine anybody coming up to where he was now. There was no reason for anyone to do so, he told himself.

He unfolded the entrenching tool and began digging a grave. It had to be an odd shape because of Rachel's bent position. The rain increased, and when he was about a foot and a half down, he thought it was enough and put her in the hole, covered it with dirt, branches, leaves, and general forest debris. When he was finished, he couldn't see it.

The walkout by compass was quicker. When he got back to the edge of the forest he stopped and just watched for a while, hidden in the trees until he was certain no one was around, then walked out onto the gravel parking lot and across to his truck. His clothes stank so he stripped and just let the cold rain cleanse his body. He climbed into the cab, pulled clothes from his duffle, and redressed. He had an overwhelming urge to drive away, but he knew he had one more thing to do.

He walked into the woods and gathered fallen pine wood, brought it back, moved the drum under the eaves of the building to get it out of the rain and started a fire in the fifty gallon drum. When it was blazing he went back to the truck, got Rachel's mummy bag, took it out of its little sack, dowsed it with some white gas from his little backpacking stove and threw both bag and sack into the fire. It smelled awful for a while but burnt down to nothing very quickly. When it was down to ashes he looked around and saw nothing that said he had ever been there. He took a rag with a little more gas and wiped down his trucks interior, then threw the rag into the fire.

When it was gone he dragged the drum back where he found it, and let the rain put out what was left of the fire.

He climbed into the truck and started the engine. But to go where? He hadn't thought about that.

As he sat in his truck, he told himself no one knew he had come into the forest with a body. No one knew it was buried hours into the woods. There was nothing to be paranoid about. But that didn't solve what he now saw as his main problem. Where was he going to go? Having grown up in the Amish world he had not travelled very much and had no social contacts outside of that world, except the motorcycle guys he had known after he had left the community and the men he had served with, now scattered across the country or still in the service.

The more he thought about this, the more he thought he could turn his isolation to his advantage. Anywhere he went would be a clean slate. No one would know him, no one knew his story, so he could say whatever he wanted without fear of someone coming forward to contradict him. He thought about going north, but as he worked through that he decided that he wouldn't like the weather. Despite what he had told his father, going west seemed too far away; a world about which he knew nothing, and anyway he didn't think he had enough money to go that far. He would go south, he decided. He went back down a chain of county roads out of the forest to where he connected with Interstate 80 and started what he now thought of as his new life.

Five hours later, when he was in Virginia and saw signs for Hollins, he got off the freeway and drove into the town. By the age of the people he saw on the street, he realized it was a college center. The affluence of the town made him think about his own money, and he decided he had to be careful. Instead of going into a restaurant that looked interesting, he drove by it and stopped at another pizza joint and bar. It was packed with young women. Several wore blazers that said

"Hollins," and he decided that Hollins must be a women's college.

As he ate his pizza, he watched them and began to fantasize about capturing one of them. One slight blonde-haired girl, looking younger than the rest, reminded him of Rachel. As she and her friends laughed and talked, he imagined tying her to a bed, spreading her legs. He imagined the feel of her breasts. He imagined the slipperiness of her vagina as he felt her with his hands, and it gave him an erection.

The girls began to notice him noticing them, and he caught that. A policeman came into the pizza place, and Noah thought it was time to go. He still had several slices of pizza left, so he closed the box, stood up, left with it, and got into his truck. He saw on the map there was a state park not too far away and drove there to camp for the night.

The next morning he got up, ate the last of the pizza, drove back to the interstate and continued heading south down Interstate 81. As he was skirting the city of Blacksburg, he began to hear a noise coming from his clutch. It wasn't much more than a soft sound at first, but it began to get louder. By the time he saw signs on the interstate for Rural Retreat, he knew he had to stop and deal with it.

He took the Rural Retreat exit, not having any idea what Rural Retreat was like, and drove into what he quickly saw was a typical small rural Virginia farming town. The buildings were mostly red brick or wood, with a railroad running through the town. The only really attractive building he could see was an old-fashioned green and white wooden railroad station with a green metal roof, clearly from a past when people travelled on trains. "Rural Retreat" in big green letters was painted on the end he could see, and the whole building looked newly restored. There were a few nice old-fashioned houses back a few streets from the railroad station, but mostly the town was modest and rundown, with empty shop fronts.

He turned onto Main Street and saw a NAPA auto parts store, a Subway sandwich drive-in, and a farmers' Southern States Co-op. A little further along, in a row of rural brick buildings, there was a wooden one that looked like an old barn. Noah, remembering the Amish world, thought it must once have been the blacksmith and carriage repair place. Over the big doors that opened onto the workspaces was a fading red sign with white letters reading, "Seabuckle Motor Repair," and under that in smaller letters, "Cars, Motorcycles, and Trucks".

He pulled into the parking area in front of Seabuckle's. As he got out of his truck, a swine-like man with a shaved head, maybe forty, came out of one of the workspaces. He was about six feet with a hairy chest revealed by a partly unbuttoned too small blue denim shirt.

"Can I help you," he said to Noah.

"Something is wrong with my clutch."

"We can't do it today, but we could tomorrow afternoon."

Noah thought quickly, and said, "I have limited funds, and I know how to do this. Could I pay you to work in the space?"

"Where did you learn how to repair clutches?"

"I learned about motors working at a motorcycle repair shop, and I learned about trucks in the Army."

"You're a vet?" the man asked, as he looked down at Noah's rear bumper and saw the Army sticker. Noah hadn't put it there, but he hadn't taken it off, and he was glad of that as he saw where the man was looking.

"Yeah, Afghanistan."

"What was your unit?"

"First Battalion, 17th Regiment."

"Me too," the man said putting out his hand. "Al Seabuckle."

"Noah Ebersole," Noah answered. He had thought about changing his name, but he wasn't exactly sure how the law worked on such things, and he was afraid of making a mistake. Besides, he thought, why would anyone connect him to Rachel? Accepting that made him relax, and he smiled and shook Seabuckle's hand.

"You know, I wouldn't normally do this, but yeah, you can use that bay and the tools. Give me fifty bucks."

Noah pulled the truck in and set to work. He was about to walk down the street to the auto parts store when Seabuckle came by. "I'll sell you the parts for my cost plus fifteen percent; it'll be cheaper than NAPA."

"That would be great, thank you," Noah replied.

As he worked, he noticed that Seabuckle kept an eye on him. At the end of the day, just as he was finishing the job, Seabuckle came over to him.

"Where are you going?"

"I lost my job... in Baltimore, and I just want to go somewhere new, somewhere that's not a city, somewhere rural. I lived on a farm growing up, and that's what I like."

"You looking for a job?"

"Yes. I've been traveling around and my money's running low."

"You drink a lot?"

"No. An occasional beer, and I don't smoke either."

"Are you a believing Christian?"

Noah looked at Seabuckle, frightened for a moment that there was still something Amish about him. But that wasn't it.

"I am, yes. I take my faith very seriously, as my father does, and his father."

"Well, how about Rural Retreat?"

"I don't understand."

"You're in southwestern Virginia in the Blue Ridge Mountains; doesn't get much more rural than this. And I need a mechanic who can work on cars, trucks and motorcycles. Not easy to come by, and you can do that. I'll pay you twenty-one dollars an hour."

Noah looked around him, put down his tools, and put out his hand. "I'll do it if you know an inexpensive place I can live."

Seabuckle shook his hand, saying, "As it happens, my sister's husband's sister has a single-wide up the mountain she's trying to rent. Nothing fancy, but warm and dry." He looked at his watch and said to Noah, "Are you finished?"

"Yes, I just got done."

"Well tonight's my wife's Bible study group, so let's go down the street to the Country Kitchen. They have the best food in town."

"Let's do that, and I'll drive; I want to test it."

Seabuckle locked up and they drove two miles to the restaurant, which was as modest as the town but centered like the Amish diet on meat, simply cooked vegetables, and potatoes. As soon as his Dutch oven baked brisket with roasted potatoes and boiled cabbage was put before him he felt a sense of good will and luck. He liked the place and he liked the food.

During the meal Seabuckle told him there was good hunting, and as they ate he began to speak about the Primitive Baptist church to which he belonged. How helpful the community was, how important a part of his and his family's lives. It all sounded very comfortable and free of judgment to Noah.

"I would very much like to come to your service, Al. If I am going to be here, a faith community will be important to me."

"Well, it's done then," Seabuckle said with a smile, and they shook hands. He drove back to the shop, where Seabuckle picked up his own truck, and followed him out of town and up a county road into the mountains. About five miles up Seabuckle pulled off the road, down a gravel lane to a hillside with a shabby green single-wide trailer home. Noah liked it immediately. There was a view across the valley, it could hardly be seen from the dirt road; it was very private.

Seabuckle had a key, and they went into it. It was sparsely furnished, almost like an Amish house, with a wood stove for heat and a propane one for cooking. The walls were covered with inexpensive sheet wood paneling.

"I talked to my sister's husband's sister, and they'll rent it for three hundred a month."

Noah did quick math in his head and realized that two days out of thirty would pay for it, and quickly agreed.

"It has its own well and septic. You'll have to turn on the electricity and phone in your own name."

"Could I stay here tonight?"

"I suppose so. There's no sheets or anything though."

"I have a sleeping bag. Not a problem. And I have light. I've been camping to save money."

"Okay, here's the key," Seabuckle said, handing it to him. "We start tomorrow at eight a.m. We'll do all the paperwork then."

Noah walked out with Seabuckle, and as soon as he left, got his sleeping bag and the rest of his gear from the back of the truck. He built a fire in the stove and, when it was going strongly he sat in one of the room's two chairs looking at the flames; he could not believe his good luck. After a while he gave himself over to reliving sex with Rachel and her death, masturbated, and went to bed.

The next morning he showed up ahead of time and was immediately put to work on a Harley motorcycle, then a farm truck that needed brakes. He walked down with Seabuckle to the Subway, and over their sandwiches they did the paperwork. He had thought about it before he went to bed and again when he drove in, and he had decided to keep the smallest possible footprint. He asked Seabuckle if he could be paid in cash because he had no bank account, to which Seabuckle agreed. He had already decided he would not turn on either the electricity or the phone. He had grown up without them and would not miss them. He would just need to buy a small propane generator to run the water pump. The simplicity of the little single-wide trailer with its plain wooden furniture was what he was used to, and it had indoor plumbing. After work he went down to a church thrift store he had seen and bought two sets of worn cotton sheets and two cotton towels. He already had a pillow.

He stopped at the Marathon station and filled up the propane tank that would supply his stove, refrigerator, and the generator, paying cash for everything.

On Wednesday, Seabuckle suggested Noah go to the farmer's market at the train depot, so he went down to see what was going on. It was the last market of the year and there wasn't much produce left, but there were still some cakes and pies, and he bought several; like all Amish he liked home baking.

As he walked around the restored depot, one of the most appealing places in the town, he was struck by how easily his presence was accepted. No one was judging or shunning him. He sought no contact, nor did the others around him. They just let him be, and that was what he needed.

On Friday, Seabuckle asked him to sit with his family at church on Sunday, and Noah was glad to accept. He wasn't very clear on what they believed, but it didn't really matter. As he sat through the service, he liked the music. Looking at the Bible he was handed, he saw the Primitive Baptists used the English King James Bible. The Amish used the German Martin Luther one. He didn't know what the difference was, but it didn't matter. The community attitudes were not that much different, except here he had never been shunned.

After the service, there was a potluck communal meal just as there had always been in his Amish community. While he sat there eating, a girl about Rachel's age caught his attention. He watched her move and imagined feeling her naked body. His reverie was interrupted when he heard the woman sitting next to him turn to her husband and say, "He seems nice, but he is very shy. Doesn't say much."

A woman on the other side of him said, "Noah, do I have that right? You're working for Al Seabuckle? Oh, I'm Sally Wilson"

"Noah, yes, that's right. I just started working for Mr. Seabuckle."

"He said you are a vet and were in the same something or other in Afghanistan."

"Yes, I am, and we were. Who could imagine?"

"Where are you from?" she asked, and to answer her Noah told a story of growing up on a farm and joining the Army after high school. It was all sort of the truth—close enough, Noah thought, to keep straight.

As he was finishing, Seabuckle and the pastor came over to where he was sitting.

"Care to join us? We were going to step out for a little air," Seabuckle said. Noah knew they wanted to talk about something, and he agreed.

They went outside, standing on the grass not far from the doors, and the pastor said, "I'm Reverend Matthew Willard," putting out his hand, which Noah shook.

"I want to extend to you an invitation to join us, join our congregation."

"I would be pleased to do that," Noah answered.

"We're fundamentalists and evangelicals. How do you see your Bible?" Willard asked.

Noah wasn't sure he even believed in God anymore, but he knew what the answer was to that question. "I'm a Bible man. I think the word of our Lord is made clear in the Bible. I do not doubt that."

"Well, Al," Willard said, looking at Seabuckle. "It seems you were right. I am glad to have this brother in our house."

"I told you. Noah, glad to have you" he said shaking Noah's hand.

He went home feeling secure. He understood the questions he had been asked. In the Amish community they would have been phrased differently, but the impulse would have been the same. Are you one of us? Do you belong? As he stoked the fire in his stove he thought, I've found a new home. His thoughts gave over to his erotic images of the girl he had seen at the dinner, and he masturbated sitting in his chair with the images of the new girl blending with Rachel's naked body on the bed.

CHAPTER FOUR

For a month, Michael and Gilbert ran session after session using targets that had been assigned a rating based on their numinosity. They were testing Michael's idea that intentioned focused awareness added information to the nonlocal informational architecture of the target. It was Michael's hypothesis that higher numinosity, particularly when heightened emotion was also involved, made the target easier for the viewers to perceive.

The day before Michael was due to leave for the War College, he was sitting in his office working on the PowerPoint to go along with the briefing, when Gilbert knocked on the door frame and came into the office.

"I just finished the analysis, and I think we've got it," he said.

"Tell me," Michael said.

"Just as you thought. If a location has been the focus of reiterated intentioned focused awareness, particularly if there has been a strong emotional component to the awareness, it becomes easier for the viewers to see it. The effect is particularly strong when the acts of observation occur over long periods of time. Let me show you," Gilbert said, as he turned on the large screen on the wall in Michael's office and took up his tablet.

"The series we did using cathedrals and warehouses of the same size around the world really shows it."

An image of the medieval Chartres cathedral in France and a large warehouse about the same size appeared on the screen.

"What struck me, Michael, was not just how many people had worshipped at Chartres in the centuries after it was opened, but also the building of the thing. They started in 1145 and it took 26 years to complete it in 1194. Imagine how much focused attention must have been directed at the concept of that building during the course of its construction."

"That's a good point, Gilbert," Michael said, nodding. "It has to be part of the calculation. This is all information in nonlocal non-physiologically-based consciousness being assembled through intention."

"Yes, I think that is what the data is telling us," Gilbert responded.

"This just makes your point stronger, Gilbert," Michael said. "If size alone were the factor the warehouses would be easier to see…"

"Yes, and they aren't," Gilbert finished the sentence. "Warehouses don't attract much attention…

"…Who looks at warehouses," Michael said with a laugh. "But there's more to it, as you've just said. Warehouses are also assembled as quickly as possible. This warehouse is the antipode to Chartres."

"Right," Gilbert said. "We know that both physical and informational entropy makes a difference."

"It could explain how people see ghosts," Michael said.

"What? How would that work?" Gilbert responded.

"A murder or any death, but particularly a murder or violent event, is a short-term high entropy event A physical life ends. Anyone whose attention focuses on the building, particularly if they expect something to happen, can become resonant with the information structure of that event. While I'm away, see if there's anything in the brain data."

"That's the other thing I came up to tell you," Gilbert said, taking off his glasses and wiping them with a little cloth he took out of his pocket.

"Well, don't make me wait," Michael said with a grin.

"The cingulate. It shows up in the therapeutic intention work. You remember Jeanne Achterberg?" Gilbert asked.

"Yes, a very nice person, and a very good researcher."

"She reported the cingulate in her fMRI study. And there are four or five other studies in different disciplines."

Michael looked at his watch, saying, "Listen. This is exactly the conversation I have been waiting to have with you, but I have to cut it short. I have to get this PowerPoint done."

"For the War College presentation?"

"Yeah." Michael answered. "But let's schedule a good block of time when I get back. We're onto something important."

"I agree. I'll leave you to it. I can do any afternoon but Tuesday. How about walking up to Dumbarton Oaks if the weather's fine?"

"You're on," Michael said, and went back to work.

Four hours later, he was finished. He packed his messenger bag with his laptop, closed everything down, and walked out of his office. Karen had already gone. As he was about to leave the building. he remembered that Barbara would be back in a week. An image of her formed in his mind—the wheelchair-bound Nobel Laureate physicist who had a garden apartment in the Hill Institute's basement and was a sometime partner, sometime viewer, and frequent mentor. He locked the door and went down the stairs and out to the brick Georgetown sidewalk that led to his house two blocks away.

Michael had had an extraordinary stroke of luck. One of his most gifted viewers, a French widow whose husband had been an international diplomat, had died, and to his complete surprise she had left him her house. She had no relatives in America, few she knew who were still alive in France. She had noticed that he loved her small eccentric house and had left it to him.

As he came up to the house, he realized his rose bushes needed attention. Because the house was smaller than its neighbors, although the lot was the same size, there was space for a garden in front, on one side, and in back, which was one of the things Michael appreciated most about where he lived. The house itself was a simple white wooden structure with green shutters, dating back to colonial times. The second floor covered only the back half of the house. Michael had put in a white fence and a gate with a rose-covered arbor opening to the small front yard. Fred, the maintenance man and master gardener at the Sacred Heart Girls School, had taught him how to look after them.

He went to the kitchen, took out some organic apple juice, and poured himself a glass. Next he got out some cold grilled chicken breast, made a salad and added the chicken, and carried it over to a dining nook. Opposite the nook was a TV screen, and he turned on cable news. He missed Tracy and her young daughter, Sarah, who was staying with Tracy's brother in Charlottesville, Virginia, and going to the Waldorf School there.

Tracy had been in the Amazon for several months. In preparation she had volunteered to be a remote viewer; that was how they had met. Tracy's interest was the anthropology of consciousness, and in order to experience an altered state of consciousness similar to the ones the shamans described, she had sought out Michael. She had become convinced shamans were actually into something real, and she realized she would not understand it unless she experienced it. Michael had taught her remote viewing; she was good at it from the start, and he asked her to become one of his viewers.

It made Michael smile that when she had shown the tribal shamans what she was doing at the Institute, they had accepted her in a way few outsiders would ever experience. He was convinced the book that would come from her months in the Amazon was going to make her internationally recognized for her anthropological research. He had encouraged her to go, but he missed her. Her satellite phone connected them, but not often. Tracy was immersed in her work and seldom reached out to the twenty-first century.

He got an early start the next morning. The Army War College was only a two-and-a-half-hour drive, but he had to be there for lunch. As he was driving out of town on the George Washington Memorial Parkway, Jake Garth called him; they hadn't talked in several months. Since Garth worked for Sam Kassimir, Michael didn't take it as a social call. Garth had been one of the agents he and the lab had worked with when they stopped the terrorist attack. He had liked Garth at first, and then not liked him. But since the event Garth had gone out of his way to be helpful, and the rift had healed. Michael also felt a sense of obligation. He was sure Kassimir had arranged for several of the grants the Institute had received from the National Institutes of Health, and Health and Human Services.

"What's up Jake?"

"I know you're off to the Army War College…"

"I gather they checked with you…," Michael responded.

"They did, and I'll let you know what the feedback is."

'Thanks, I'm on my way up there now. So what's up?"

"Sam would like you to come see us when you get back. We have a problem; we think your group's unique talents may be able to help us, and we might need some of the officers you are about to brief. That's why Sam wanted you to do it."

Wheels within wheels, Michael thought. He knew there was no point in asking for further information over the phone, so he just said, "I'll have Karen call you and work out the date and time."

After he hung up, for several minutes he couldn't stop thinking about what Kassimir wanted. Whatever it was, it was in that secret world where nothing was quite what it seemed.

His thoughts gradually moved on, and as he drove up PA-94 guided by his GPS, what he mostly thought about was what they were learning from the research. He was deep into numinosity and entropy as he drove down Pitt Street through the gates of Carlisle Barracks, the Army's War College, a graduate school for men and women the Army thought were destined to become its generals.

Once on the base, a combination of the college and the town around it, he parked in front of Theodore Roosevelt Hall. It was an enormous impressive structure of brick and light tan stone with a rotunda above an entrance which had a large stone eagle and the words "National War College" in the arch.

As arranged, Michael texted the number he had been given to signal his arrival and walked up the wide steps into the hall. A tall man with short blonde hair, a major in Class A greens, saw him and walked across the floor, putting out his hand. "Robert Barry, Dr. Gillespie, so glad you could drive up. Was everything okay?"

"No problems at all, pleasant drive. Now what?" Michael asked.

"Let me take you for lunch at the officer's club," Barry responded, steering Michael back outdoors. As they walked across the campus, Barry said, "To get briefed I read the media about what you did, and how your team found the bomb and kept it from exploding. It made me think about Afghanistan."

"Something you experienced while you were there?"

"Not me, but there was an E-6 in my company; I was a newly minted captain," Barry said with a smile. "Anyway, this sergeant was known to everybody as the guy to lead a patrol. He just seemed to know where the bad guys were. It was uncanny. All my men wanted him to lead because fewer of them were injured when he led. When I asked him how he knew, he said there was a kind of glow to the information. Impressions just came into his mind when he was focused on leading the patrol. He told me, 'I get a sense of how many of them there are, and what they have by way of weapons.'" Barry's manner was matter-of-fact.

"I have heard of something similar. Back in the 1970s, during Viet Nam, the Marines ran a study and found many examples of the same thing. I found the study when I started doing my research."

"Really, I had no idea; it was just something I experienced," Barry said, as they entered the officers' club dining room. As they sat down, he added, "How does this relate to your own research?"

"It's another form of nonlocal perception, akin to the remote viewing research we're doing," Michael explained.

The conversation continued throughout the meal, and Michael was surprised by how open Barry was to the idea of nonlocal consciousness. He'd seen it work; it was not an abstraction to him. He saw it pragmatically like a soldier would, and he was uninterested in materialist objections.

At two they walked back to Roosevelt Hall, and Barry took him into a handsome rather formal lecture hall. There were about a hundred men and women, all in uniform, already seated.

Barry took Michael up to a colonel who introduced himself as Colonel Randall Bishop. "Glad to meet you, Dr. Gillespie. Jake Garth speaks very highly of you. I understand you are going to brief us on your remote viewing and consensus methodology."

"I'm going to try," Michael said, and once again felt himself being submerged into the world of the military and their interest in the tactical applications of his work.

Colonel Bishop introduced Michael, and for the next hour he walked his audience through his research, describing the sessions, how he and Gilbert did the analyses, how in the applications studies independent experts were used. He illustrated all his points with pictures and videos of actual remote viewing sessions, the targets matched with the drawings of the viewers. He could hear the rustle of murmured conversation when the officers saw the high degree of correlation.

When he was finished he answered questions for another half hour, then there was a break and the audience filed out. As Michael was closing his Mac laptop, Barry reappeared with a very strange look on his face.

"The district attorney of the county and the commanding officer of the state police are outside. They want to see you… they say it's urgent."

Michael could tell the major was not sure how to take what he was saying.

"Did they tell you what is was about?" Michael asked.

"No."

"Well, I haven't been here long enough to have done anything wrong," Michael said with a laugh, "so it must be something else." Barry relaxed slightly, then led him out of the hall, where a man who looked to Michael like a conservative Washington politician was waiting. Standing next to him was a state police colonel in uniform.

"This is Dr. Gillespie," Barry said by way of introduction.

"My name's Gordon Baskerville," the district attorney began. "This is Colonel Tim Johnson," he said, indicating the trooper commander.

"A pleasure; what is it you need from me?"

"We need some help, and we think you might be able to provide it. Is there someplace we can go and talk, Major?" Baskerville asked.

Barry led them down the hall to a room set up for small meetings.

"In here; I'll see you're not disturbed," Barry said, closing the door as he left.

Michael, the trooper, and the district attorney sat down around the small conference table.

"A young Amish girl has gone missing," Johnson began.

"She's just short of fifteen," Baskerville added, reaching into his suit jacket for a manila envelope from which he took a snapshot of a young girl, and slid it across the table.

"Gosh, she's good looking," Michael said, looking at the picture.

'Yes, she is," Baskerville responded. "Unusually so, I think."

"And she has disappeared? Maybe she just ran away," Michael said.

"Amish girls don't run away," Baskerville responded. "There is a period called Rumspringa, when they can choose to leave, but few do," Baskerville explained. "But that usually doesn't start until sixteen, and it's not a surprise; the family and the community know their plans. The Amish live in very tightly knit communities in a way it is hard for us English to understand."

"English?" Michael asked.

"Their name for all non-Amish people," Johnson answered.

"So, what do you think happened?" Michael asked.

"She disappeared a month ago without a word," Baskerville said. "That just doesn't happen, and the community is very agitated about it. They are pressing very hard for us to do something... to resolve this."

"We have searched every place we can think of, done hundreds of hours of investigation," Johnson added.

"The Amish are a significant presence in this county, as you may know," Baskerville said. "They want this resolved, and we've run out of ideas. That's why we wanted to talk with you."

"We've read about you, of course. We know about the nuclear bomb," Johnson continued.

"We learned you were coming to speak here..." Baskerville added.

"And you thought we might be able to help," Michael said, looking at the two men.

"Exactly. What do you need? The briefing book..."

"...Nothing…"

"Nothing. How can you possibly find someone with nothing?" the colonel said in a challenging tone.

"You're right; I could use that picture," Michael said, pointing to it.

"You don't even need her name?" Johnson asked incredulously.

"No. The picture will be enough, although it will stay sealed in its envelope. I do not cue the viewers with any information, just ask them what is the current location and condition of the individual pictured in the sealed envelope."

"You don't tell them it is a girl?" Johnson tried once more.

"No, I don't tell them anything. Can I have it?" Michael asked, putting out his hand.

"Can I have that as well?" Michael added, indicating the opaque manila envelope Baskerville still held in his hand. He passed it over to Michael, who put the picture back into it and put the envelope in the pocket of his tweed jacket.

"When are you going back?" Johnson asked.

"My plan was to drive back now. I'm at Georgetown University, as you probably know. I'm the Director of the Lynn Hill Institute for the Study of Human Capacities."

"Where will you start?" Johnson asked.

"We'll start with Lancaster County and expand if we need to. You really think something untoward has happened with this girl?"

"As I said, Amish girls don't run away; they don't just disappear with no word. So yes, we think something has happened to her. One possibility is she has been kidnapped. We had trouble with a gang of methed-up city boys from Philadelphia who terrorized and molested Rachel and some other girls earlier this year."

"I understand the urgency. How do I get in touch with you?"

Both men took out cards and wrote on the back. "These are our private numbers," Baskerville said, "as well as our direct emails. How long will this take?"

"I think seven sessions should do it," Michael answered, "so say three days, and another two days to do the analysis. Early next week I think."

"What will you give us?" Johnson asked.

"I don't know. But it won't be general, it will be very specific. Remote viewing is not a search technique, it's a find technique. I'll be giving you her present condition..."

"Alive or dead?" Baskerville asked.

"Yes, alive or dead. I believe you'll get a very specific place to search, also what I think the session data is telling us is to be found there, and why she is in that place in that condition. But we've never looked for a missing child before, so this will be a first."

"I'll be honest," Johnson said. "If it hadn't been for the nuclear bomb thing, I wouldn't believe a word you're saying."

"I understand. But there is the nuclear thing," Michael responded with amusement.

"Yes, there is that," Baskerville responded for both men.

"Well, let me get to it," Michael said, standing. The others stood when he did, and they walked out of the little conference room together. Baskerville and Johnson went on, and Michael went over to Major Barry, who was sitting on a couch waiting for him.

"How did that go?" he asked Michael.

"A missing child," Michael answered. "We've never done anything like that, but we'll see."

Barry walked him out to his car but asked no questions, which Michael appreciated. He had already begun to think about how to do the probe, and all the way back he thought about the girl and worked out the way to find her.   The

Institute had never deliberately undertaken a criminal case. But, reduced to its essence, the Amish girl probe, as he had decided to call it, was just a form of outbound target protocol. They had done that hundreds of times. Over and over he had asked viewers to describe where someone was located at the time of the session, something neither of them knew intellectually at the time. Viewers gave him detailed descriptions. It worked no matter how far away they might be. It was one of the ways his experiments had taught him that in nonlocal consciousness, space and time were information points but not limiters.

As he pictured the girl in the context of her life and what Baskerville had told him, he realized that this time there was a numinosity factor that should help him. An entire Amish community held this girl in focused intention. They wanted her to be found. He realized he was assuming she was alive.

CHAPTER FIVE

As soon as Michael got back to the Institute, he began planning the seven sessions. He rang Karen and asked her to book them, and she got back to him an hour later to say the first was the next day with Weldon Shelcraft at ten a.m.

That evening he had the feeling they were embarking on something bigger than he knew. The next morning as he walked into the Institute he felt the same way, and was eager to get started. He found Weldon waiting for him in the kitchen, having a cup of coffee with Karen.

Weldon was a powerfully built Black man in his late twenties with a shaved head, who moved with the grace of a pro-athlete and had an easy going kind of charisma. He was seven feet tall, and impossible not to notice. As usual, he was dressed in white painter's overalls with his name stitched in red over his left breast pocket.

"Good morning, Karen, and you too Weldon. How goes it? Good to see you," Michael said.

"No complaints, Boss. Barbara just sent me an email last night saying she's going to China next week."

"Yes, she sent me the same."

The Barbara being referenced was Barbara Strickland, who was also a Nobel Prize winner. And quite flamboyant. She and Weldon made the most improbable couple Michael had ever seen, but from the moment they met they had been inseparable. Barbara had played a big role in Michael's life as well; she had gotten him the initial money to create the Institute from the Hill Family Foundation.

"What have you heard from Tracy?" Weldon asked as they walked up to the egg.

"She's having a good summer. Her altered states research is going well; she thinks it will be a series of papers and then a book."

"Like that Castaneda guy you knew?" Weldon asked.

"Yes, good comparison. We can only hope her book does as well as *Yaqui Way of Knowledge* or *Journey to Ixtlan*," Michael said with a laugh.

"May it be so, Boss," Weldon replied as they settled into their chairs in the egg.

They each put on their biometric helmets. Michael logged in the session, they meditated for twenty minutes, and then he handed Weldon the same opaque manila envelope Baskerville had given him. It was sealed, so the picture could not be seen.

"Weldon, in this sealed envelope is the picture of a human being. I would like you to go over the map on your tablet asking the question, 'Is this individual within the area depicted by this map?'"

Weldon ran his large hand an inch or so above the tablet.

"I don't think so. I think this person is a female and she is not in the area this map represents."

"Okay. Can you please describe this individual, and tell me about her present circumstances and condition?"

Weldon sat in thought for a moment, then began to speak with pauses in his speech. "This woman... no not really a woman. A girl, but becoming a woman. Fourteen...fifteen... very pretty White girl. But she's dead," Weldon said, and looked up at Michael. "You didn't know?"

"No. I have been assuming she was alive. Tell me about her."

"She was part of some kind of religious community. A man... she knew him... she went with him voluntarily. I get a sense of confusion on her part, then clarity. It wasn't what she expected... but then it was too late," Weldon said, rubbing his hand on the envelope. "He raped her... it didn't start out as rape, but that's how it ended. He put a sock in her mouth, so she couldn't cry out."

Weldon looked Michael in the eyes then said, "There is something wrong with this guy. He gets uncontrollably angry… very confused in his head. Not stupid, quite smart actually, but angry and confused. After it was over he was very sorry, but it was too late."

"How did she die?"

"Several things. The sock in her mouth, but he also hit her."

"Then what?"

"When he calmed down he was very scared. He stared at her body for a long time," Weldon said, then shook his head. "This is nasty stuff, Michael. This is a bad dude, not stable."

"Where is her body?"

"Outdoors."

"You are life-sized standing near the body; what do you see?"

"Trees. I'm in a woods; no that's not right. This is like a forest. There's a stream nearby. I hear running water. There's also a big wall… no maybe it's a cliff."

"How did her body get there?"

"He put the body in, I think it's a pick-up truck, but with a cab… He drove around… This is weird Michael, but I think he got hungry and ate something."

Michael fooled with his tablet and called up a map of the eastern United States which also appeared on Weldon's tablet.

"Weldon, I know the scale is too large, but we have to start somewhere. Can you locate the body and make a circle as tight as you can? We'll have to do other sessions, I know."

"I can try," Weldon said, and began to pass his hand over the table.

"What are you looking for?"

"Barbara showed me; I'm looking where I feel a sense of warmth. Here," he said, and made a circle. It was still in Pennsylvania, but north and west of Lancaster.

"That's it, Michael. I'm losing focus."

Michael logged out of the session and wondered what Gilbert and Coyote would get in their session. As he and Weldon were coming out of the egg, he saw them coming down the hall. They all exchanged greetings, and Gilbert and Coyote went into the egg, taking their place.

And hour later Gilbert came into Michael's office.

"I think the girl is dead."

"That's what Weldon thought as well."

"It was a guy; he raped and killed her."

"Ditto again."

"I'll get started getting it transcribed and broken into concepts, and start the analysis to find the patterns," Gilbert said. "Who are we doing tomorrow?"

"I've got Jefferson Yu, and you have Constance in the afternoon. Karen checked your schedule and booked her for four-thirty."

"All right. I'm going home," Gilbert said, and left. Michael went out into the walled garden the Institute shared with Barbara. Ivy-covered walls edged a brick patio. A fountain softened the street noise, and a red Japanese maple graced the back. Michael had just sat down when his phone rang. It was Tracy, and he immediately went back inside, answering as he walked.

"How are you, my love? How are things going?"

"I'm just back at my tent from a coming of age ceremony for four kids in the tribe. It was fascinating," Tracy answered as he got into his office. "What are you up to?"

He told her of his trip to the Army War College and the Amish girl, and was about to tell her what the viewers had told him and Gilbert, when Tracy interrupted, saying, "I'd like to do that. In fact, I have an idea..."

"You're in the Amazon in Brazil. I don't see how it would work. It would cost a fortune to do a session on the satellite."

"That's not what I had in mind. I will work with the tribal shamans and call you back with the data. I won't be the viewer, they will; I'll conduct the session. What are you using as a target?"

"I have a picture in a sealed envelope. I could take a picture of the envelope and send it to you with the Xgate satellite data service."

"That works. Do you have a map?"

"The one we started with isn't big enough, so I'm now working with a much larger scale; it will take several sessions to pin it down. Do you have a printer down there?"

"Yeah, I do. You remember the portable one I bought? And I have that folding solar panel to power everything. Send both images down."

"Alright, we better hang up, this costs what, six dollars a minute? I'll call you back as soon as I have everything ready."

As soon as they hung up, Michael went down to the egg, retrieved the envelope, and took a picture of it with his iPhone. Then he went back to his office and did a screen capture of the eastern U.S. map.

He called Tracy back and uploaded the two images.

"How are you going to do this?" he asked.

"I am going to invite the shamans to do a ceremony with me. I'll present the protocol as a ritual. They'll be very comfortable with the idea, because they have a similar ceremony to communicate with other tribal groups with whom they are allied."

"Fascinating. It's brilliant. I've never heard of anyone doing anything like this."

"We'll make a paper of it," Tracy said, and they laughed together.

"I love you," Michael said.

"I love you to too. I'll call back with what I get."

The next morning Michael did a session with Jefferson Yu, a slender middle-aged second-generation Chinese-American whose family had escaped from China in 1965 during the chaotic period called the Great Leap Forward. He and his wife owned a hardware store in Bethesda, Maryland. They had seen Michael on a television program and had sought him out because of Jefferson's strange precognitive hunches, one of which had saved his family.

Michael was not surprised when Jefferson's session went much like Weldon's and Coyote's. But he took particular note that, like Weldon, Jefferson thought the killer had stopped for a meal with the dead girl's body in the back of his truck, and he drew a picture of a little stylized castle that he associated with the restaurant.

He had just returned to his office when Karen buzzed him to say Jake Garth was on the line.

"What can I do for you, Jake?" Michael asked when he picked up the phone.

"Sam wondered if you could come out to Langley this afternoon? We'll leave a pass for you at the gate."

It wasn't really convenient, but Michael felt he owed Sam and agreed.

After lunch he drove out to the CIA, got through security, and went up to Sam Kassimir's office on the executive floor.

Kassimir greeted him and they went into his office where, besides Garth, Herbert Waterman and Stanley Potter, Kassimir's principal deputies, were also present. Both Waterman and Potter, Michael had learned after the nuclear bomb event, had initially been skeptical of the Hill Institute's remote viewing program. But they couldn't argue with the results, and when he had seen them once or twice over the subsequent months they had been supportive.

"Oh dear," Michael said with a smile when he saw them. "If you two are here then something alarming must be up." He went over and shook hands with each of them, then sat where Kassimir indicated.

"You're not wrong," Kassimir answered, wiping his hand over his heavy features. "We need to find something."

"What's gone missing?" Michael asked.

On the large screen on the wall Waterman called up a PowerPoint; it displayed the image of a large missile.

"Okay," Michael responded, his confusion evident.

"We have reason to believe," Kassimir began, "the North Koreans, in a month or maybe a few weeks after that, are going to fire a ballistic missile like this one."

"They've done that before," Michael responded. "What's different this time?"

"This is strictly classified, you understand, Michael?"

"Of course."

"It is not the missile that is the issue, it's the warhead."

"What about the warhead?"

"It's a MIRV," Potter answered.

"A MIRV, what does that mean?" Michael asked.

"Multiple independent reentry vehicles. That means it's not one warhead but several."

"That sounds ominous," Michael said.

Potter got up and walked over to the screen. He pointed at the top of the missile, saying, "We think that under this shell are three warheads, each of which can be targeted for a different location."

Waterman took off his rimless glasses, polished them with his tie, and looked at Michael. "We need to recover this missile before anyone else does," he said emphatically.

"Michael," Kassimir said, looking directly at him, "could your viewers tell us in advance where this missile is going to come down so that we could position a recovery team near that location and find the missile and at least one of the warheads?"

"Well, we've never done anything like that before, but conceptually, at least, it should be possible, yes," Michael answered, looking at each of the men in turn. "There are no guarantees of course. You *do* understand that," he said with emphasis.

"Yes, of course," Kassimir responded. "But your track record is pretty good, and we don't have a better option," he said, then added. "Let me stress again how highly classified this is."

"I assumed that," Michael replied.

"What do you need?" Waterman asked.

"As tight a map as you can provide."

"Tight?" Potter asked.

"We'll start with the smallest landing area, however big that is, and work our way down through several sessions. You know how it works," Michael said. "It would also be helpful if we could have a picture of the missile."

"That's rather difficult, for reasons you surely understand," Potter said.

"If the issue is people seeing the picture, that's not a problem at our end. You could put it in a container sealed up in some way that makes you feel comfortable. Doesn't make any difference to me."

"Why does the picture matter, anyway?" Kassimir asked. "If I understand your protocol you don't show it to the viewers."

"It's hard to explain, Sam," Michael answered. "Start with consciousness as the fundamental, spacetime as a manifestation of intentioned consciousness. The picture plays no visual role, the sort of thing you would expect. Rather think of it as a search term in a Google search."

"Then why can't you just say, 'missile'?" Waterman asked.

"The research evidence tells us that this is all an information phenomenon," Michael answered, with an encompassing gesture. "The missile is an information architecture that has been defined, so the more closely we can do that the better; that's why the picture matters. The selection of this particular missile from all the missiles in the world is made concrete by that picture. The viewers aren't looking at the picture, they are opening to nonlocal consciousness guided in part by your intention and interest in this particular missile, as defined by the unseen picture. That state of consciousness is what guides the viewers. Just as a search term does on Google."

"I have an idea," Waterman said. "Does it matter what form the image is in?"

"No. In the earlier remote viewing research they reduced the lat-long coordinates of locations to code and put that information on a microdot, an image about the size of a period at the end of a sentence. Didn't change results," Michael answered.

"Then suppose we give you the image on a thumb drive with a password. If you put in the wrong password the data on the drive self-destructs. I will put the map on another thumb drive that is unsecured. We don't know the location yet, but we should in a few days. We're waiting for some... data. So, thumb drives, would that work?" Waterman asked.

"Nobody has ever done that experiment," Michael answered, "but conceptually it should. It's like the lat-long experiments I told you about. I'm willing to try."

"Good, thank you, Michael," Kassimir said. "Jake, set that up with crypto and get it to Michael as soon as we have the map data, will you." It wasn't a question.

"Of course, Sam," Garth answered, then looking at Michael, "I don't know how long it will take to arrange this, but I will bring it by the Institute when it's ready."

"Works for me. Is that all, Sam?" Michael asked, and when Kassimir nodded affirmatively, Michael got up, shook hands with each of them, and turned to leave.

"When can you start?"

"Right now we are doing another first-time effort," Michael said, then explained about the Amish girl project.

"Interesting." Kassimir responded. "Keep us apprised about that as well, if you would," he said as Michael got to the door.

As he drove back, Michael began planning the protocol he would use for what he now thought of as the Missile Probe. He had learned that naming projects from the start helped everyone involved to hold the common intention that was so critical to success.

CHAPTER SIX

By late that afternoon, everyone had gone home except Michael. He was going over the first take of data on The Amish Girl Probe, as it was now officially logged into the database, while he waited for the government car to bring Barbara Strickland in from Dulles Airport. She had been in China for the last two weeks as part of the American delegation representing the National Science Foundation, and she texted him while driving back to ask him to dinner.

When he heard the elevator, he knew she was back. Twenty seconds later the elevator door opened, and Barbara came rolling out. She was in her fifties, not so much beautiful as intriguing. She had thick red hair and large green eyes. She came across as very physical in spite of being in a wheelchair that looked like something created by German racing car designers. She was sexy. Barbara had been severely injured in a car accident, t-boned by a drunk driver just after she had returned from Sweden with her Nobel.

"How are you, dear boy?" she said as she rolled into his office, speaking in her distinctive Louisiana Bayou accent.

Michael got up and went over to her, leaning over and kissing near both of her cheeks.

"Good. How was the trip?"

"Quite interesting. I'm having the food brought in so let's go down to my place."

He walked down the stairs and she took the elevator, and they went into her apartment in the basement of the Institute. They each got an iced tea and were sitting in the windowed conservatory at the end of the building, overlooking the walled garden. The conference had been in Shanghai, and Barbara was describing the stunningly modern skyline when the doorbell rang. Michael got up and answered the door, taking the food packages from the courier. When he got back, Barbara had set the table.

"I ordered those grilled shrimps you like, grilled asparagus, and iceberg wedges with blue cheese dressing."

"A woman after my own heart," Michael answered, and sat down at the table. By now it was dark, and the garden was lit by a full moon. They began to eat in silence, then Barbara began talking about her trip again. But after a while, she said, "What's happening with you?"

Michael told her of his experience at the Army War College, but then said, "I don't want to tell you anything more. I'd like you to do a session."

Barbara looked at her phone and said, "Can you do it at 11 a.m. tomorrow? I'm staying home tomorrow to catch up on emails, phone messages, and read the papers from the conference. Will that work for you?"

"Absolutely," Michael said, logging in the appointment on his phone so Karen and Gilbert would know not to book that time in the egg.

"Then help me clean up, dear boy, and I am off to bed. My body is not quite sure what time it's in."

When they finished he left, walking back to his house, thinking about both the amish girl and the missile project.

Promptly at eleven the next morning, he and Barbara settled into the egg for their session.

After the log in and the meditation, Michael gave Barbara the task instruction, "Please describe for me the present circumstances and conditions of the individual pictured in this sealed envelope."

Barbara was silent for a moment, then began. "This is a woman... no a girl... no a child. Maybe fourteen or fifteen. She's very pretty. Very attractive to men, even though she is really a child." Then Barbara stopped. "Michael, this child is dead, she was murdered."

"Before we go there, tell me about her."

"She was part of a very strong community. Religious... I think. They wore distinctive clothing. This is very sad, Michael. This is just awful."

"How did it happen?"

"He got her to go away with him. She didn't really understand."

"He?"

"Yes. The killer is a he. Early twenties. He does and does not belong to this community. I don't know what that means," Barbara said, looking into Michael's eyes.

"What can you tell me about him?"

"He's damaged. I mean literally. Something is wrong with his brain. I get a sense of explosions, several of them. I'd say this guy was in the service, but I debrief that as analytical overlay," Barbara said, making the debrief because it was an analysis statement, not a nonlocal perception.

"Okay. How did this come to happen?"

"They went off together. This boy had serious lust in his heart. He was obsessed with her. He groomed her. He taught her something, but he is not a teacher."

"And?"

"They went off. There's a truck involved. A good ole' boy truck. Dark color. Has a cab on the back. He just couldn't control himself. I keep seeing her naked for some reason. I don't know why. They were in a motel... Cheesy looking. There was an odd chemical smell in the room. He went for her. At first it was just kissing, and she could handle that, but it got out of control."

"Are you okay about going on, Barbara?" Michael asked, concerned that the imagery might be too unpleasant.

"Oh yes, I want to stay with this. Very much. I want to catch this guy. This almost happened to me when I was about this girl's age."

"I understand. Go on."

"She was a child really. At some point he pulled off her shirt, then her pants. I'm not quite clear on the sequence here. It's like I get flashes. High emotion moments," Barbara said. Then, "Pay attention to that, Michael."

"I did. High numinosity events. While you were gone Gibert and I have been working on this."

"Good. Let's go back."

"Target."

Barbara closed her eyes for a moment, took a breath, opened her eyes and said, "I'm sure she fought back and screamed. He took one of her socks off and stuffed it in her mouth. He took her belt off and tied up her hands. I'm not even sure he was dressed. He penetrated her, but she still kept fighting. She kicked him in the balls, and he fell off her.

"It was very painful, and he was filled with rage," Barbara said, and at this point she was almost in a trance, lost in the vision that filled her mind. "He took the handpiece of the phone and smacked her on her right temple. It knocked her unconscious. It broke something. He raped her again, and when he was done he realized she was no longer breathing, and he panicked."

"Go on."

"He sat for a long time and stared at her. I have a sense of water. I think he bathed or showered. I just have this sense of him being in water. He cleaned up the room and carried her down. I get a sense of a small metal space, so I'll debrief to say he put her in the cab of his truck."

'Then what?"

"He didn't know what to do. He drove around with her body in the back. He put her in something flexible. He drove around for quite a while, then headed out of town. He hadn't had breakfast, though, so he stopped someplace. He ate a hamburger. No maybe more than one. It was some kind of fast food place. Hard surfaces, shiny metal. While he was eating he came up with a plan. He drove out of town up into a wooded area."

"You are with him, you are life-size, what are your perceptions?" Michael said, restating the intention task.

"There was a building. On the left as he went up a hill into the woods. I don't sense other people. It was abandoned, boarded up. I'll make a drawing," she said, and did so on her tablet. "He pulled behind it and got out her body... Put her over his shoulder. She was a slender girl... didn't weigh much." Barbara stopped, and Michael saw that tears ran down her face.

"We have to get this bastard. At first I felt sorry for him, there's something wrong with his head. But this is cold-blooded."

"Do you want to stop?"

"I do not," Barbara answered emphatically, and sat with her eyes closed for a moment. Then she began again. "He took her out into the woods. He carried her until he got tired. He is a strong sturdy man. Six feet. He suddenly came into focus for me. He's in his twenties. He does a lot of physical work. He also smells of oil or grease."

"Then what..." Michael asked to encourage Barbara to keep talking.

"He got tired and laid her down on the ground. He'd brought some kind of shovel. Short. It folds. Here, I will make a drawing for you," Barbara said, and sketched out a short-handled shovel. "He dug a shallow grave and put her body in it, then covered her with some dirt, leaves, branches," Barbara said.

"Look at this map," Michael said, and on her tablet a map of Pennsylvania and its adjoining states came up. Barbara looked over the map and marked a quarter sized circle.

"It's there, and I am wrung out. This kind of viewing is very tough, Michael."

"I can see that. So, let's close," and he logged out.

"We have to find this man, Michael."

"Both the police and the district attorney seem highly motivated."

"Oh my, look at the time. I have to go. They are sending a car for me, and it should be here in about ten minutes. Let me know if I can help any further," Barbara said, taking off her helmet and turning in her wheelchair as Michael opened the door.

When he followed her out, Gilbert and John Sacks were just coming into what had been the house's dining room.

"Let's get together at four, if that works," Michael said after greeting John, a very elegant man who was the most sought-after interior designer in the District.

"Okay. I'll see you then, and I will get my session analysis done as soon as we finish," Gilbert responded.

"I'm going to go upstairs and do mine," Michael said, and went up to compare Barbara's session with what they already had. A picture of what happened was emerging, as well as where the Amish girl's body was.

At four, Gilbert knocked as he always did on the jam of Michael's office door.

Across the three screens they called up the data from two sessions at a time, looking for consensual images or comments.

"I don't think there's any doubt that this girl is dead, do you agree?" Michael began.

"She was killed by a man, older than herself. She is almost fifteen. Agreed?" Gilbert asked.

"Yes."

As they spoke, they manipulated the data into the hypotheses the fieldwork by the police would test.

When they overlaid all the location choices, a consensus zone like a Venn diagram emerged in something called Pennsylvania Game Lands 159.

"What are game lands?" Gilbert asked.

"Haven't a clue, except I think it probably has something to do with hunting," Michael said as he did the search. "Yes, these are lands reserved for hunting and fishing in that state. Let's see what Google Earth can tell us."

"Oh, it's all forest wilderness," Gilbert said when the image came up.

"Yeah, that's going to be very tough to search, and the circles cover what... four square miles?"

"More, I think," Michael said measuring, "maybe six."

"I think we ought to take a team up there and fine tune it," Gilbert suggested.

"We haven't been asked to do fieldwork, only provide location information."

"Why don't they want us to do the fieldwork?" Gilbert asked.

"I don't think they want people to know how they're getting the information."

"Well then, you're right; it's going to be a lot of work and take a lot of people."

CHAPTER SEVEN

Deep in the Amazonian rain forest, so far from modern civilization that it seemed more a dream than a reality, in a small clearing along the bank of an unnamed river that fed into the Rio Negro, Tracy was preparing.

She was living with a tribe she had sought out after reading about them in two papers published in journals an anthropologist would not normally look at. Although similar in many ways to other Amazonian tribal groupings, these people had a deep spiritual belief that they guided another tribe they called the younger brothers, that at some distant time had broken off and left the area. It was this belief that had been the focus of the first paper she had found in a psychology of religion journal.

A year later, in a neuroscience journal, she had found the second paper. This one was about a tribe in Columbia, hundreds of miles away from the first. This group, the paper recounted, believed they were guided by another older tribe they had never seen, but upon whom they could call for help whenever their need was real.

Neither research team had made the connection between the tribes, not only because the papers were written by researchers in different disciplines, but because neither of them accepted the idea of nonlocal consciousness and so never took either tribe's beliefs as anything more than myth and magical thinking. However, the anthropology of consciousness was Tracy's field, and she saw the connection immediately.

What had caught her attention in the two papers was that both tribes recorded their experiences in their imagery. And the imagery was the same in very specific details across both tribes. To her, the connection was obvious. Something real was going on.

Tracy remembered Carlos Castaneda from her graduate school reading. As a young Hispanic anthropologist interested in shamanism, he had challenged anthropology's assumption that shamans were just individuals who were ambitious to achieve status in their tribe, and so through mastery of their tribe's beliefs and a kind of performance magic, they achieved their goal. Castaneda presented the case for shamans being individuals who worked with altered states of consciousness through disciplines like meditation, often along with the use of psychoactive substances, in order to experience nonlocal awareness. In those states, processes like healing through conscious intent could be achieved. In the 1970s, Castaneda's challenge that to understand a shaman one had to walk a shaman's path tore anthropology apart. Tracy was a child of anthropology's next generation.

Before attempting to contact either tribe she felt she needed to experience nonlocal awareness, to open to the altered state of consciousness shamans described. She wanted to objectively verify under rigorously controlled circumstances what was real. She had sought out Michael because his remote viewing research was the closest experience she could find to what she saw in the two papers.

She was awarded a Richardson Fellowship that same year, and it gave her enough money to go into the Brazilian state of Amazonas. It took six more months to get permission to contact the tribe, which had only had the one previous contact by a Brazilian missionary who had written the first paper she had come across. Finally, though, permission came through, thanks to some help from Barbara Strickland, whose name carried a lot of weight with the National Science Foundation.

Getting there had been a trip out of a novel for her. A tale of ever smaller airplanes, arriving finally at Santa Isabel do Rio Negro, a town of less than eight thousand deep in a jungle of more than two million square miles. Then from there by water in smaller and smaller boats, until she arrived in one of the Amazon's distinctive sharp-bowed canoes at the tribe's river encampment.

She remembered how alone she'd felt as the canoe pulled away and went back downriver. She had contacted the original researcher and learned from him that the tribe was untouched and peaceful if not threatened. Her instinct was that a lone woman would not be threatening, and so it had proved. Initially the tribe had treated her with bemusement and a polite uninterest, except for the shaman.

He had come to her that first day, as soon as she was given permission to stay in the village by the tribal elders. A man about forty years old, trim and fit like the rest of the tribe, wearing nothing but a loincloth. He was heavily decorated with totem objects and body paint, and both ears were pierced.

They had begun a series of exchanges, part pantomime, part spoken because they shared no common language. Over the following weeks, though, they had worked out a patois. She had done her best, in answer to his questions, to share what she had done in Michael's experiments. Had given him a demonstration by accurately describing something he had hidden, in the process showing him how her tablet worked. The exchange had given them a bond, and she realized her demonstration and questions had given her authenticity that the shaman recognized. She came to understand that he saw her as a colleague, a shaman from another tribe, and accepted their differences as interesting but irrelevant.

Her reverie was interrupted by the arrival of her main contact accompanied by three other shamans from villages along the river belonging to the same extended tribal family. She had met these men before but did not know them as she knew the shaman with whom she had been working, and wondered how the session would play out. She had a plan, but she knew these strong-willed men, who were used to deference, would have ideas of their own.

As they came into the clearing where she sat, she could see they were in ceremonial dress, and understood that to them opening to nonlocal consciousness was an integrated part of their spiritual culture.

They had with them some fish of a species whose name Tracy could never remember, as well as other food, and after acknowledging her they set about building a fire and grilling the fish. She understood that they were shaping the experience she had planned into their culture. Later, as they sat eating the fire-grilled fish, Tracy looked at the four shamans. As they sat on woven mats under the thatched roof of a small pavilion, its sides open to the air, she explained to them what she wanted to do.

She hadn't been sure before arriving whether she could deal with the diet but, in fact, she loved it, and saw now why Amazonian tribes have the healthiest arteries in the world. It was an active life of fishing, hunting, some simple cultivation, gathering the nuts and berries that abounded, and ritualized ceremonies centered on states of consciousness. Although superficially different than the Kung Bushmen of the Kalahari or the aborigines of Australia, whom she had previously studied, at a deeper level this Amazonian tribe had taught her that like the Kung and the aborigines these people were not primitive; they were very sophisticated, only based on a different world view. Like her earlier trips, her weeks in the Amazon had shown her there were a lot of ways to be a human, and this time, because of her work with Michael and remote viewing, she understood the tribal worldview at a deeper level.

After the meal she mimed out remote viewing and asked the men to be her viewers. They listened respectfully, then spoke amongst themselves for some minutes and countered that it was her culture, so she should be the one to be the viewer. They would, they said, help her have a stronger experience; and in spite of what she had told Michael, that is how they decided to do it.

The next day she and the others fasted, and in the early evening she gathered with the shamans around a fire. They spent the next hour chanting and drumming, which Tracy, thanks to Gilbert, knew was a sophisticated way to create brain entraining that reinforced common intention. As the evening wore on she realized that Michael was right: all such religious rituals empirically developed over generations were basically protocols for opening to nonlocal consciousness.

One of the shamans brought her a pipe made from a length of bamboo and a carved stone bowl. In it he put the crumbled leaves of what Tracy had worked out was a mix of Salvia divinorum and some other jungle herbs. He lit it for her and indicated she should breathe it in which, following his gestures, she did four times, holding her breath as he indicated for several seconds each time.

She handed the pipe back to him. As they had arranged, one of the men pushed a key on her solar charged tablet, and her own previously recorded voice gave her the task instruction. The shaman then pushed a second key to activate recording and propped the tablet up to video her. The image of a Brazilian shaman in the depths of the Amazonian jungle pressing a key on an electronic tablet made her laugh out loud as she felt herself falling under the influence of the drug. Her eyes closed as the image of a young girl came into her consciousness.

"It's a young girl... she's very pretty" she said, as the shamans around her continued a chanting drumming ritual in the background.

Then she saw the girl on the ground, her body being covered with dirt, leaves, and branches.

"She's dead. she's been murdered, but raped first," and she saw as if from the girl's perspective, the man plunging his body into hers. She felt the pain of the girl's torn vagina as he penetrated her and realized she had been a virgin. The man's smell pervaded her senses. It was as if she were in the room, and she was filled with rage and fear.

"She knew this man, trusted him, was attracted to him. But he turned into a monster. She fought him... and tried to scream. He picked her sock up off the floor and stuffed it into her mouth." Tracy was staring into the jungle darkness, but in her consciousness she was in the room with the girl, and it was terrifying.

"He kept on until he came. As he withdrew, and relaxed against her, she kicked him in the balls. The pain enraged him. He grabbed something, she never saw what, and struck her on the right temple as hard as he could. Something broke in her head and she went unconscious," Tracy said, swept away by the emotions she felt. She had curled her body into a fetal position lying on the mat.

"He got up and went into the bathroom and showered. When he came out she was dead. He became very frightened and didn't know what to do. He cleaned up.... There was a bag, canvas, I think. I get a sense of green. He carried her out as if she were asleep. It was still dark out.... He had a truck or a van. Not new. Dark. Maybe... black. He put her in the back and drove around as the day began trying to figure out what to do. He stopped to eat. Meat. I can taste it. Three." She was filling with rage again, rage and fear. Tracy stopped for a minute and looked around her. She could see the shamans in the flickering fire light. Then the drug pulled her back, and she did not resist.

"He drove around some more, then went up into a forest. Lots of trees. Very green. An old structure... he went behind it." As she was talking the Salvia divinorum began to wear off, and Tracy came back to the jungle and the night. She became aware of the four men sitting around her silently. Tracy took the tablet, called up the map and drew a circle where she thought the girl's body was located, then closed the session. She looked at her watch and realized it had only been thirty minutes, but she felt as if she had been away on a long trip. It was disorienting, and she was not altogether clear what she had said. It was like remembering a dream. She had never had an experience like it before. She went back and sat down for a few minutes just processing what she had experienced. She got up and went to each of the men, thanking each one, then went off to get some sleep.

The next morning she was up with the rest of the tribe at dawn. Strangely, Washington. D.C. and the Amazon were in the same time zone, and as soon as the lab was open she contacted Karen. Michael wasn't in yet, but she uploaded the files. Karen, who didn't look at them, responded with friendly talk, then said, "I think it's weird talking to you in the Amazon jungle and me at the Institute in Georgetown. Very weird."

"I agree," Tracy responded. "Say hi to everyone," she said as she hung up.

When Michael got in, Karen told him about the files. He immediately went up to his office, downloaded them and watched them, and then transferred them into the transcription program. He was fascinated by what he saw, the chanting and drumming in the background, and to imagine Tracy in that jungle clearing along the river. She had sent him some shots, so he could picture where she was. As he was finishing, Gilbert came up to his office, and Michael told him to download Tracy's session and watch the video as he read the transcript, then ring him and they would go for lunch.

A while later, Gilbert called and they walked down to M Street for lunch at a new Portuguese restaurant known for its fish dishes.

As they ate and shared some wine, they went over the session and found they were in close agreement.

"Both of us have been getting very detailed information. Unusually so, and I think this is because the target is highly numinous and there is a lot of informational entropy," Gilbert said, using a piece of bread to wipe up the wine caper sauce on the fish.

"I agree. The death of the child. What could be more emotionally compelling, more numinous than that? Death is a high information entropy transition."

"Yes, I agree," Gilbert answered. "Have you looked at Tracy's map? I think we have a consensus zone," Gilbert said, and pulled up the master composite map on the tablet he had brought with him. Looking Michael in the eye, he said, "That has to be one of the strangest remote viewing sessions ever done," he continued, pushing his glasses back on his nose.

"Definitely a singleton," Michael responded.

"Okay, I'll get everything together. How about we meet tomorrow, say eleven?"

"Perfect," Michael said as he paid the bill. "I have to get back to start on the Missile Probe. I haven't done much on it since we got embroiled in this. God, this is an awful business," he said as they left the restaurant. When they got back to the Institute, Gilbert went to his office and Michael to his.

He found it difficult to concentrate on the Missile Probe, but finally settled into it and decided that in nonlocal terms it was a pretty straightforward precognitive project. Where would the missile come down? The trickier part was when.

At the end of the day he called Jake Garth. Knowing that Jake would say nothing on the phone, he simply asked if the paper work was in order yet.

"As it happens, it is. Suppose I come over tomorrow and bring it to you?"

"I've got a busy morning, but if late afternoon works, that would be fine."

"I'll stop by on my way home," Jake replied, and they hung up.

At five thirty the next day, Jake walked into the Institute just as Karen was getting ready to leave. She alerted Michael and told Garth to go on up, then left. When Garth got to his office, Michael asked him to sit down, saying, "What have you got for me?"

"I brought another thumb drive with a map of the area where we now think the missile will go down. But I don't see how it is going to help much; it is just thousands of square miles of Pacific Ocean"

"That doesn't matter. If I understood you and Sam and the others at the meeting, you want us to tell you where this thing is going to go down in the area covered by that map. Is that right?"

"Yes, exactly. We want to position a recovery team so we can get the warhead and see if it is indeed a MIRV."

"MIRV is what again?"

"Multiple, independent, re-entry vehicle."

"Are other countries looking for this thing as well?" Michael asked.

"You bet. The Chinese, the Russians and, of course, the North Koreans themselves," Garth answered.

"Don't they all already know where to go? I mean, they're allied with North Korea in various ways."

"That's why we need you and your team. The others have a general idea, at least we think they do, so they will be positioned to make the recovery. But it is a big area. That's why your team's fine-tuning is so important."

"Okay, let's take a look," Michael said, as Jake handed him the drive. He booted it and got the sign-in, and Garth read out a long string of letters, symbols, and numbers. On the central of Michael's three monitor screens the Pacific Ocean appeared with Japan on the left.

"We think they are going to overshoot Japan to make a point. They've done it before, but not with a MIRV warhead."

"Do you need any information about the MIRV part?" Michael asked.

"Mostly what we need is the location, but sure, if you can tell us in advance anything about what we are going to bring up, that would be interesting. I confess we still don't have a very clear understanding of what you can discover with remote viewing."

"I'm not sure I do either," Michael said with a laugh. "But so far the only limits are things which require analysis, cognitive thinking, names, numbers, identifying by name what something is, that sort of thing. It might help if we had a date..."

"Sorry, we don't know that. Only that they are very close to doing this launch," Garth answered as he got up. "I've got to go. My wife has her sister coming to visit, so I have to get back."

After Garth had left, Michael sat for a while in his office thinking about how much his life had changed, and how much his research had shifted, since Tracy had had her first vision on the balcony.

CHAPTER EIGHT

Gordon Baskerville was clearing his final action items for the day before leaving for a political debate. He was up for re-election, and his Democratic opponent was running ahead of him according to the private poll he had commissioned. He began thinking about issues where he would be vulnerable and was sure the case of the missing Amish girl would come up. It had provoked outrage in the Amish community. He knew it was not just the girl herself. The response also arose from a growing grievance amongst the Amish that their children, particularly their girls, were not being adequately protected from non-Amish teenage boys and men when they went into Lancaster or any of the malls in the area. It was a problem that had waxed and waned for years, but with the rise of social media and the growing nativism, this kind of public thuggery had gotten worse.

He had talked with the Lancaster police and the state troopers, and had his prosecutors focus on it. But in politics nothing was more important than the immediate optics, and several recent events and now this missing Amish girl had become major issues.

Gordon had been District Attorney for a decade, inheriting the job from his father. The Baskervilles had a history in Pennsylvania that dated back to colonial times; they were a presence in the county and a force in Republican politics. On the walls of his office were pictures of Gordon and his father with American presidents going back to Kennedy. This was the first time he had felt seriously threatened politically.

As he drove to the high school where the debate would take place, Gordon thought about what was going to happen.

What should he say? What could he say? He thought about that and decided he would focus on his increased emphasis on the issue, citing Tim Johnson, who would back him up. Could he mention the Hill Institute, he wondered? No, he decided; it could be seen as bad judgment or dabbling in witchcraft, or worse, trafficking with Satan. He told himself that if Rachel Swayze's disappearance came up, he was just going to have to take what Don Schmidt threw at him. That made him think, when was he going to hear from Gillespie, anyway?

He got to the gym and was met by his campaign chairman, but just as they began to talk, a group of three Amish leaders walked up to him.

"Mr. Baskerville. Could we have a word with you," one of them said. In their broad brimmed black hats, starkly plain black suits, staring at him with very serious expressions, they were a presence.

"Bishop Fisher, Bishop Zook, Bishop Beiler. Nice to see you all. I am sure you want an update on Rachel Swayze. We have contracted with some specialists to try to locate her," Baskerville said as they shook hands. "But I must tell you, if something has happened to her... if she is dead, you have my commitment that the investigation will continue until we find who did such a heinous deed."

"That is very good to hear," Bishop Zook replied, a hard-faced man from another age, Baskerville thought.

"I will have more to say about this in the debate, but I must get on gentlemen... the schedule... you understand," he said to the bishops as his aide led him away.

"Of course, and thank you; that is exactly what we wanted to know," Bishop Beiler responded.

The gym was crowded with people, more than usual, more than he had expected. Many were Amish.

Schmidt spoke first and began his attack immediately.

"Perhaps Mr. Baskerville will tell us what he is doing about the opioid crisis that has so affected our county because of inadequate law enforcement."

Twenty minutes later, as the debate was coming to an end, Schmidt took his last shot; he brought up Rachel Swayze and challenged Baskerville with the same issue the bishops had raised. As soon as he did, Baskerville could feel a shift in the room.

He took a deep breath. How much could he say? How much did he trust Professor Gillespie? At least he had Tim Johnson's statement; he was so glad he had pressed for that meeting. He looked out and decided to go with his gut.

"I'm glad you asked that, Don. I was going to hold a press conference tomorrow. Now I can get it out a day in advance. Let me deal with it in sections. First, as to the Amish girls and young women being bothered when they go out to shop. I have met with Colonel Tim Johnson and Chief Weirtzer in Lancaster. It began a week ago. We didn't talk about it at the time, because we wanted the kind of people who do such things to get arrested and word to get back to Philadelphia and the other cities where these men and boys come from, that people were getting arrested. Nothing is better than word of mouth. I can tell you also that we have put officers in place, both uniformed and plain clothes, to stop incidents from happening in the first place; and if they do, to expeditiously arrest the perpetrators, prosecute them, and send them to jail."

Looking around the room he could see heads nodding, and added, "In addition to all that, we are also consulting with appropriate specialists in our search for Rachel." He could feel the room shift again. "And I want to state this commitment publicly. We will not stop until we know what happened to Rachel, and if she has been harmed, we will pursue and capture whomever did it." He looked at the faces and knew he had won the evening. As he stepped down from the podium and people began to come up to him, he knew his election had hung on that answer.

That same evening, as Baskerville was in his debate, Michael and Gilbert were carefully going through the session data in the Institute's conference room, putting the remote viewing drawings up one by one on the big screen along with the data that had been analyzed and processed into its patterns.

"The girl is dead, agreed," Michael said.

"Yes. Murdered, by a man who was a 'teacher but not a teacher. Jefferson, Barbara, Constance, and Tracy all agree on that."

"Yes, and when they are saying it, the biometric data we have, on everyone but Tracy, correlates with past accurate observations, so we have high probability."

"What does it mean, though?"

"I don't know, some kind of instructor but not a formal teacher?" Michael answered.

"Okay, as to location. Six of seven of the viewers say the body is in a woods or a forest. Look at these drawings," Gilbert said, and called up a sequence of drawings all showing multiple trees.

"I agree. But there is something official about these woods, I think. Three sessions make that point."

"It's state game lands, I believe. When I saw the consensus zone, our most likely location..."

"...Yes, four of the seven, but we take all the identifying information off the map, so how do you know?"

"I brought it up on Google Earth; it's obvious why he would choose one of them."

"And there is some kind of an abandoned roadhouse or building off the road a bit. One storey building," Michael said as he called up the images. "Looks like something built in the 1950s."

"Yes, he parked behind the building and took her body out of his truck, I think, although it could be a van. But I think a truck because three of the viewers mention a cab."

"Agreed," Michael said, nodding his head for emphasis.

"He dug a shallow grave, put the body in and covered it with dirt, branches, and leaves," Gilbert went on.

"Should be easy to find, I would think," Michael said, sitting back down. "And we're agreed about the sock in her mouth, and the man striking her on the right zygomatic arch."

"With the phone..."

"...Yep."

"And let's not forget that weird low a priori business about his stopping to eat hamburgers..."

"... Three," Michael added. "With the girl's body in the back of the truck. What do you make of that?"

"That this is a guy who has gone numb, who is damaged in some way. So, what now, great leader?" Gilbert asked.

"I wish you wouldn't call me that."

"I'm only half in jest," Gilbert said, looking Michael in the eye, which made Michael blush.

"We are agreed, then, so I'm going to write up the report and send it to Baskerville," Michael answered, without commenting on what Gilbert had said.

It took most of the next day, but Michael finally got the protocol and hypotheses document completed. It described in detail what they had done, how it had been done, and the hypotheses developed from the session data to be used to guide Baskerville's fieldwork. Looking at the final .pdf he was going to send, the thought occurred to him that it really was a double-blind, really almost triple-blind, experiment, as rigorous in its execution as anything they did in the laboratory.

He composed his email, added the .pdf attachment, and sent it off to Baskerville and Johnson.

CHAPTER NINE

Baskerville came back from the courthouse to find Michael's email and its attachment in his inbox. He immediately downloaded it and printed it out, cancelled his appointments, and began to read it.

He was amazed at the detail. How could people in Washington, D.C. know about events weeks in the past that took place hundreds of miles away? He didn't really know how to process that, and he began to get nervous. How could he possibly explain this to other people, the religious community particularly? Had he made a terrible error?

He reached for the phone and called the one person he could talk to, Tim Johnson at state police headquarters.

"Tim. You remember going over with me to the War College?"

"To meet that professor? Of course. I'm glad you called, I was going to call you. I just got an email and an attachment from him. What's going on?"

"Have you read it?"

"Not yet, Have you?"

"Yes, but I'm not really sure what to make of it. I'd like you to read it before I say anything."

"Glad to..."

"... then let's talk... and Tim, I think we should hold it just between ourselves."

"I understand. I can't do it right this minute; unfortunately, I've got a staff meeting, and then I have to inspect the new station. But I will read it tonight and get back to you first thing."

Tim Johnson printed out the report before leaving his office. He preferred reading things on paper.

He had lived in Lancaster all his life except for his time in the military police in the Army. His dad had been a policeman, and so had his grandfather. He knew Lancaster was a conservative world. One of the reasons he thought he and Gordon Baskerville got along was that they were men following family traditions dating back generations. Just as his family was in law enforcement, a Baskerville male in each generation served the county in some legal capacity.

It was Marge's craft group night, so after work, instead of going home, he treated himself to the Gibraltar Grille in Washington Square, his favorite because they served wild caught seafood. Once there, after asking for a glass of the craft brewed beer, he started with the chowder and ordered the wild Alaskan halibut with Jerusalem artichokes, scalloped potatoes, and asparagus. As soon as the chowder and beer arrived, he propped the Hill Institute report up on an overturned peppershaker and began to read, keeping at it as he ate.

The protocol of using multiple viewers reminded him very much of his own work. Interview multiple witnesses, as not everyone saw everything, and everything they saw they did not accurately report or just missed altogether. But by putting things that were similar together one could get a pretty good idea what happened.

The location part and the map had nothing comparable in his world. But the scenario the viewers provided made sense to him. This was a damaged man; over the years he had seen a lot of people who became uncontrollably angry and acted out. About a third of policework revolved around that.

He wondered if the killer could be a vet, and then considered what that would mean. It eliminated anyone in the Amish community. That immediately put him in mind of the meth-heads and gang boys who had been causing problems.

The next morning he called Baskerville, and they set up a time to meet at a conference room in the courthouse. When they got together, Baskerville asked him, "What do you make of this?"

"I called the FBI earlier and asked them if they knew anything about remote viewing. They didn't really say very much, except that if it was done correctly it could be useful. I asked them if they knew a Professor Michael Gillespie and the Hill Institute, and they told me they were aware of him, and that he, the Institute, really, were receiving government funding. And they reminded me about the nuclear incident. On balance, I think we have to take this seriously."

"I agree. The location is out of the county, though, so I will have to..."

"...Not a problem," Johnson said. "My jurisdiction covers it. How do you want to do the search?"

"Police. Fire fighters. State rangers."

"Agreed."

"It's not going to be easy, though. Those game lands the state runs can be rugged. Heavy forest. A lot of manpower is going to be required."

"Can the county cover the cost?"

"I don't see any way around it, so yes," Baskerville answered. "Do you think we should use the Amish?"

"Highly motivated. What would we tell them?"

"We had information."

"From an informant?"

"Yeah. It's the truth... always the best way. We just don't say they're psychics," Baskerville said, smiling at Johnson, and they both laughed.

"Thank God, at least it's not hunting season yet," Johnson responded.

That same morning, following Michael's meeting with Jake Garth, Michael came into the office and told Karen to begin scheduling sessions. Having sent off the Amish Girl report, it was time to move on.

After lunch Karen came up to his office, telling him, "I've got seven sessions set up as you asked. The computer has randomly assigned you to Weldon, John Sacks, and Jefferson Yu. Gilbert will take the other four. You can't do any more sessions because you have to be at NIH for the neurobiology seminar."

"Oh God, I had completely forgotten about that because of this business with the Amish girl," Michael said.

"I'll post the schedule to everyone's calendar. You start with Weldon tomorrow at eleven. Oh, and thank you by the way. The little Waldorf doll was a great success. Susan carries it everywhere." Susan was Karen's eighteen-month-old daughter. Michael had given the child the little knit doll stuffed with lambswool when he had gone over to have dinner with Karen and her husband, Jeff, a newly minted neuroscientist who had participated in several of Michael's fMRI studies; that was how he and Karen had met. She had just graduated from Chapel Hill and had come up to Washington, where a placement agency had sent her to the Institute. She and Michael had hit it off immediately, and she was now the office manager.

As soon as Karen left, Michael called Garth.

"We're ready to boogie," he said when Garth came on the line. "I'm asking you for a final check for time," he added.

"As of today, six weeks; I just got that by the way," Garth responded.

"Got it, six weeks it is," Michael responded. Garth said goodbye and rang off, leaving Michael once again feeling as though he had gone through the looking glass into another world. Part of it was that Garth would say never say anything specific on the phone, so their conversations were always truncated and cryptic.

Gilbert came up late in the afternoon to go over the new project. Michael told him, "The best date they can give us is six weeks, but honestly, Gilbert, I think that's the weak link."

"Why?"

"They have arrived at their window based on some kind of intelligence and rational analysis. You agree?"

"I would assume so, yes."

"What if they're wrong? I mean, if you think about it, what's the real point of this drill?"

Gilbert thought for a moment, and answered, "Where it comes down."

"Yes."

"Okay, let's focus on that, then let's try to get the date through a second set of sessions using the Associated Remote Viewing Protocol."

"I like it. But in the first sessions let's get an approximation; it will make things simpler the second time."

"Yeah, I agree. Let's do that."

The next day, Weldon came up to the office at eleven and they went down to the egg. Once there, they meditated and prepped for the session. Michael gave Weldon the task instruction: "Weldon, contained within this thumbdrive is the picture of a missile. When it is fired it will come down somewhere. Your first task: Will it come down in the area depicted by this chart?"

Weldon slowly ran his hand over the tablet. He didn't know how it worked but he had learned from Barbara that when his hand went over the requested target location he felt a very slight warmth. With his hand flat and his fingers together, he moved slowly from top to bottom, left to right. Then just to be sure, he went through the whole routine again.

"Yes. It comes down in the area covered by the chart."

"Would you please pinpoint it as closely as you can?"

Without hesitation Weldon moved to an area of ocean east of the Japanese islands, and taking up the stylus he drew a circle a little smaller than a quarter. "Here," he said.

"Alright," Michael said. "You are life-sized; you are standing next to what goes into the ocean. Where are you?"

"Underwater. But it's weird, I am on top of a mountain," he said with a kind of bemused look on his face.

"Look at whatever it is. What do you see?"

Weldon closed his eyes for a moment, then opened them and looked at Michael. "Something went wrong. I feel like this thing was supposed to break into pieces. It didn't. There are..." he counted them off on his fingers, a trick viewers used because getting numbers was too analytical and cognitive; they were rarely right. But by visualizing first one part, then another, bending his fingers one at a time could produce the number. "Four pieces, I think. But still together. But not secure. It's caught at the top of the mountain. But if something jarred it, it would slip off and slide into a deep hole."

"Could you make a drawing of this thing? Look at it and please sketch it for me." Again, Weldon closed his eyes and sat silently for a moment. Then taking up the stylus, he called up a new page and began sketching, talking to himself as he did so.

"There are four tube shapes. There is a metal cover over the whole thing. It was supposed to blow off, but it didn't. There is an electronic box at the core of this thing, whatever it is. Something went wrong, it didn't work; that's what happened."

"Do you have any sense of when this will occur, Weldon?"

"Very soon. I'll debrief two weeks."

Michael was stunned by his answer but said nothing.

Weldon put the stylus down and looked at Michael. "That's what I get. I'm losing focus."

Michael nodded, logged the session out, quickly looked through the biometric data, and thought it had been a good session. "It looks good, thanks Weldon."

"No problem. But it is not going to be easy to get this thing. Warn them it is right on the edge of a big drop-off."

Two hours later, Gilbert was in the egg with Coyote. After the preliminaries and the task assignment, Coyote looked at the tablet showing the chart. He just sat and stared at it for quite a while in silence. Gilbert watched the biometric data. Suddenly there was a spike in the cingulate area of the Native American's brain, and he leaned over and drew a small circle.

"You're life size," Gilbert said. "You're standing at the site. What images come to you?"

"I'm underwater... deep underwater. But I am also on a precipice. The seafloor is far beneath me."

"Can you make me drawing?"

Coyote sketched a mountain. "It's seems weird, but I am on a mountain."

"Can you see the thing in the thumbdrive?"

"Yes, it's pointed, looks like the top of a missile, but that's a debrief," he said, and drew a cone shape. "Something's wrong with it."

"Can you expand on that?"

"I feel like this thing was supposed to break into pieces, but it didn't; it's still all together. It's wedged between two rocks... no, not rocks, bigger than that. One piece is part of the mountain, the other is like a boulder," he said, and made another simple drawing. "I think this thing could fall off the mountain. If it does it will go much deeper."

"Any sense of when this will happen? Don't try to analyze, just your gut answer."

"Soon. I think everyone will be surprised. I get the sense there's a lot of pressure to launch this thing. An urgency. I don't know why, but that's the sense I get."

"Okay, anything else?"

"Yeah; whoever we're doing this for, tell them this thing could explode."

At the end of the day Michael went down to the kitchen at the Institute and was pouring himself a cup of coffee when Gilbert, who had just completed a session with Constance, came into the room.

"You want to talk about it?" he asked.

Michael responded by going over the highpoints of his session with Weldon, and Gilbert listened quietly until he was finished.

"We have three of the seven sessions, and it is already clear, I think, there is a lot of consensus, and a considerable sense of urgency. What stood out for me beyond that was the warhead did not function properly..."

"Yes," Michael agreed, "that's my take as well. The MIRVs were supposed to separate, but they didn't, and there are four of them, not three as I was told. Let's go to the conference room; there's something I want to show you."

They walked over to the conference room and called up the sessions, one on each screen. "This thing is on top of a mountain. The chart has no details, but I looked up the location on Google Earth. It's the Kita Koho Seamount."

"For now," Gilbert answered, getting up and pointing to drawings from all three sessions. "All three sessions describe it as being on a mountain, but they also say it could fall off."

"Yeah, I got that," Michael answered, then circled transcribed statements from all three sessions. "Look at this. All three suggest this thing is going to launch in two weeks or less. That's radically different from the time frame Jake gave us."

"Yes, I noticed that as well. But the biometric data suggests they're right. What are you going to do?"

"I'm going to take Jake to breakfast tomorrow."

"All right. We've got four more to go, so things could change, but I think that's a good move. They should have a heads up. It will take time to get things in place."

The next morning Garth and Michael met at the Georgetown Inn on Wisconsin Avenue for breakfast; Michael liked their eggs benedict.

Jake listened without interrupting as Michael went through what they had so far.

"But the big issue, and the reason I wanted to get together with you even though we're not even halfway through, is that we have a location consensus, and all three of the sessions we did yesterday had a really strong consensus on the timing."

"What do you mean?"

"You gave me a six-week window. The viewers all see this happening in two to three weeks."

"What!" Jake exclaimed, looking up from his meal to stare at Michael.

"We had two two-week predictions and one three-week prediction. And the biometric data gives a high probability of accuracy based on past success patterns. I was sure Sam would want to know."

Garth gestured for the check and paid it, even though Michael had not finished and neither had he. "Finish your breakfast, Michael, but I have to go. I have to get this to Sam immediately."

"Here's a thumb drive with all the session data including the charts. I wouldn't normally give it out at this point, but when I thought about the logistics involved to get recovery ships in place, I thought it best to do it now. We have four more sessions to go, though; remember that. We are going to do them as soon as we can, and I will call you as soon as we've done them. You should also stress with Sam that it looks like the warhead is on a seamount, a word I just learned by the way. We looked it up on Google Earth; it's called Kita Koho, east of Japan."

"Thanks Michael," Jake responded, taking the thumb drive from Michael's outstretched hand. "I gotta go," and he quickly left the restaurant.

CHAPTER TEN

Tim Johnson was just coming back from lunch when his adjutant caught up with him in the hall. "A ranger from Game Lands 159 thinks he knows where that roadhouse is. It's in the circled area," he told Johnson, who kept walking into his office.

"Come in," he said. "How does he know?"

"Let me show you. First, it's within the circle. Second, look at the drawings. Here's the picture the ranger took with his phone when I asked him to," he said, showing his commander first one and then the other. They both looked at them in silence for a moment, and were struck by the similarity.

"Okay. I see the connection. Alert everyone. We will search on Saturday. If we begin at o-eight hundred, will that give people time to drive to the site? Are the buses scheduled to pick up the Amish?"

"It's about an hour drive for most, so yes sir, I think that is a good time, and yes the buses are set up," the adjutant responded, and got up and left the office.

Two days later, deep in the woods of the Game Land 159 forest, at a weathered boarded-up brick roadhouse back about fifty feet from the road, over a hundred men and women gathered. The morning was damp and chill; it was late fall and it had rained overnight and threatened to begin again.

Johnson spoke through a bull horn. Media cameras were pointed at him, and two helicopters hovered above them.

"All right. As you have been briefed we will form a line, not arm-to-arm but close enough for adjoining men to see each other's area. Make sure you have water and your lunch. We will go to sixteen hundred unless we find the girl, breaking at twelve hundred for lunch."

The men began to sort out by groups in a line along the edge of the forest behind the roadhouse, tightly together at first and spreading out as they entered the forest. Group leaders along the line stayed in touch by radio as the cohort of men moved through the trees.

They searched until noon with no success, ate the generous sandwiches church ladies had made for them, and at one began again. At two thirty, when they were about three miles in, it started to rain. By four when they started back, even in their raingear they were damp. They were back in the abandoned roadhouse parking area at sixteen hundred having found nothing.

As the men stood around, the team leaders came over to Johnson and they went into the bus.

"How many more searches do we do?" one of them asked Johnson after they had debriefed.

"You're a better judge of that than I am. You're the ones who have walked the territory. That's the main reason I called you together. If we assume he parked his truck behind the roadhouse and carried Rachel Swayze's body... we're told she weighed about one hundred and eight pounds...and started from here, how far could he carry her before it became too much of a burden?"

"This was a man in good shape?" one of the team leaders asked.

"Yes," Johnson answered, but he did not want to be questioned about where he had gotten the information, so he quickly carried on, "I don't know... let's suppose he was say, six feet and in good physical shape. What do you think a man would do in such a situation? That's the perimeter of the area we will have to search."

The team leaders, five men and three women, talked amongst themselves and walked over to the map on the large screen on the back wall of the bus. Finally, a red-headed forest ranger who introduced himself as "Eric," about thirty-five, who seemed to have been elected their leader, turned to Johnson, and said, "We think it will take two more searches like today. We think he wouldn't have taken her body out front and across the highway where he could be seen. Why do that when the woods were right there? The problem is, even if he started from behind the roadhouse, we don't know which direction he went. We had a hundred people today, and we still couldn't do everything. It's gonna take two more days. I don't see any way around it," he said, and the other team leaders nodded their agreement.

"All right, we'll start after church tomorrow, and oh eight hundred Monday. Can you all hang on to your people?" Johnson asked them.

Eric answered, "We'll lose some, but may gain some when these people go home and talk about what they did."

"District Attorney Baskerville arranged for everyone who works for the government to be put on temporary orders."

The Amish leader, who had been silent, said, "We will be here; this is important to us. Many of us, like myself, knew this child. How sure are you of the information you received?"

"Ebenezer, I'll tell you the truth," Johnson replied. "I'm not sure how good this is, but neither you nor I have a better option. Correct?"

The Amish man, dark-haired and also in his late forties with a salt and pepper beard, took off his hat, wiped his scalp with his hand, and said, "Yes, Colonel. I think that's correct. I just pray we get some answers."

"Let's do that," Johnson said as he closed his laptop.

Even more people gathered after church on Sunday from both the "English" and Amish communities. Spaced close enough together that they were never out of touch, the line moved out into the northern section of the search area drawn by the remote viewers. An hour later it began to rain again. It didn't change the search, just made it more miserable. By three they had found nothing and turned around, moving faster but still very aware of their surroundings as they trickled out of the forest into the gravel lot behind the road house. The first ones out found Baskerville and Johnson talking under the roller awning that ran down the side of the command bus. When everyone was gathered in the gravel lot, the team leaders came forward and went with Baskerville and Johnson into the bus.

"Nothing," the Amish leader said, and his statement was echoed by them all.

Eric looked at Baskerville and Johnson, and asked, "How good is this information?"

"It comes from a confidential source," Baskerville responded. "We had reason to believe it was credible, or we wouldn't be here. Also, candidly, the only other thing we can think to do is tear up the dump."

"Tear up the dump?" the Amish leader said in horror.

"Yes. When Colonel Johnson and our staffs worked this through, there were three scenarios. First, Rachel left willingly and is alive somewhere, not wishing to be found. As you know, the thinking in your community is that this is extremely unlikely, and I completely understand that. Second, she was kidnapped and is being held captive in some human trafficking scenario. We are pursuing that through the FBI, but it has been unproductive so far. Third, that someone caught her when she went on an errand, which was the last time her family saw her, put her in a car, and took her someplace to rape her. Ended up killing her and then had to dispose of her body and chose this forest as the easiest solution. It's not yet hunting season, so except for a few backpackers and hikers there's no one here. Being observed wouldn't be likely. The roadhouse doubled that by giving him a place to hide from the road. To us that made the most sense and was most consistent with how people who do these sorts of things behave."

The team leaders listened very closely to Baskerville, clearly understood what he was saying, and by expression and gesture made their agreement known. After a moment, Baskerville began again. "There is a fourth scenario that we have now begun to consider. That he killed her and somehow got himself and her body over the fence and into the dump, where he buried her body."

Eric, shook his head, "Oh my God, that would take weeks to search and cost a fortune."

"Exactly," Baskerville answered.

"Well, let's not get ahead of ourselves," Johnson said, taking command of the space with tone and body posture. "There is still a lot of forest to search; it's going to take most of Monday, maybe all of it. So let's go home, get a warm meal and a good night's sleep, and reconvene at o-eight hundred tomorrow."

They all filed out of the bus, went over to their teams and briefed them, and by six thirty, as it was getting dark, the lot was empty.

The next morning everyone had the drill down. The sky had cleared and the crowd shared a sense of determination. The search was easier because the weather was better, although the terrain was steeper. By two thirty, according to GPS, they had covered everything, and by four were back in the lot, discouraged that it had all been a waste of time. Media vans lined the other side of the road. Reporters accompanied by camera and sound crews were spaced all over the lot.

Baskerville and Johnson came out of the bus, and the TV crews moved in. They went over to the microphones the media had set up.

"Colonel Johnson and I would like to thank each one of you. You heeded the call and turned out to help our community and this girl. I just want to say that we will not end our search for Rachel Swayze until she is found. I'm sorry this didn't work, but that is often the case in investigations. I thank you personally," Baskerville said, and yielded the floor to

Johnson, who echoed his words. The group of searchers began to pack up their gear as reporters fanned out amongst them for human interest interviews, asking people what the search was like and how they felt about it. While this was happening, other reporters came over to Baskerville and Johnson for an impromptu presser.

"What's next, District Attorney?" the CNN reporter asked.

"We not sure yet. But we're not giving up."

"We're going to redouble our efforts to find something in Rachel's life that might give us a lead. We'll re-interview people," Johnson added.

After the TV crews were gone, Johnson and Baskerville sat in the command bus with the few close staff who were left.

"How sure are you, Tim, she's not in those woods?"

"As sure as I can be. They searched. They wanted to find her. Some of them knew her."

The two men sat for a moment in silence, then Johnson asked, "What do you think about Gillespie and the remote viewing?"

"Tell you the truth, it's weird," Baskerville said pouring himself a cup of coffee. "You want anything, Tim?"

"No, thanks."

"What I think," Baskerville continued, "is I've never seen anything like it. They were correct about hundreds of details. The roadhouse. It's description. The highway. The forest. Even the rain. It was extremely plausible but..."

"...it's wrong."

"Yes, it's wrong. How could so much be right and yet be wrong. As I said, it's weird."

"What about Gillespie"

"I think they did the best they could. They didn't cost anything, and they worked very quickly. I don't think they're frauds. I mean, they did do the nuclear bomb thing. But this time they're wrong."

"What are you going to do?"

"I'm going to call him and tell him that, if he hasn't already heard about it on television," he said, getting up. "You want to go back with me or with the bus?"

"I have to start the report, so I'll stay with the command bus, thanks."

As he wound down the mountain, Baskerville thought about what had just happened and how he felt about it. He accepted that Michael Gillespie was sincere, and apparently other scientists held him in high regard. There was also the nuclear bomb business. He couldn't just write him off. Also, he didn't really see how all the odd details that were correct could be so by chance. But as he thought about it, that really didn't matter. They had searched Game Lands 159 in the area selected by the Institute team and had found nothing. When he got to that, he called.

The phone was ringing when Michael got home from presenting at the NIH symposium. He knew nothing of the search. It had been swamped out by the two big stories of the last four news cycles, an earthquake in Northridge, California, that was so big it had damaged Los Angeles, and the murder of a Supreme Court justice in his RV at a park in Florida. Except for local coverage, the search in rural Pennsylvania for fourteen-year-old Rachel Swayze, if it was mentioned at all, was thirty seconds going into the break. He was completely unprepared for the call.

"Michael, I wanted to get to you as soon as possible. Have you seen television news?"

"You mean the earthquake and the justice?" Michael asked, confused.

"No. We did the search of the consensus zone you described."

"How careful was the search, and what happened?" Michael said, putting down his bag and sitting.

"The roadhouse your report describes was recognized by a ranger who sent in a picture. It was dead on. Really. Little details, like the decayed drainpipe in the back, were there. We had about a hundred searchers: it took three days... I'm sending you pictures now."

"...and what did you find?"

"Nothing. I'm sorry Michael. We found nothing."

"I'm so sorry, Gordon. It's research; sometimes it works and sometimes, and this apparently is one, it doesn't. I am very surprised, though, that so many details were correct, but the central task was not. It doesn't usually happen that way. But it's research; it is what it is," Michael said, then added, "I am sorry... on several levels, that this did not work. I know it was expensive, and one hundred searchers must have been a complicated operation to coordinate. You have different issues but, for me, studying what went wrong is as important as studying what worked. I hate to ask, but I would really appreciate you and Colonel Johnson giving me as much concept-by-concept accuracy assessment as you can. It may seem an imposition, but that's how we learn."

"I understand, Michael. Neither of us question what you did. We'll do that. And I want to be clear that I appreciate what you did, and I hope you will thank all the viewers. I know everyone did the best they could."

"I appreciate that, Gordon."

"If anything else comes up I'll get in touch. I'll talk to Tim, and we'll do the assessment. Take care," Gordon said, and rang off. Michael stood in the hall at the entrance to his library. He decided to put aside what he had just heard and not think about it. He went into the room and turned on the lights, walked over to the fireplace, laid a fire and lit it, then went back to the kitchen and got himself some fresh-pressed apple juice. Once he was back in the library, he sat looking into the flames and gave himself over to what Baskerville had told him.

He let his emotions of failure and embarrassment sweep over him, and just sat with that. After a while the emotion drained away, and his analytical mind came into play. He took the tablet he kept in his library, linked with the Institute, and called up the session data and the analysis. He had no prior precedent of a consensus zone defined by five of seven viewers being wrong.

The next morning, before he even went in, he called Karen and told her to get everyone involved with the Amish girl probe assembled as quickly as possible.

By the time he got to the Institute, Karen was already on it. Before going to lunch she came into his office and told him that everything was set up for five o'clock, and within a few minutes of five, everyone was in the conference room.

"I have feedback from Gordon Baskerville," Michael began. Then he replayed what he had been told. "I must tell you," he said, standing at the briefing podium, "Gordon sent these pictures to me when we talked. This is really the only part for which we have detailed feedback, except, of course," he said ruefully, "not finding the girl's body."

"Can you give us the girl's name now? I think we'd all like to know," Constance said, and heads nodded around the room.

"Yes, I guess so," Michael said. "This probe seems to be finished. Don't call us, we'll call you. Her name is Rachel Swayze. Here's her picture." The image of a young girl with a white, pleated Amish kopp on her head, wearing a simple dark crimson dress appeared.

"Oh, my God," Weldon said. "She's a child."

"She was fourteen years old, not quite fifteen, just as you thought."

"I don't think this is right, I don't care what they say," John Sacks said firmly.

"I agree," said Coyote. "I saw that girl's body in those woods."

"Yes, exactly," Jefferson Yu agreed.

"It is strange," Michael said, "that so many details are correct, at least as Gordon noted them, and as you can see in these pictures." As he talked Michael put up the image of the roadhouse on the big screen along with the session drawings. The transcribed descriptive statements from the sessions appeared on the other two screens.

"Start with the fact that there was a roadhouse at the consensus location. Then details like the gutter," Michael said, calling up that image. "This is the first time we have ever done a study where the details are correct and the central task is not. I don't know what to make of this. What do you think, Gilbert?"

"I think we don't want to get ahead of ourselves," Gilbert responded, pushing up his glasses. "I don't want to draw any conclusions until we see the feedback document that Baskerville and Johnson are preparing."

"Point taken," Michael acknowledged, "but what is your first impression?"

"That something is wrong. The biometric data associated with past success is present on both location and description of surroundings. I agree with Weldon as a first impression, but I want to see the feedback," Gilbert said, speaking with emphasis.

"You're right. It didn't work; we need to see if we can figure out why."

"There is another scenario," John Sacks said. "And I think it is the right one."

"And that is?" Constance asked.

"That we are right, and they just didn't find it," Sacks replied.

"Have you considered us going up there?" Coyote asked.

"Yes," Michael responded. "But right now, I don't think it's a good idea. We were specifically not asked to. If we went up there without checking in with Baskerville and Johnson, and they found out, it could get embarrassing for the Institute. But if we were ever asked, absolutely. I went through it all last night and came to the same conclusion. I think John is right. I wanted to see what your consensus was without biasing it."

CHAPTER ELEVEN

The next week started with a call from Sam Kassimir asking for a meeting, and Monday afternoon Michael drove out to his office, wondering what was going on. When he got there he found Kassimir, Jake, and Kassimir's deputies, Herbert Waterman and Stanley Potter.

"Come in, Michael. Sit down. Can we get you anything?"

"No thanks. What's going on?"

"With the help of the Oceanographer of the Navy, we've located the Kita Koho Seamount, and we've moved ships into position. It all has to be done very carefully. The Chinese Navy is carrying out operations in the area."

"Yes, I saw the BBC report on how the two destroyers almost collided."

'This is being done as an oceanographic research project," Kassimir explained to Michael.

"That's great. I assume they will use some kind of submersible. The viewers thought it was very deep, even though on top of a mountain."

"We're not sure yet; that's part of why I wanted this meeting."

"I'm all ears. Maybe I could use a cup of coffee," he added.

"Me too," Potter said, and Waterman nodded agreement.

A steward came in, took the order, and came back with the coffee. When they were resettled, Waterman looked at Michael, saying, "We're looking for something quite small which, according to your viewers, is lodged in a crevice on a mountaintop thousands of feet under water."

"Even your consensus zone, small as it seems on the map, in place, is fifty miles across; that's almost two thousand square miles in area," Potter said, picking up from his colleague.

"We want you to design something that can get us closer," Kassimir added. "Remember, this thing is going to come down, and there will be several countries interested in finding it. We're not going to have much time, which is why we are moving the ships into position now."

"Do you have any better sense of the timing?" Michael asked. "That was almost a week ago, and we thought it would happen in two weeks, maybe three."

"Yes, we do," Kassimir answered, then turning. "Stan, tell him."

"Everyone in the world except the North Koreans and your viewers thinks this launch will happen in six weeks to two months. That works for us, because it makes the cover story plausible. An oceanographic ship doing research weeks ahead, who cares. But once it goes off a lot of people care. It takes time to get ships in position, though. We have a small window. But it would be very helpful if we could narrow the search area down."

"I assume no one, even the Koreans, has any idea that the MIRV warhead isn't going to function properly?" Michael asked it as a question.

"Of course not, how could they?" Potter replied.

"Can you do this?" Kassimir asked, looking Michael in the eye.

"I don't know," Michael answered, "and I have just experienced something that has made me very unclear."

"The Amish girl project," Waterman said as a statement.

"You already know about that?" Michael said, suddenly feeling things were going on that he did not understand.

"Of course, Michael," Kassimir said. "Anyone who can do things that aren't supposed to be possible attracts attention.

Surely you expect that. Your media experience over the past months, I am sure, made you aware of that."

"So, am I under surveillance, then?" Michael asked, beginning to become irritated.

"You mean, are we bugging your phone, putting sensors in your lab? No. This is not personal. You're not under suspicion or surveillance, at least by us. You and your Institute are just the focus of some attention, and there is a difference," Kassimir answered.

"I have your word on that, Sam?"

"You do," Kassimir said. "I understand your reaction; don't worry about that. Now, can you do it?"

Michael thought about that for minute, went through how it might be done in his head, and finally said, "We can try. I see how to do it. We'll have to go out there."

"You mean on the ship?" Potter asked.

"Yes. I'll take two viewers with me. When do you want us to do it?"

"The day after tomorrow," Waterman answered. "We'll arrange to have you picked up and taken to Andrews. You'll be flown to Yokosuka, Japan, where the Seventh Fleet is based, then taken by plane to the carrier Nimitz, and from there helicoptered to NOAAS' Harold Edgerton. She's a two hundred and seventy-four-foot state of the art oceanographic research vessel. Massive displacement. Whatever is required, they can do. You, the chief scientist, and the captain will work out what that is. She'll be on station by the time you arrive. Here," Waterman said, "is a briefing book. What you tell your people is up to you. But please remind them we operate under very strict secrecy, well above Top Secret."

"They know that; everyone got very clear when we went through the clearance process. No worries. Do I have a budget?"

"Of course," Kassimir answered. "You know the drill. Spend what you need to, keep records of everything, we'll work out the paperwork afterwards."

"Then I'd better get out of here," Michael said, putting down his cup and standing up. "Given the logistics of this, I will be taking Coyote and Weldon. You've met them."

"Oh yes, the Native American DJ and the African American house painter," Potter said with a laugh. "You couldn't make this stuff up."

Everyone chuckled. Michael waved and left. As he drove back to the Institute, he thought about what was going to be involved. He was pretty sure, but not absolutely certain, that Coyote and Weldon could do it and would want to, and he had a budget. Then he realized he had never really been told how long to plan for, and that it was being left up to him. After thinking about it, he decided to assume twelve days including travel, but possibly less.

He pulled over in a picnic grove on the George Washington Parkway and got both Weldon and Coyote on a Facetime call and asked them if they could go.

"Make a carrier landing in a jet. Are you kidding, Boss? Of course, I will go," Weldon said.

"Me too," Coyote said, laughing.

"I have a budget, so you'll get paid the standard consulting rate."

"Then no problem at all. How about going down in a submarine, do we get to go down in a submarine?" Weldon asked.

"Probably, one at a time. I have worked out the protocol for doing this, and that is the way I want us all to think of it. As an experiment it's triple blind; nobody, not even the Koreans, knows the answer. Only the actual launch of the missile and where the warhead comes down will reveal it."

"Love it," Coyote said. "And I want to go on record, Michael, that I still think we're right about the Amish girl. I don't care what they say."

"Me too," Weldon added.

"We'll figure out a way to check, but for the moment let's stay focused on this missile." Michael went on to share most of what he had been told. He liked blindness in experiments, triple blind if possible, but he wasn't big on secrets from his team mates when it wasn't necessary.

An hour after he got back to the Institute, he got a call telling him it had all been arranged. They would be separately picked up and taken to Andrews Air Force base for the flight to Japan. Each in his own way spent the next day getting ready, and the following morning cars picked them up and took them to Andrews where they were put aboard a C-130 Hercules filled with vehicles and supplies. It reminded Weldon of his two tours in Afghanistan and put him in an odd withdrawn mood that didn't change until they landed in Japan.

They were put up in the bachelor officer quarters and fed breakfast at the officers' club. Michael felt like some anonymous particle caught in the ebb and flow of people, planes, supplies, and weapons that moved through the Yokosuka base like a tide and spread out across the world. Coyote, who had grown up on the Hopi reservation in Arizona, was fascinated by the tribal quality of the experience; it was a world within a world, like the reservation.

At nine that morning they were taken out to the airfield where they checked in with the dispatcher behind the counter. Half an hour later they were called on a speaker and told to walk out to a Fleet Logistics Support Grumann Hercules parked on the revetment.

"I thought we were going in a jet; this is a prop plane," Coyote said when he saw the aircraft. "And it's so big. How can that thing land on a ship?"

"With great difficulty," a sailor walking past them answered.

They climbed aboard and found themselves in a stripped-down version of the economy section on a commercial flight. The bulkhead was a kind of dirty tan, as were the frames of the seats which were covered in a blue fabric. The front of the aircraft on both sides had other minimalist seats along the bulkheads, while chests lined the aisles, some styrofoam, some metal, each securely strapped in with blue nylon belting.

Five others were on the flight with them, three men and two women. They reminded Michael of commuters doing something very familiar. Two of the men were officers and aviators, as Michael could tell from the wings on the left breast of their jackets, and they seemed to be friends who had gone to a training together. The other three were enlisted sailors in their early twenties, lost in stories about what had happened to them during their shore leaves.

The flight took just over two hours, then the captain announced they were landing. The other passengers stayed relaxed in their conversations, just business as usual, while Michael, Coyote, and Weldon had their faces pressed against bulkhead windows. At first as they looked down, they saw nothing but ocean, but as the plane continued its descent, at what seemed to Michael a dangerously high speed, Nimitz appeared suddenly, about half the size of a postage stamp.

"I can't believe how fast we are going," Coyote said as the plane continued to descend and the ship grew larger by each second. He was sitting in front of one of the aviators, an athletic looking man in his early thirties with close cropped brown hair who, hearing Coyote's comment, turned to him and said, "We have to keep the speed up because if the landing doesn't work you have to have enough speed to get into the air again. Otherwise you roll off the end of the deck and fall into the sea. We try to avoid that. The aircraft are very expensive."

"You do this?" Coyote asked.

"Most days, yes, but in an F-35... different beast," the aviator replied with a smile.

"Very cool, dude," Coyote responded.

In the time their brief exchange had taken, the ship had become enormous, and the plane seemed to be headed for a crash into its deck.

"Sit straight in your seat," the aviator counselled Coyote and the others. "It's going to get physical."

Just as Michael was convinced they were about to crash, the aircraft leveled out and rolled a short way down the deck and was jerked to a stop, which pressed them back into their seats.

As soon as the plane came to a stop, deck crew wearing different colored vests and cloth helmets ran over to the plane and opened the door. The passengers filed out as the crew went aboard and began to unload the chests. There was a choreographed quality to the entire exercise. Once they were on the deck Michael realized for the first time how enormous the Nimitz was. Their bags were brought to them by one of the crew just as a lieutenant approached them, a tall Black man in his twenties.

"Professor Gillespie?" he asked.

"Yes."

"I'm lieutenant Daniel Bowser," he said, putting out his hand to shake theirs, starting with Michael. "Would you and your men please come with me." It wasn't really a question. Michael and the others followed the lieutenant through a steel hatch into the ship's interior. As they went through the hatch, Weldon suddenly stopped. "We used this ship as a target. It came up in the numinosity study."

"You're right," Michael answered. "I hadn't thought of it, but you're right. What suddenly made you think of that?"

"Because I remember in the session seeing this door and the people coming out of it." Weldon answered.

They entered a world of steel walls and ceilings, and tile covered floors; it was at once claustrophobic for lack of windows and enormous, seemingly endless and confusing. Everything was painted a soft gray or pale green. Corridors led off from the one they were in; pipes and armored electric lines were overhead. Sound reverberated because there were no soft surfaces to absorb it. They lost their orientation as the lieutenant led them down one corridor after another, and then down a steel staircase. They came to a hatch labelled "Officers' Country" and went into a space with faux wood paneling where a group of young officers and some men who were obviously civilians were eating lunch.

"You'll have lunch here, and at o-fourteen hundred, you're scheduled to be helo'd over to Edgerton. The steward will take your order. You can put your bags over there," he said. As they sat, a Filipino man in a white coat came up to them.

"You have servants in the Navy?" Weldon asked, leaning into the lieutenant and speaking very softly.

"Officers do, it is an old tradition," Bowser responded, and he and Weldon exchanged a look.

"Who are the civilians?" Michael asked.

"Oh, we always have a contingent of civilian engineers and technicians aboard to help us maintain all the electronics and other systems. They work for the companies that make the gear," Bowser explained.

They were offered a lunch of small sirloin steaks, baked potatoes and salad, basic mainstream American food and quite good. The others in the room, after acknowledging their presence with waves or a nod, went back to their conversations and ignored them.

After they were finished, Bowser returned.

"Would you like to see something of the ship? We have about an hour before you are scheduled to be off. Don't worry about your bags," he said, indicating them. "They'll be taken up to the flight deck."

"Lead on," Michael responded.

For the next hour the lieutenant led up and down corridors and steel staircases into the three hangars, each so large as to be intimidating. Multiple planes were spread out across the hangar decks with part of their wings folded up.

"It's enormous," Weldon observed. "How many people are on the Nimitz?"

"Right now, about three thousand two hundred," Bowser answered.

They went down to the nuclear reactor and up onto the bridge high above the flight deck where Captain James Zhou, the ship's commanding officer, shook their hands, welcomed them aboard, and then excused himself. Everywhere they looked there were monitors; being on the ship was like living inside a huge machine as it was operating.

At the end of the tour they came out onto the flight deck in time to see their baggage being loaded aboard a helicopter. They thanked Lieutenant Bowser and climbed aboard. As soon as they were seated and strapped in, the helicopter rose and began to move out over the open ocean. About thirty minutes later what looked like another warship, only this time painted white, not gray, came into view, and they slowly descended onto its landing platform. As they did so, they looked out and saw the NOAA R 111 on the side of its bow.

"What is NOAA, anyway?" Coyote asked, speaking into his headset because the copter noise was too great to permit normal conversation.

"National Oceanic and Atmospheric Administration," came from the pilot. "She's a government ship but a civilian agency."

As he answered, Michael realized that on both Nimitz and now this helicopter not a single person had asked them what they were doing at sea. He wrote it off to a norm for people living in a world of security secrets.

The helicopter came to rest, and a crew member opened the hatch to let them out. Their bags were passed down, and as soon as they were clear the helicopter rose again, leaving them standing on Edgerton's helo pad with its yellow landing markings. A middle-aged man with a beard and wearing an officer's cap came over to them.

"Professor Gillespie?" the man said with a smile, putting out his hand.

"Yes."

"Chris Reno. I am Edgerton's captain."

"A pleasure to meet you. This is Weldon Shelcraft, and this is Istaqa Chester. We call him Coyote."

"Nice to meet you... what tribe are you from, Coyote?" the captain asked.

"Hopi," he answered.

"Which Mesa?"

"Old Oribi; do you know the mesas?" Coyote asked.

"I'm from Flagstaff. We had one of your tribe on board a few years back."

"You must mean George Hania," Coyote answered, remembering from his teens a boy three years older who had gone to Arizona University and then to Scripps Institute in San Diego to become a marine biologist, an unusual thing for a desert Hopi to do.

"Yes, exactly. He came out with us twice doing his post-doc."

"He was a different mesa, but I remember him well."

"Well, let's get you set up," the captain said, leading them into the ship's interior. It was much like the Nimitz, mostly steel, but this time there were framed photographs on some of the walls, scenes of research activities. The captain led them to a series of small staterooms.

"The head is down the hall," the captain said. "Have you eaten?"

"Yes, thanks, they fed us on Nimitz," Michael answered.

'Well, why don't you just relax, and professor..."

"...Please call me Michael."

"Why don't you join me in the bridge conference room at sixteen hundred. Right now we're in the middle of a Scripps research project," Captain Reno explained, as he turned and walked away.

"How are you doing?" Michael asked.

"I could do with a nap," Weldon answered. "We've been through so many time zones I want to reset."

"Me too," Coyote agreed.

"Okay, sixteen hundred it is," Michael said, looking at a ship's clock on the wall monitor, and he went into his space and closed the door. He hadn't said anything to the others, because he did not want to create stress and performance anxiety, but as he lay down his mind was filled the idea that the United States government had moved the three of them more than half way around the world and committed hundreds of thousands, maybe millions of dollars to support them. In going through this he recognized that all this was a demonstration of Kassimir's belief in him and the viewers of the Hill Institute. But he also recognized that after the apparent failure of the Amish girl probe, if this were to fail as well, the Institute would collapse. Everyone would be very polite, he was sure, but the effect would be devastating just the same.

In spite of his emotional turmoil, the demands of his body prevailed and he slept. Half an hour before the meeting was scheduled, the alarm he set on his phone went off and woke him. For a moment he was disoriented and not sure where he was, then it all came flooding back.

He cleaned himself up at the sink in his room, put on a new shirt, picked up his tablet, and went out into the corridor as a bearded man in his early twenties, wearing wireframe glasses, was going by. He stopped when he saw Michael.

"You must be one of the guys that came in on the helo," he said. "What are you going to be doing?" he asked, then volunteered, "I'm doing a post-doc on micro-plastics in the food chain. Jon Rider, Nova University," he said, putting out his hand, which Michael shook.

"Michael Gillespie, Lynn Hill Institute, Georgetown University," Michael said. "I'm supposed to meet with

Captain Reno in the bridge conference room; can you show me the way?"

"No problem, follow me," Rider said, and led down the cream-colored steel-walled corridors and up steel staircases until they were on the bridge, behind which was another steel walled room. He left Michael at the door. A group of people were already sitting around the room's table, with Reno at its head. As he was taking his seat on one of the gray metal chairs, Michael looked around and realized Edgerton was even more austere and cluttered than Nimitz. There were shelves around the walls, full of loose-leaf binders and books. Gear was stashed on the floor.

"Professor Gillespie, this is Mitchel Farley, director of our dive operations. Naomi Peoples, senior pilot of our submersible. And Colin Whitehead who runs the ROVs. They are all part of the permanent crew, and from what I was told by Jake Garth, they may play a role in what you are here for," Reno said, gesturing to each of them as he introduced them.

"In addition, we have shifting teams of researchers from various universities and institutions who come out for a few weeks or a season to carry out specific projects," he explained, gesturing towards the other side of the table. "This is Sidney Kilgore from Nova University in Florida, who is studying microplastics; Ruth Goldstein, from Scripps Institute, who is working on ocean currents and salinity; and Sam Barber from USC Institute of Marine and Coastal Studies. His team's studying ocean ecosystems."

He looked at Michael, saying, "This is Michael Gillespie, from the Hill Institute at Georgetown University. He is here for a special project that, as I told you yesterday, takes priority over everything else." As he said it, Michael could see that the visiting researchers were not happy.

"Alright," Reno said. "Let's get down to it. We have orders from a unit of the CIA, supported by DOD and Homeland

Security, to help Professor Gillespie and his people; although I'll be honest, I don't quite understand what we are going to be doing, except it's not oceanography. Okay, Michael," Reno said in a manner Michael appreciated for its friendliness. He had been concerned as to how all this might be received and figured Garth would set it up. Now it was happening.

"Do you want to tell us what's going on? I am told you can speak fairly freely. Everyone here has been cleared."

"Of course. But first a question: what does ROV stand for?" Michael asked.

"Remote Operated Vehicle, unmanned submersibles that can be run from Edgerton or from the MIR submersible which gives us another three thousand feet of depth capability and the ability to do fairly delicate movements," Whitehead explained. He was a stocky man in his late forties, with a wild head of hair, and like many of the men aboard that Michael had seen on his way to the conference room, he was bearded.

"Very helpful, thanks," Michael replied. "Alright, I can tell from your expressions that none of you are very happy to have your projects interrupted, and I want you to know I've been there and done that, so I appreciate your feelings," Michael said as he plugged his tablet into the ship's system, bringing up the PowerPoint he had prepared.

"By way of background, I am a neuroscientist and an anthropologist. I have double doctorates. But relevant to why I am here and have two colleagues with me, I'm here to carry out a remote viewing project."

"Wait a minute," Ruth Goldstein said, interrupting him. "You're the guy who stopped the nuclear explosion in Washington, aren't you? I thought I recognized your name and your face." She was a woman in her fifties, with graying hair, who spoke with a New York accent and had a very assertive manner. "You all remember, don't you?" she said, turning first to her left and then to her right. "It was about two years ago."

"Yes, I am," Michael answered, then changed the subject. "As to why I'm here, I don't actually know very much about this project except my Institute's part in it. Mostly I know Washington has a very strong interest in finding something, and this is the only way they can do it. Do any of you know about remote viewing?"

"Is that some kind of remote sensing technology like sidescan?" Naomi Peoples asked. She was an attractive, athletic looking woman in her thirties with tattoos on her arms and short hair pinned back with two Navajo silver clips.

"That's a good way to think about it," Michael answered. "Only in this case the instrument is the human mind. The nonlocal, non-physiological aspect of it."

"You've gotta be kidding," said Sidney Kilgore, a muscular man with a heavily tanned and weathered face and a Marine buzz-cut. "That's just a fancy way of saying psychics." Then, turning to Reno, "Chris, are you telling me my project is being suspended in the middle of our collection period because of psychics? Please tell me I misunderstood."

"Yes, Sid, that is exactly what is going to happen. My orders are clear, and we are going to follow them. Michael has a four-day window, and for the next four days what he needs is what we are going to do."

They could all see that Kilgore was furious. "I planned this project for two years, and we only get six weeks on Edgerton. And now I'm going to lose four days to some kind of psychic lunacy. No. I'm going to file a complaint."

"All you are going to do is hurt yourself, Sid," Ruth Goldstein said. "Let Michael continue."

"First of all, Dr. Kilgore, I am no happier about this than you are. My research and my life are on hold to do this, and the same for my companions. This is not something I sought," Michael said flatly. "Here's what I know," he continued. "Apparently, the North Koreans are going to fire a new kind of missile. The American intelligence community takes this very seriously. It's not my field so I can't tell you why that is so, but I assure you there is no question that it is, and that several other countries, for whatever reason, have a very high level of interest in what the North Koreans are about to do. Our interest is in recovering the missile."

As he looked around the room, Michael was calibrating what to say. His instinct was that Sam Kassimir would prefer that he say as little as possible.

"We have reason to believe this missile launch is going to happen within the next four days and have a sense of where it will land in the sea. Our job is to locate it before anyone else can," Michael said, looking particularly at Farley, Peoples, and Whitehead. Then he turned on the PowerPoint, and the screen grab from Google Earth, the one he had used in the final remote viewing sessions.

"We think the missile will come down in this area," he said, as a red circle appeared on the image. "Specifically, we think it will land on the top of the Kita Koho Seamount at 26°45'N, 135° 22'E," and as he spoke an arrow on the exact location came up on the large monitor screen in the conference room.

"How could you possibly know that? It hasn't happened yet, and even I, who know almost nothing about ballistic missiles, know you can't predict their impact with that kind of accuracy," Sam Barber said. He was a man in his fifties with rimless glasses. To Michael, he looked like a stereotypical accountant.

"His psychics told him," Kilgore said in disgust.

"You mean that in a nasty way, Dr. Kilgore, but you are actually exactly right," Michael responded, and went on to show them the multi-viewer protocol he used, and what it produced.

When he was done, he could see that everyone but Kilgore and Barber was, if not supportive, intrigued.

"That's how we build up the hypotheses to guide the fieldwork," he concluded. "The next step is to find it."

"The Kita Koho Seamount is about one hundred and twenty nautical miles from our present location," Naomi Peoples said.

"At ten knots," Reno added, "it will take us until about this time tomorrow to get in position."

Suddenly Farley spoke, "Dr. Gillespie, Michael if I may, I don't understand any of this, but my crew," he said with a gesture to include Naomi Peoples, "will give it our best shot. If the government thinks this is so important that they have turned to remote viewing and arranged to get you out here, no small feat, it will not be said we didn't give you our full support."

"Thank you, I appreciate that," Michael responded warmly.

"Obviously we are going to wait for this thing to get launched," Farley continued. He was a man in his early forties with the craggy good looks of a movie star. "How specific can you get as to the location? I don't know how much you know about sea searches, but it's hard to get back to a place, even when you know where it is. A few inches, a foot, a yard, and you miss it," Farley said, and Naomi Peoples nodded her agreement. "And if this thing comes down on top of a seamount, you should think of it as coming down on the top of Mt. Everest, only with several thousand feet or more of water on top of it," he said. "Do you get the idea?"

"On the plane over I read the fourteenth meeting of the Intergovernmental Oceanographic Commission, so I know its least depth is one thousand and eighty feet, three hundred and twenty-nine meters, and another nearly five thousand feet, fifteen hundred meters to the seafloor."

"That's more than I know," Farley said with an easy laugh. "What do you think, Naomi, Colin?"

"It will be much easier if it stays on top of the mountain," Whitehead answered, and Peoples nodded her head in agreement.

"What does the weather look like, Chris?" Peoples asked.

"Excellent question," Reno answered. "Authorization zero zero one, put up on monitor three current weather charts and read-outs." The computer complied, and a weather map with read-outs running down both sides of the screen appeared.

"Center on coordinates, 26°45'N, 135° 22'E," he said, and the chart moved.

"Identify Kita Koho Seamount." A label appeared.

"Looks clear at the moment," Michael said.

"Yeah, well, for a few hours anyway." Peoples said. "Look at the upper right corner."

"She's right," Reno replied. "Project storm course in twelve hours." As he spoke the chart began to move again, and it showed the storm was going to verge to the right and miss the seamount by the time they got there. The windspeed read-out on the side began to flash red, showing one hundred and five miles per hour.

"We wouldn't be able to operate in that," Reno said. "So we've had a lucky break."

"What's the plan, then?"

"Here's what I propose," Reno responded. "We get as close as we safely can. Side-scan will show us the seamount. As soon as we get word that the missile has launched, we wait for it to sink into the ocean.

"I will work with my viewers to fine-tune the location," Michael said.

"It takes hours to search the sea, Michael. It's all going to get down to how close you can get us."

"We could use pingers," Peoples said to Farley.

"I'm sorry, I don't know what a pinger is," Michael responded.

"It's a radio homing device. We'll rig a buoy with a reel of line long enough to get to the top of the seamount, and the pinger at the end. Your guys can drop one, and it will unspool. Then we can use either the submersible or the ROV, or both, to home in on the pinger and make the recovery. But are we talking an entire missile? That could be a big factor."

"The viewers describe just the warhead, which has become detached from the missile. It's the warhead they want. They don't seem to care about the missile itself, and if they separate they may not come down in the same place anyway."

"How can you all sit and listen to this?" Kilgore asked in anger. "Psychics say a missile will be fired in four days and say exactly where it will come down. Nobody knows the answer to that question until it happens. And trying to find something the size of a warhead more than a thousand feet underwater is absurd. We all know how hard it is to find something at depth in the sea even when you think you know where it is. This cannot possibly work," Kilgore continued. "I'm not going to listen to any more of this. I can't stop it, it seems, but I don't have to be party to it. What about you, Sam?"

"Well, I have no role to play in any of this, so I'm going back to my lab to finish some work there," Barber answered. Both men got up and left the room, leaving only Goldstein, who stayed where she was.

"Sorry about that, Michael," Reno said, "but I suspect it isn't the first time you've had that reaction."

"It isn't, and I don't care. They're right; they have no role to play in this. I'm sorry though, Chris. It's not my intention to create problems for you. I'm doing what I have been asked to do. You all are doing what you've been told to do, so let's just get on with it. What you are telling me about the weather suggests that it's going to be a near thing," Michael said, suddenly exhausted by all the travel, the time zones, and the hostility he had just experienced.

CHAPTER TWELVE

Michael got back to his cabin; the others were asleep, and he soon was as well, as Edgerton steamed at ten knots to the Kita Koho seamount. He, Coyote, and Weldon were just going into the dining hall in the morning when they ran into Captain Reno.

"We have some bad news. The storm has increased in intensity, and its path has changed. It looks like it is now going to go directly over the seamount. And it is going to be so severe that we're not going to be able to get into operation today, and maybe not tomorrow. We'll just have to see."

"Whoa, that's going to cut it pretty close," Michael answered.

"Yes, I'm afraid it is. Are any of you subject to seasickness? We're looking at fifteen-foot waves even at some distance from the seamount, so it's going to get rough. If it's an issue, go over to the doc there," Reno said, indicating a middle-aged woman with deep auburn hair pulled back in a bun who sat alone reading a book and eating at a nearby table. "Grace Reynolds is her name," Reno said, beginning to move. "Sorry, I have to get up to the bridge."

The three men looked at each other and without a word walked over to the physician.

"You boys looking for a little help?" Reynolds asked, looking up from her book and gesturing for them to sit down.

"The captain told us to see you about something for seasickness."

"You want drugs or holistic?" she asked.

They looked at each other, and Michael said, "I think we'll start with holistic."

"Good choice. As it happens, I've come prepared; Chris warned me earlier. Here are some Chinese plum ball tablets," she said, handing them each small plastic bags filled with little purple balls. "Suck on several" she explained as she handed them over. They thanked her and walked out of the dining hall and out of the ship's superstructure onto the rear deck to see what was going on.

Naomi Peoples and Mitchell Farley, assisted by two other men, were carefully checking the MIR II submersible in its cradle on the rear deck of the ship, testing how securely it was tied down. On the other side of the deck a team of women were doing the same thing with a large inboard orange tender.

Michael went over to Farley and Peoples, saying, "How can we help... willing but untrained hands."

"Two of you go down to the catwalk. They can use some help. And one go forward. Look for Jon Rider, he'll tell you what to do. This is going to get rough, Michael."

"So we've been told," Michael said, going back to where Weldon and Coyote were standing.

"You guys go down to that catwalk structure on the stern. I'm going up to the bow; I've already met the guy who's there."

They split up and spent the next three hours going through the ship with everyone else, securing everything in anticipation of the rough seas. Michael had found Jon Rider notably cooler than at their first meeting, but given who he worked for, this did not surprise him. As the day went on and he interacted with more people what did surprise him was that everyone aboard knew details he thought were private. It was just like the Institute.

While Kilgore, Barber, and a few others on their teams were cold, unfriendly, or even angry at having their work interrupted, the majority of the post-docs and assistant professors, as well as the ship's crew, seemed fascinated. He could tell from the comments he heard and overheard that

Weldon and Coyote were no one's idea of a psychic, and what they were doing had energized and intrigued the ship family. He was glad for that. Collective intention toward success was an important variable in the nonlocal domain.

Not long after lunch, the weather changed, and Michael began to feel queasy, although sucking the plum balls helped. Coyote, who had never been on a ship before, went back to his stateroom, having thrown-up over the ship's side twice. Weldon was completely untouched by seasickness, and that plus his great size and strength made him an asset and a character; Michael saw several women engage with him.

"I'd love to hear how he tells them about Barbara," Michael thought. A twenty-eight-year-old house painter, special forces vet, whose best friend, a Nobel Laureate physicist in a wheelchair, was also a viewer. Imagining that made him smile.

All that day and most of the next the storm raged. Reno kept Edgerton at its edges, her bow rising and falling as she headed into the waves, some so strong and high they washed over her bulwarks, seawater running down the walkways on either side. Every so often a wave took the ship broadside and she rolled from side-to-side.

At one point, as Michael stood talking with a group explaining what they were going to do, he suddenly had to turn and vomit over the side. When he stood straight again, someone handed him a bottle of water, he washed out his mouth, spit it over the side, took a drink, and handed the bottle back. No one said a word about what had just happened; the conversation just kept on going. A few minutes later it happened again, but this time the person vomiting was one of the oceanographers.

As they stood on the rear deck, one of the ship's crew came pounding out of the superstructure.

"Come quick, they've launched. The captain wants you on the bridge," the man said. "Follow me," and he turned and ran back with Michael.

When he got up on the bridge, Reno, Farley, Peoples, and Whitehead were clustered around a monitor.

"Seventh Fleet notified us, gave us the data. It will be about thirty minutes," Reno said, then pointed at the twenty-five-mile radar screen. At its upper left edge, they could see small white outlines representing other ships.

"Do you know who they are?" Michael asked.

"The upper one is Chinese, the one at three o'clock is Russian." A chime sounded, and on a third screen an image from a satellite appeared showing the ships from an altitude of thousands of feet.

"The Chinese one is a warship," Farley said.

"Yes, a destroyer," Reno said, concurring. He clicked on a link and an image of the ship came up. It was very sleek with a sharp bow.

"A type 055 destroyer," Farley read off the screen.

"Is it alone?" Peoples asked.

"No, but the other ships must be out of range. Destroyers are usually part of a carrier group, just like the Nimitz carrier group you flew out from," Reno said to Michael.

"What's the other one?" Peoples asked.

"A Russian oceanographic ship."

"I presume they're looking at us?" Michael asked.

"I'm sure they are," Reno answered. "But they have no particular reason to think we are here for anything but oceanography, and Edgerton is well-known in these waters. It's only because of Michael and his people that we know to be here. They can't know that."

"So, if you just go about your usual evolutions, we shouldn't draw any particular attention," Michael put forward.

"Do you think the Russians or the Chinese knew there was going to be a launch and where it will come down? Are they just here for other reasons?" Whitehead asked, looking between Reno and Michael.

"I've no idea, do you?" Reno asked Michael.

"None."

"Okay, so what's the plan?" asked Farley.

"This is your call, Michael."

"I think the way to go is what I said earlier, and based on what you just said, Colin, it is just what would be expected. The hidden variable here is the remote viewing and what it has told us, and that's not something they would even consider. I assume the Koreans pushed the day up, what is it, thirty-six hours into this storm, so it will be hard to track the exact impact location, and even harder to find it. They don't want it to be found because of the warhead."

"What about the warhead?" Peoples asked, and Michael realized he was at a line he had not intended to cross. They all looked at him, and he had to decide. The success of the project depended on these people. In nonlocal consciousness work the best option was always common intention. These people had to be included.

"I don't know a lot about warheads. No, scratch that, I don't know anything about warheads; but what the viewers describe is what I am told is a multiple independent re-entry warhead. A MIRV, I was told it's called. The American government apparently had no idea the North Koreans could do this, had this technology. But when we analyzed the data and showed it to some people, that's how they interpreted it. As I understand it, the missile head is supposed to break into several warheads, each with its own target. From what I understood from the people who asked me to do this, I don't think it ever occurred to the Koreans that it could be recovered, or that it would not separate as it was intended to. They just launched it, and that's what they expect to happen. Only the viewers think that doesn't happen. The warhead comes down intact in this location. That's what got everyone so stirred up."

"Recovering the whole warhead so they could see how it was constructed. I get it," said Farley.

"So, these other two ships, and there may be more, may not be in the same part of the ocean we are for the same reason," Whitehead commented.

"Yes, but they're going to be notified, or even see the missile come down, and then the game might change," Reno pointed out.

"As soon as the missile is down, can we launch that orange tender and do what Naomi said, about the pingers?" Michael asked.

"Already have them set to go," Whitehead answered.

"It will take two trips. I take Weldon first, then Coyote. I hope he's up to it."

"While you're doing that," Reno said, looking at Farley and Peoples, "we get ready to launch the MIR II submersible. Since Michael says the warhead's going to end up in a crag on the seamount that may be too small for the MIR to get in, let's set it up for ROV operation," he said. Looking at Whitehead, "Can you see to that?"

"I can."

"All of this, of course, is dependent on this storm going down," Reno said.

Colin looked out the bridge windows, and said, "As if that's not enough, there's a fog coming in." When he said it they all looked up.

"I don't think we are going to see this thing come down unless it is very close. Your viewers are the only way we will ever find it."

"We'll do our best."

"Okay, then let's get at it," Reno said, and they broke up.

Michael went down and found Coyote shoveling down a breakfast of scrambled eggs, a small steak, and toast while an attractive and engrossed blonde-haired woman cook sat talking to him.

"The nearly dead have arisen," she said, as Michael sat down.

"So I see. How are you doing?"

"I went to the doc again, and she gave me something that seems to have worked. Also, I'm not being bounced around like a sock in dryer," Coyote responded.

"Good. You ready to work?"

"Yes, and we've got to hurry."

"Why?' Michael asked.

"This thing's been launched."

"You know that how?" Michael asked.

"I felt its release," Coyote answered.

"You're right. I just learned that from a more traditional source," Michael said with a laugh.

"That's not all," Coyote answered.

"What else?"

"This thing gets caught on a crevice of the mountain... you remember, from the session?"

"Yes, of course."

"The storm has changed things, or maybe I'm just more aware cause I'm physically proximate. Anyway, it's going to balance there very delicately."

"What in the world are you all talking about?" the blonde cook asked. "It's about the Korean missile, right?" she added, proving, as Michael had expected, that the ship's grapevine had spread the headlines of the story.

"It's why we're here," Coyote responded.

"You feel strongly about this?" Michael asked.

"I do," Coyote answered

"We think the missile comes down, and instead of falling thousands of feet deeper to the seafloor, it is caught in a crag," Michael added. Getting up, he said to Coyote, "The missile is going to land in about fifteen minutes. We're going to fine tune the location."

"You got it, Kachada Cheveyo."

"What?" the woman asked.

"White Spirit Warrior," Coyote said. "In Hopi, my language. The remote viewing I was telling you about, Michael's the White shaman who makes it work."

The woman looked at both of them and got up, "Cool," she said, and walked back to the galley.

"Here's the plan," Michael said. "As soon as the missile is down we launch, and Weldon will go first. That will give you another hour, when they tell me things will be even calmer. The front is moving on."

"Thanks," Coyote answered, "but I'm okay now. Are we going to be able to see this thing land?"

"I don't think anyone knows, exactly. There's a dense fog coming in," Michael answered as they walked onto the rear deck, where they found Weldon talking with Peoples.

"Will we be able to see this thing go into the water?" Michael asked her.

"No way to know. We don't have great visibility, as you can see," she said, waving her hand across the vista they saw from the stern. "I would guess not. But we will know the time from one of those agencies you work with. They'll tell Chris; he'll know. We're in, what did you call it, the consensus zone you picked. The tender can cover the area you've picked."

The minutes went by, and the sea did calm, as they stood there talking while all over the ship people carried out their assigned tasks. Suddenly, Reno's voice came over the PA. "The missile is down, could anyone see it?" When no one called out, Reno said, "Then by appearance it's a normal day, commence operations."

The ship's crane lifted the orange tender off its cradle and lowered it slowly into the sea on the ships' starboard side where there was an opening in the bulwark. As Weldon and Michael put on anoraks and safety vests, a man and a woman they hadn't met yet lowered steel dive steps and climbed down and into the boat.

Colin Whitehead came over and handed Weldon what looked like an orange basketball tethered to a yellow cylinder by a thin line.

"You're going first, right?"

"Yes," Weldon answered.

"Okay, here's the drill. Just give the crew the direction you want to go. Michael explained to me what you're going to do, so when you get to the spot, just drop it overboard. The pinger is the cylinder; it will spool out a thin line in the buoy. There is enough to get to the top of the mountain. When it lands, the pinger will be released and begin broadcasting its location and depth. We'll pinpoint the tender on the radar. That will give us a three-dimensional fix. Then a signal from the boat will turn off the pinger."

Turning to Michael, he said, "As soon as we have fixed the location, the buoy will reel up its line. Since you don't want Coyote to know the site Weldon picked, you'll pick the buoy up, come back to Edgerton, and we'll do the whole evolution again. After each, we'll turn the pinger off. When we have the locations from each of you, we'll turn the pingers back on and home in on them with your guidance. Based on what we find we will turn them off again and leave them down there. The salvage group can reactivate them using the coordinates we'll give them. Does that do what you want?"

"Perfect," Michael answered. "Thank you very much."

As Michael was finishing, Farley walked up and listened to the conversation, then added, "When that second evolution is finished, we'll put the MIR II in. Are you guys ready?"

"Yes."

"Well then, good hunting. Mind the ladder going down, and time your drop into the boat when it's coming up."

Michael and Weldon each climbed down, and once in the boat, the man who had the wheel introduced himself as Clarence Ryan, "They call me Buddy." The woman put out her hand and introduced herself as Cindy Ludivic. Both were doctoral students in their early twenties. Michael explained what he wanted to do, and they cast off.

Weldon sat silently, holding the orange buoy as they pulled away from Edgerton. After some minutes he spoke, "Go to the left more," and Buddy complied.

"A bit more. That's it, stay on this course."

The boat with the four of them in it cut through the waves which were growing smaller as the wind calmed. They had gone about four nautical miles and could no longer see Edgerton because of the fog, when Weldon stood up, holding on to the safety bar attached to the wheel pedestal where the navigation, engine read outs, and communications were housed. Michael was videoing and recording all of this.

"Turn right a little bit... no too much, come back a bit. There..." he said. They went on another few hundred yards, when he said, "Can you slow down... a lot?"

"Sure," Buddy answered, and a few seconds later Weldon dropped the buoy over the side.

Buddy leaned over and said quietly to Michael, "We are just one side of the seamount. Look," he said, indicating the echo sounder screen where Michael could see a rough outline.

As soon as the buoy hit the water the pinger descended, and Buddy steered the boat a few yards away, put the engine in neutral, and waited for Edgerton to get a clear fix on the location. There was a pause, then over the radio they heard, "Edgerton to tender, we can't see you, but we have the location by radio, radar, and depth. Activate retrieval." Buddy picked up the radio mic and answered, "Copy that," pressed a radio control, waited a while as the line coiled back into the buoy, and then reached over with a boat hook and snared the buoy. Once it was aboard, they started back to the ship.

"I feel good about it," Weldon said to Michael, and Michael could tell from his smile that he did.

When they got back to Edgerton, Weldon climbed up the ladder, and according to the protocol, walked back to his stateroom. When he got there he picked up the phone and called the bridge. "This is Weldon, I am in my room; notify Coyote he's on."

Coyote's phone rang, and a minute later he was going down the corridor to exit onto the deck. He was excited and had a good feeling about things. One of the crew pointed out the ladder, and he climbed down to find Michael, Buddy, and Cindy, to whom he was introduced. The buoy and pinger were already aboard.

Michael explained the protocol, and they cast off the mooring line and headed out. By now the sea was much calmer, for which Coyote was very grateful. He had never been to sea before, and being in the small tender was different from being on the ship, intimate with the sea in a way he had never experienced. He relaxed into his feelings. It was all so unlike anything in his desert home in Arizona, and yet he felt the forces of nature were familiar. For the first time since he had arrived on Edgerton, he felt empowered.

"Keep going, but go maybe five degrees to the right."

The fog still hung heavy in the air when Coyote suddenly said, "Turn left about ten degrees, and slow down." After a moment more, he said, "Stop."

The small tender coasted on a few more feet, and Coyote stood up and dropped the buoy over the side, watching as the pinger spooled out. Once again, the tender bobbed in the water until Buddy received notification that Edgerton had the location.

Buddy then sent the signal to recoil the line and engaged the prop. Cindy Ludivic used the boat hook this time to snare the buoy and bring it aboard. Then they pulled away and headed back to Edgerton. As they were returning they looked to starboard, and on the right, saw dimly in the distance the Chinese destroyer.

"Edgerton, this is the tender," Buddy said into the radio mike. "Do you see what we see, the Chinese destroyer on the horizon?"

"We do, tender, and they have contacted us by radio. Just keep coming." As they steamed back the fog began to clear and both the Chinese warship and the Russian oceanographic vessel could be seen at a distance.

The tender pulled up to the side of Edgerton, and everyone got out except Buddy, who rigged the lifting harness to the crane before he climbed out and came back aboard.

As soon as he was on Edgerton's deck, Michael went up to the bridge where he found Reno, Farley, and Whitehead. Reno was on the marine radio, this time talking to the Russian oceanographic ship.

"Yes, Vladimir, we're doing microplastics right now, but we are going to be lowering the submersible in a few minutes. What's up with you?"

Over the speaker a heavily accented Russian voice came back, "Edgerton, yes, Chris, we're focusing on changing water temperatures right now."

Michael was surprised that the two captains seemed to know each other and that their exchange was so chatty. He gave Reno a quizzical look, and the captain responded, "It's a small world, Michael. There aren't very many oceanographic ships, period, and far fewer of the Global class like Edgerton and the Yakov Gakkel. Vladimir Gorskov and I have known each other for years."

"Gakkel to Edgerton," the speaker announced. "Would you like to come to dinner?"

"I'd love to Vladimir, but we picked up a very nasty flu in the Philippines. I've got a number of folks down with it, and I'm not feeling so great myself. I would hate to bring it aboard Gakkel, but certainly the next time," Reno adlibbed.

"Understood. Have the Chinese contacted you?"

"Yes. I told them the same thing, minus the dinner discussion, Vladimir. Apparently, they are part of the Liaoning carrier group which is headed this way."

As he spoke, Michael could see that on the deck Sidney Kilgore and his team were lowering a piece of yellow equipment into the water with the crane, and he guessed that to the Chinese and the Russians everything would look like business as usual.

"Grakkel to Edgerton. Chris, the Chinese destroyer is headed your way," the Russian captain said, and as he spoke they could see on the radar that the destroyer was moving in their direction.

"If this is what you look like under normal operations, then let's keep going."

"I agree, but the Chinese can get aggressive, so we must take care," Reno said, then picked up the radio mic and said, "Edgerton to Grakkel. Thank you, Vladimir. You take care. I hope our voyages cross paths again soon, and we can do that dinner. Back to work. Edgerton out," he said.

"Is the Chinese destroyer going to be an issue?" Michael asked.

"Hard to tell," Reno answered, "but it is not that simple. Just before you got here I got an encrypted message saying the Nimitz group is headed our way to make sure no one bothers us. I'm not sure that's a good idea, but I wasn't asked. So this could escalate. I suggest you all get going."

"Let's not get ahead of ourselves," Farley said. "How close were the two, what's the word, viewers?" he asked, looking at Michael.

"Yes, viewers, and that is the question I was about to ask."

They walked over to the chart table where Reno had laid out a paper chart.

"As the tender was coming back, I calculated that," he said. "The two viewers were twenty-eight feet apart."

"Are you serious?" Farley asked.

"Twenty-eight feet, I don't see how that is possible," Peoples echoed. You know how hard it is to locate something under the sea."

"I can't explain it either," Reno answered, "but that's how it worked out."

He turned to a crew member and said, "Quarter speed ahead." The ship's engines engaged, and Edgerton began to move. Farley worked at one of the monitors, and suddenly they could hear pings coming from the devices Coyote and Weldon had dropped.

Fifteen minutes later, Reno said, "Full stop," and the ship came to a halt facing into the waves that were now just two or three feet.

CHAPTER THIRTEEN

"Okay. Let's launch," Reno said.

Farley, Peoples, and Michael left the bridge, going down to the rear deck where the crew was preparing the submersible. There was something oddly familiar about MIR II's form. The craft was shaped like the egg in his lab, only on its side with the large end forward. It had two mechanical arms and a large bubble window in the front. At the small end of the egg in the back was a prop and a small fin. Underneath, it had skids. It was one thing to see a picture of a submersible like the MIR II, he realized, quite another to be about to get into one to and go thousands of feet down into the sea.

"How many people can go?" he asked Peoples.

"Three. You, me, and one of your viewers. I assume you want to video the entire thing inside and out, right?"

"Exactly, thank you. That's precisely what needs to happen. I was just about to ask you how we could set it up," Michael said, then added, "Can I tell you how much I have enjoyed working with you?"

"This is the craziest thing I have ever done," Naomi answered with a smile. "And I want it to succeed. And we get two tries."

Michael was filled with appreciation for Naomi, the ship, the crew. Even the people that didn't like him. It kept him sharp.

"I'm going to talk with Weldon and Coyote. I'll be back with one of them in a minute," he said, and went back into the superstructure. Because his was the last in the line of staterooms, they gathered in Weldon's room.

"We have to arrive at this amongst ourselves. Which one of you wants to go first?"

Weldon and Coyote looked at each other, then hugged.

"It doesn't matter to you?" Weldon asked.

"No, and you should know that your buoys were only 28 feet apart."

"Yes!" Coyote said, looking at Weldon, and they high-fived.

"Let's see if we get an answer," Michael said, and put out his hands. They joined hands, and Michael said, "Who should go first?" They stood there with eyes closed for several minutes, then in unison their eyes opened.

"Weldon," Coyote said.

"I agree," Michael said, then to Weldon, "It might get chilly; I'm going to bring a sweater."

Weldon reached into the tiny locker that was his closet and came out with a blue hoodie. The three of them looked at one another for a moment and stood in silence, then they left the room. Michael and Weldon walked over to the MIR II where Peoples was waiting. When she saw them coming, she spoke into her shoulder mic. Control of the ship had now passed to the stern bridge overlooking the rear deck, where the crane could also be operated. "We're ready to boogie," Naomi said, and they climbed a ladder to the top of the MIR, went through the hatch and down a ladder into a large titanium sphere. When they were in, a crew member dogged down the hatch into the sphere, and Peoples mirrored this from the inside.

It was a small space filled with instruments, reminding Michael of the cockpit of a 747 Boeing aircraft or pictures he had seen of a space craft, only more so. It was packed with instrument read outs and screens. Peoples went forward and sat on the left at an angle. She reached out her right hand and gripped the joy stick that gave her control of the craft. Michael and Weldon sat behind her, hunched slightly forward because of the curve of the sphere. Peoples put on a head set and spoke into it, "We're in place."

The crane came alive and lifted the submersible from its cradle, pivoted, and slowly lowered it into the sea a few feet out alongside the ship. As they bounced up and down with the sea, Peoples and Farley went through a lengthy checklist, and finally the submersible was free.

"MIR to Edgerton, we will go out five hundred yards and submerge."

"Roger that, MIR."

"How deep can this go, Naomi? And who builds these things?" Weldon asked.

"The Russians designed the MIRs. This is a second generation, and we can dive to twenty thousand feet." She turned and looked at Weldon. "We can go anywhere you want, Weldon, down to the bottom, which here is about five thousand feet. But to start we're going to home in on the pinger," she said.

Inside the sphere all they could see was the ocean outside. Peoples engaged the prop, and the craft began to move forward. When it had gone only a short way, she stopped.

"MIR to Edgerton, we are diving and tracking the pingers," she said as she manipulated the controls. Slowly the MIR began to sink, and she turned on the prop again so that there was a decline rather than a straight drop. It was a slow but steady descent, and a large white dial tracked their depth. As they descended, Peoples turned on a receiver, and they began to get steady pings from the two devices; she navigated by their signal. Initially they were too far from the bottom to see it; they only saw occasional strange fish. But slowly it became clear that they were beginning to go over a mountain, part of a range. To Michael it was like looking down from a drone.

The shape was familiar, but the surface was completely different. Instead of ice and rocks, this mountain was covered with various forms of plants; there was a fuzzy quality to the landscape. At this depth the sea was dark, but the small submersible's five-thousand-watt lights lit up the sea. Out of the large bubble window they saw a strange blue-green scene.

"It's like being on another planet," Michael said, and Weldon agreed.

After about half an hour they were at fifteen hundred feet, a few hundred feet below the top of the Kita Koho Seamount. There were folds and crags in it like any mountain, only softened by the marine life that lived on every surface.

"Okay, this is about as good as the signal will get," Peoples said.

Weldon looked at Michael.

"Weldon, let's begin," Michael said.

The two men sat opposite one another, closing their eyes. Peoples watched this, not sure whether she should join them. She decided not to; it would be too dangerous. After a few minutes, Michael said, "Weldon you are life-size, you are standing next to the warhead. What do you perceive?

"It's lodged in a crag, as I said. I can see it." He opened his eyes and said, "Naomi, go around that outcropping to the right of us."

Peoples complied, and slowly the MIR followed his directions.

"Now go deep into that cleft or whatever you call it. That's it. Now down lower. More. Now further in."

In the arc of light put out by the MIR there suddenly came into view something clearly man-made. They began to cheer, but as they came closer to it, they could see it was part of the missile, not the warhead.

Weldon sat down, closed his eyes and sat silently.

"Give me the task instruction again," he said, finally.

"Weldon you are life-size. You are standing next to the warhead. What do you perceive?"

For a moment there was silence, then Weldon said, "We have to go up and further to the right. Not far, around this fold."

Peoples maneuvered the craft as Weldon directed, and they rose up a short distance and moved around the fold in the mountain. As they came around, just on the edge of the light, they caught a flash of metal. Its foreignness more than its shape caught their attention. They came in closer and could see a heavily damaged cone shape.

"That's it," Weldon said. Michael and Naomi both looked at it for a long minute and agreed, and once again they cheered.

"I am so glad that I have seen this," Naomi said, "because if I hadn't, I wouldn't believe it."

She continued to slowly shift the MIR's position until she was close enough to extend the craft's arm.

"No one has said anything about this, but is this thing armed?" she asked.

"I asked that question," Michael said, "and the best judgment seems to be no, because this is designed to be a nuclear missile, and they don't have a bomb of the right size yet. But if it was still intact there might be a charge to separate the warheads."

"Good to hear," Peoples replied, as she brought the MIR in even closer until the mechanical arm on the front of the craft could touch the elongated cone, which was painted black. Hanging a short distance above it was one of the pingers.

"Could you have found that with electronic survey techniques?" Michael asked Peoples.

"Virtually zero chance because of where it is located," she replied.

Peoples pulled the MIR out of the mountain fold, and Michael asked, "Can you notify Edgerton?'

"No, unfortunately we have no radio contact at this depth," Peoples answered, then pulled back on her joy stick and the submersible slowly backed up. Weldon looked at the clock and asked her, "We've been down about four hours; how long will it take to get to the surface?"

"Probably another hour and a half," Peoples told him, and she moved the stick so that they slowly began to rise to the surface. As they were rising, Weldon asked, "Can you get back to it?"

"Oh, yes, no problem thanks to you and Coyote." Peoples replied, smiling at him, putting her hand on his arm. "We have a fix on it. We'll turn the pingers off, so we are the only people that will know, and I have the only track of how to get there. We're not really equipped for this kind of salvage operation. We need to get a ship out here that's set up to make such a recovery, and they will reactivate the pingers and follow the track."

As soon as they broke through the ocean surface, they saw a small boat was positioned between them and Edgerton. Standing in its open stern was a squad of heavily armed Chinese men in uniform. There was a frame across the boat, on top of which was a heavy machine gun, pointed at them. They could not hear the men, but they could see their agitation as they broke through to the surface.

"Whoaa, what's been going on while we were submerged today?" Naomi exclaimed. She quickly adjusted the radio and said, "MIR to Edgerton, come back."

"Edgerton to MIR. We see you. We will come to you; it's getting complicated," Reno said.

"What about these guys between us?"

"The Chinese navy have been shadowing us all day while you were submerged. We're a recognized U.S. government research vessel, and we're in international waters so they can't board us. How did the new technology work?"

"Squared away. You'll be happy."

"Well, that's good news."

"We're coming to you," Reno said, and inside the MIR they could see the ship begin to swing around. So could the

Chinese, and they moved out of the way at the last minute. It took forty minutes for Edgerton to get close enough for the MIR to steer alongside where the crane could reach and lift it back on deck. Michael was struck by how slowly everything moves at sea. As soon as it was in its cradle, they opened the hatch and climbed out. As Michael stood on the MIR before climbing down, he looked around and really appreciated for the first time that there were warships a short distance away.

"What did you find?" Reno, Farley, and Whitehead stood together, and behind them on deck was nearly everyone else in the crew.

"We found it," Peoples told them, then looked at Weldon, who towered over her. "I don't know how he did it, but once he and Michael went through a little ritual he just seemed to know where it was. We can't bring it up, though. It's going to require a ship equipped for salvage."

"No clapping," Reno said to the assembled crew, then "Come on down," to those with the MIR. "Let's go up to the bridge and you all can debrief. Everybody else just go about your business; remember, you're on candid camera," he said, gesturing towards the Chinese warships.

While crew members washed the MIR down with fresh water and secured it, Reno, Michael, and the others went up to the bridge. From that greater height they could see several more Chinese ships, and the twenty-five-mile radar showed even more.

They went to the conference room and were joined by Coyote. Goldstein smiled at Weldon, while Kilgore and Barber looked uncomfortable. The room crackled with excitement.

Peoples began, "We homed in on the pingers, even saw one, and Weldon guided us the rest of the way. I've got video of the whole thing,"

"You've actually found this thing?" Whitehead asked, amazed.

"Yes, thanks to these guys we know exactly where it is. And it is intact just as they said it would be. I will tell you quite honestly, if someone told me this story at, say, a conference, I wouldn't believe it. But look at it, here it is," Naomi said, and called up the video file, found her place, and put it on the big screen. The image was split, one side inside the MIR with three of them clearly in the picture. There was also audio, so that everything said inside the sphere could be heard. The other side was what was seen outside the craft in the arc of its six lights.

The room was silent as they first saw the missile part come into the light, and then listened as Weldon told them to move around the mountain fold where they would find the missile head itself. When they did so, there it was. "Look," Goldstein shouted. "The pinger is hanging from the rock above," and she pointed at the screen.

Peoples stopped the video and looked around the room. Everyone except Kilgore and Barber was looking at Weldon, Coyote, and Michael. Naomi waited a beat, then picked up the narrative.

"Everything was just as we were told it would be. I have no explanation for how this could be so, but there it is. I certainly will never forget this. That said," she said, reversing the video back to the first images of the warhead, "although Chris and Mitchell may feel differently, I don't think we're equipped to make a thirteen-hundred-foot salvage recovery of an object this size; it must be almost six feet."

Reno and Farley leaned towards each other and spoke between themselves for a moment.

"We agree," Reno replied. "Edgerton is not set up for that as presently configured. It's just as well, frankly. The Chinese have come very close and seem to be getting more agitated. The Russians left this morning. We've been trying to keep appearances calm and ordinary looking. While you were down, I sent out the tender with Ruth and some of her team, and so they watched her and saw nothing more than standard oceanography. Then you came up, and nothing is unusual," Reno said. "I am sure the Chinese videoed your surfacing and everything else we've been doing all day and are beaming it back to China for evaluation. So, we're going to get underway, as if we are finished here, which in fact we are," Reno said with a smile, looking around. "The Nimitz carrier group knows what's going on and they are headed this way, so we are going to let them sort it out with the Chinese. They're waiting to hear from us," he told them. Then he reached for a clipboard and read his notes.

"Sidney, Ruth, Sam, we'll move on to our next scheduled area. Michael, Jake Garth is waiting for an encrypted satellite call from you... Mitchell, can you show him how to set it up?"

They all looked out the bridge windows and back at the radar, and Reno said, "Okay, then we're getting underway. Michael, you need to make your call."

Farley led Michael over to a satellite phone different than any he'd seen before.

"It's the encryption circuitry," Farley said, then dialed in the code. Jake Garth answered. "What's happened? You can speak on this connection." Michael described what had happened. As he spoke, Farley whispered, "Tell him we're going to upload everything in a couple of hours, then tell him we are going to change position, and why." Michael did that as Garth listened quietly.

Then he said, "Okay, I will tell Sam. You have no idea what this means, Michael. Please thank your guys. Since nobody else knows, and you tell me it would be virtually impossible to find using electronic survey techniques, we're going to let things cool down. Then pick it up. I will arrange for a helicopter from the Nimitz to pick you up tomorrow. Then it's just the reverse of what you did to get there. Bravo Zulu, Michael, Bravo Zulu. We'll connect as soon as you are back," he said, and rang off.

"We're going to have a little celebration dinner tonight," Reno said, when Michael told him of his conversation. "Let's enjoy some downtime. I suspect your next few days are going to be very busy."

Michael and Weldon went back to their staterooms, picked up towels and their toiletry kits, and went down the corridor to the shower. Coyote had discovered the ship had a DJ set-up, and immediately volunteered to do the dance the crew was organizing for after dinner. Even though Chinese warships were on the radar, the whole ship had a sense of downtime and success. Michael got a cup of coffee from the very active galley, where fresh caught fish was being grilled, and went back out onto the rear deck. The Chinese ships were even closer and there were more of them. Just on the horizon he could see the carrier steaming towards them. A ship's tender with armed men came cruising by less than fifty yards from Edgerton, and he put up his hand and waved at them. To his surprise several waved back.

The ship's bell announced the meal and he went back in, joined the line, and filled his plate with the fish, a cabbage slaw with a miso based dressing, and browned fingerling potatoes with thyme. Weldon and Coyote, who had gone ahead of him, were sitting at a table surrounded by young scientists, mostly women. It made him laugh. He sat down at one of the metal tables, and Ruth Goldstein came over. "Can I join you?"

"Of course," he answered, and pulled out her chair, then sat down across from her. They ate in silence for a moment, then Goldstein said, "It's really good, isn't it? Jerry Reynolds is the best chef I've seen on a research vessel in thirty years. Chris is a foodie; he's not going to sea for weeks eating slop."

"A man after my own heart," Michael replied.

"Okay. How did you do it?"

"Do what?"

"How, out of thousands of square miles of ocean did you locate something that's six to ten feet long and six feet around? Or something like that. How did you do it?"

"Yes, I'd like to know that as well." Sidney Kilgore said, sitting down at their table.

"Okay. I'm happy to tell you. You won't believe a word of it, Professor Kilgore," Michael said, looking at him. "You start with Max Planck..."

"...The father of quantum mechanics?" Kilgore asked.

"Yes. In an interview he gave to the British newspaper in 1931, Planck was told, 'You and Einstein are the most famous scientists in the world. What have you learned?' Planck thought a moment and answered, 'I regard consciousness as fundamental. I regard matter as derivative from consciousness. We cannot get behind consciousness. Everything that we talk about, everything that we regard as existing, postulates consciousness.'"

"And your point is?" Kilgore said, in a challenging tone.

Michael ate another forkful of fish and thought how to answer and decided to focus on remote viewing as a technology. He put his fork down and continued, "My point is that I have developed a remote sensing technology that uses consciousness as you all use side-scan sonars or proton-precession magnetometers. Put the materialism versus consciousness debate aspect aside and just think of it as an application technology. There are the same issues."

"How could that be?" Goldstein asked.

"You are in one domain, and your instrument and target are in another domain, right?"

Goldstein thought for a moment, then said, "Yes. I am on the ship above the sea, and I am towing a device that is in the sea."

"You have an information-to-noise problem."

"Yes."

"You have to develop a skill-set so you can understand the information. Right?"

"Yes."

"You have to honor the limitation of your system, right?"

"I don't understand..." Goldstein said, and Kilgore sat with his arms folded.

"You have to see that your computer has a stable power source. You have to keep the temperature of your computer under control so it doesn't overheat, right? You have to understand the language your sensor system uses, correct?"

"Okay, I see where you are going with this," Goldstein answered.

"That's what I do. I have to create the right environment. I have to understand how to read the information I am getting from my instrument, in this case the human consciousness of my partner, the viewer. I have the same problems you do. How to distinguish good information from noise. Basically, remote viewing in this context is a remote sensing application technology. However, if you really want to understand what I am doing you have to begin with Planck's dictum: consciousness is the fundamental. Like everything else, the processes of nonlocal consciousness operate according to certain rules. You just have to learn the rules. That's what most of my research is about. How does it work? What are its limits?"

Suddenly the room was filled with music as Coyote went to work as a DJ. The young scientists got up and began to dance.

"I'll have to think about that, Michael," Goldstein said. "There's no question that you and your associates found the missile and the warhead. There is no denying that. Even you have to admit that, don't you Sid?" she said, looking at her colleague who sat there stony-faced.

"It was found, yes," he said begrudgingly. "How it was found is not clear, and I am not prepared to jump to any conclusions," Kilgore stated, as if testifying.

"A pleasure to talk with both of you," Michael said. "I'm going to go dance," and with that he picked up his dishes, took them over to galley window, sorted them out, left them soaking in gray plastic tubs of warm water, walked over to the dancers, and joined in.

CHAPTER FOURTEEN

The next morning the three of them were up early and in the middle of breakfast when Reno, Farley, Whitehead, and Peoples came over.

"The helo will be here in thirty minutes," Reno said, "but we wanted to come over and tell you how much we have enjoyed working with you all. I don't pretend to understand how you did it, but there is no question that you did. You're welcome back anytime."

Peoples handed Michael a 5TB flash drive memory stick, saying, "Here is the full record, everything," she said, looking at him. "Thought it best not to put anything online, so it's all here on this drive. I included my accuracy assessment, concept by concept as you showed me. On your four-point scale I make it eighty three percent correct or partially correct but still operational. Five percent wrong, and I can't evaluate eleven percent. I'm like Chris; I don't pretend to know how this worked, but it did, and I feel honored to have been a part of it."

They sat as a group, talking, until it was time to go. The helicopter touched down exactly at nine. As they climbed aboard the entire crew gathered and cheered. It made them feel wonderful, and the glow lasted the full ninety minutes it took to get back to the Nimitz. When they landed on the carrier's deck and got out of the helicopter, they noticed a Grumman C-2 was being made launch-ready. The same Lieutenant Bowser who had met them the first time came out again.

"Welcome aboard, but it will only be for a few minutes. Let's go down to the Grumman."

"When will it take off?" Michael asked.

"It's been waiting for you. That's why it's here," he answered. Michael, Weldon, and Coyote took that in and looked at one another. Michael had the same feeling he had had when they first landed on Nimitz; they were in the system. Things were being moved, not on some established schedule, but simply because moving them where they needed to go was a priority. Michael shared his feelings with the other two, and Coyote said, "It's like making friends with a scary rich giant."

"So right," Weldon responded.

The lieutenant saw them strapped in, said goodbye, and for the first time in days they were alone.

"I gotta tell you. I'm glad this ended better than the Amish girl probe," Weldon said. "I don't think I could have stood two failures that were that public."

"Me neither," Coyote agreed.

"Yeah, I feel the same; it would have been grizzly," Michael added. "You both made it happen. Twenty-eight inches apart. I mean, come on," he said with a laugh, and they joined in.

Two hours later they landed in Yokosuka, where they were met by another young lieutenant who introduced herself as Sally Harwig.

"I'm supposed to see that you get a decent meal, and Professor Gillespie, I have an urgent message," she said, handing him an envelope in which was a pink telcon note telling him to call Karen at the Institute. Harwig led them to the VIP lounge area, which made Weldon laugh as he thought about his time as an enlisted man in the service, and how he had travelled then.

There was a kitchen in the lounge, and since it was lunch time, a buffet was laid out.

"Take your time. When you're ready, a plane will take you back to the States."

"Just us?" Coyote asked, amazed.

"Yes. You all are very important; did you not know that?"

"No, we didn't" Michael responded.

"Well, you are," Harwig said, and laughed. "They didn't tell me why. Would you like to make your call before or after your meal, professor?"

"Now, please. Guys get started, I'll be back in a minute. Since it's on our schedule, relax, take your time eating."

Harwig led Michael off to an office and told him, "Just put in the country code and the number. Do you know the code?"

"001. Thanks," Michael said, sitting down. He looked at his watch, calculated the time difference, realized it was eleven a.m. in Washington and that Karen would be in her office. She was and picked up the phone immediately.

"So good to hear from you. What's the news?" she asked, carefully wording her question.

"Couldn't be better."

"Oh, I am so glad to hear that," and he could sense the relief in her voice.

"I'll tell you all about it when I see you. What's going on at your end?"

"The reason I marked my message urgent is that Gordon Baskerville called you yesterday afternoon."

"What did you tell him?" Michael asked.

"I said you were out of the country travelling and that I had no way to get in touch with you until you checked in."

"Perfect. What did he want?"

"He asked me to have you call him urgently as soon as we made contact. He wouldn't say anything else."

"I wonder what he wants. Well, he's in the same time zone as you, so I should be able to catch him. They're holding a plane for us."

"Really. Wow. Oh, Jake Garth called and asked me to call him as soon as I heard from you, and he would call you. But he said it might be a few days. They're waiting to get everything and process it, and he said to tell you they are planning the follow-up."

"So I've been told," Michael responded.

"Other than that there is nothing that can't wait."

"All right let me call Baskerville," he said. "Take care." He hung up and dialed Baskerville's number. His secretary answered and passed him through.

"What's up, Gordon?" Michael asked.

"I owe you an apology," Baskerville answered.

"Why?"

"Because it seems you were right after all."

"I don't understand."

"It's hunting season, and a deer hunter was up in your consensus zone. He found the body."

Michael felt a frisson of excitement pass through his body. "Well, that's great," he said enthusiastically.

"There's only one problem. He can't find it again. It's way off trail, and he had never been there before. It took him two hours to walk out, and now he can't get back to the same place."

"Put out a search group, like you did last time," Michael said.

"We did, and we couldn't find it either. I know this is an imposition, but could you come up here with a couple of your viewers? I remember the protocol you explained to me."

"We're in Japan right now..."

"Oh, I had no idea," and Michael could hear both the question and the disappointment in his voice. "Do you know when you are coming back?"

"As it happens, today. We're in transit."

"Are you in Tokyo?"

"It's a little more complicated than that."

"Could you do it?"

"I would have to talk with Weldon and Coyote; they're with me. It would depend on how they feel," Michael explained, "and you would have to pick us up wherever the plane is going to leave us and get us back home, of course. Wait a minute," Michael said, and went to the office door and saw the lieutenant waiting for him.

"Where is this plane taking us?" he asked.

"Where do you want to go? I don't think it matters," she responded.

"Oh. Then Harrisburg, Pennsylvania."

"Yes, sir. Harrisburg, Pennsylvania. I will tell the pilot and the tower."

Michael went back in and picked up the phone. "As it happens, they will fly us to Harrisburg, I think that's the closet airport to you.

"Yes, it is. You have a private plane?" Baskerville asked.

"Something like that."

"When are you scheduled to leave?"

"When we want to," Michael answered. "If you don't hear further from me, assume Weldon and Coyote are game. We will leave here in about an hour. I don't know how long it takes, but I will call you when we get in. You'll have to have someone pick us up and make arrangements. Also we're going to need some clothes and boots. Wait. Maybe we can do that here."

"Okay, thank you Michael. I'll cover whatever costs you have, and I really appreciate this," Baskerville said, and they hung up.

Michael left the office and found Harwig waiting.

"Is there a PX on the base...there must be," he asked.

"Yes, of course. Do you need something?"

"We need to buy some different clothes and hiking boots. I assume we could get that sort of thing. We have a new assignment."

Harwig looked at him in an appraising way, then said, "I'll drive you there. No, even better, I can get them out of stores. I am sure the admiral would approve."

They went back to the dining area, where he found his friends deep in conversation over a roast beef luncheon. He went over to the buffet, put together a plate, and sat down with them. Feeling it would be polite, he invited Harwig to join them, but was glad when she declined, saying, "I've already eaten, and I need to get a car and arrange everything."

As soon as she was gone, he turned to the other two, saying, "Major news. I talked with Gordon Baskerville, and they found the body where we said it would be."

"You puttin' me on, dude," Weldon said.

"No. They found it. Only they've lost it again."

"What?" Coyote said putting down his silverware. 'What does that mean, they've lost it. How could you lose it after you've found it?"

Michael recounted what Baskerville had told him. "He wants to know if we could come up and find it for him."

"Hey, why not? What do you say, Coyote?"

"Works for me. How do we get there?'

"The plane will fly us to Carlisle Barracks."

"How do you know that?" Weldon asked.

"Because I asked them to."

"They'll just fly us wherever we want to go?" Coyote exclaimed.

"Yes, they will."

"Wow, I could get used to living like this. This must be what it's like to be rich," Coyote responded.

Michael explained about the clothes and boots as they ate. They had just finished when Harwig reappeared.

"If you'll come with me," she said, and they followed her out to a car driven by an enlisted woman. They drove across the base to a supply building where they were fitted out with underwear, socks, camo, field boots, and Michael was given binoculars. As this was going on, Weldon regaled them with stories of his very different experiences as an enlisted man getting fitted out to go to Afghanistan. Then they drove out onto the revetment where there sat a large private jet.

"What kind of plane is this?" Coyote asked.

"It's a Bombardier Global 8000," Harwig answered as they reached the steps leading into the plane. They thanked her, went up the steps and buckled in. They were the only passengers. A young man in uniform came over and asked if they needed anything and handed them blankets and pillows. They told him no, so he went forward and the plane began to taxi down the runway. When it got to cruising altitude, they took off their shoes and tipped their chairs back until they became beds. Coyote put in his ear buds to listen to music, and within minutes all three were asleep.

Michael woke up first. He brought his chair back up, took out his laptop, and put the flash drive Peoples had given him into the USB port. As the others slept he went through the data, reliving things and seeing them in more detail than he had the first time. He was very impressed with how thoroughly Naomi had documented everything, particularly the search in the MIR. After about an hour he switched to going through the Amish girl data. It seemed a long time ago since they had done that project.

About ninety minutes later, Weldon and then Coyote woke up. The steward came down the aisle and set up a breakfast of scrambled eggs, toasted bagels, fresh squeezed orange juice, and coffee on the table at the plane's rear. The table had a white table cloth, proper silverware, plates, and white cloth napkins with the Navy seal on them.

"I'm loving this life," Coyote said as he began to eat.

Michael briefed them on what they would do. This time Coyote would be the first viewer.

It was just before ten when they landed at Harrisburg, and to their surprise both Baskerville and Johnson were waiting for them.

"How did you know when we would arrive?" Michael asked.

"Your plane filed its flight plan and someone called my office and left a message." Baskerville said, looking at the sleek jet as they came down the stairs. "You are the only three passengers," he said appraisingly.

"Yeah," Michael answered, and to change the subject and avoid questions, added, "You seem pressed."

"The hunter who thinks he found the girl is from North Carolina, and he has to be back at work," Baskerville explained as they walked into the officers' club bar, where they sat down and ordered coffees. "It's going to take a couple of hours to get there, say noon. Could you guys do it today, while we still have him?"

"We don't need him. In fact, I'd prefer that he not get involved," Michael said.

"What do you mean you don't need him?" Johnson asked, outraged at the idea of giving up the only man who had seen the body.

"Just what I said, Colonel. Get us to the consensus zone behind the abandoned road house, and we'll take it from there. Coyote and I will go first."

"Are you sure about this, Gordon?" Johnson asked.

"The hunter couldn't find it the last two days we went out, Tim, so I'm not sure what he adds; and I have to admit that so far everything Michael's team has told us has checked out. I think we go with what he wants."

"Alright. It couldn't get any crazier, why not."

"Gordon, I'd like to take this day off," Michael said. "We've been through a lot of time zones. I don't know what time it is for my body, but we are out of synch."

"Tell you what," Baskerville replied. "I'll put you up in the Brattlestone Inn; it's been there since the Revolution. And you can walk around Lancaster and get a sense of the place."

"That would be perfect," Michael said, and Coyote and Weldon nodded their agreement.

"The inn's food is notable." Baskerville said, and got up as they all did and walked out to his car. They drove to

Lancaster through Amish farms, then stopped in front of an eighteenth-century colonial brick building painted white with dark green shutters. It had a small garden and white fence at its front. Baskerville checked them in then pulled Michael aside, "I'll come by and get you in the command bus tomorrow morning. Would you object if a couple of Amish elders joined us? I don't know how this works."

"Gordon, from a science point of view this is a very rigorous experiment. Only the killer knows where this child's body was buried, and if it is as hard to locate as you describe it's very possible that even the killer couldn't find her. That makes it a sort of triple-blind experiment. I'd like to have the whole thing videoed, and I would like you to evaluate everything in a way that I will explain as we drive up. It's a concept-by-concept assessment as to the accuracy of the nonlocal perception data. And I would like Tim to do the same. That's the deal."

"You're that sure you'll find the body?" Baskerville asked, genuinely puzzled.

"No, you miss the point. I want the record and the assessments no matter what happens. None of us have ever done this before; I want the data. As to the Amish elders, no problem."

"Alright, I'll pick you up at eight thirty. The restaurant is taken care of," Baskerville said. He shook Michael's hand and walked down the lobby.

Once they had left their luggage in their rooms they walked out of the inn and down the street. At a corner they saw a group or Amish teenagers, easily distinguished by their starkly archaic dress. As they walked towards them, along a street of historical architecture, Michael had the sense he had moved in time. A horse drawn buggy went by and made the image even stronger. Then it was broken by a motorcycle roaring down the street. They stopped at a shop and looked in, but really looked at the teenagers. Weldon and Coyote were mesmerized.

"That's what I saw," said Coyote. "I never understood until now. The old-fashioned cloth has a quality you don't see in modern clothes. You see it on the res, though."

"This guy came from this," Weldon said.

"Wait," Michael said, taking out his phone, setting it on record, and giving their location, who the viewer was, and the time and date.

"The killer came out of that community," Weldon said, pointing at the teens. "He was one of them, but something went wrong. That's it," Weldon said.

The moment was broken by the noise of several more motorcycles going by.

When they got back to the inn, they went into its colonial dining room and ordered dinner, rehashing everything that had happened as they ate, and then went to bed. The next morning they were up, dressed in the tactical marine camo gear and boots supplied at the base.

The blue command bus was right on time. In addition to Baskerville and Johnson there was some kind of aide, a videographer and her assistant, a three-person bus crew, the driver, and two Amish men.

"My goodness," Tim Johnson said, as they climbed onto the bus. "You all look like a tactical ops team."

"We are," Weldon answered. "I wish I had had them with me in Afghanistan. If I had, several of my friends would have come home alive."

The comment shut Johnson down, and in the silence Baskerville introduced Michael and the team to the two Amish men, Samuel Yoder and Jonathon Schrock. Both were middle-aged robust men with the strange Amish beard down the sides of their face and under their chin, but with no moustache or facial hair on the front of their faces. Each was dressed in a black suit. On their heads were wide brim black Amish hats.

As they pulled away from the inn and settled down for the drive to State Game Lands Number 159, Yoder turned to Michael and asked him, "Can you assure us there is nothing demonic, no trafficking with spirits in what you do? Attorney Baskerville has explained a bit about you, but I don't understand, and this is important to us."

"Mr. Yoder," Michael answered, "this has nothing to do with either demons or spirits, nor is it religious. This is a normal human ability. Some people are better than others, to be sure, just like any other human ability. It's just that most people don't know that and never train for it. I gather you and Mr. Schrock are going to go into the forest with us, so you'll watch it happen."

Yoder looked at Coyote. "You're Indian. Where are you from?" It was such a blunt question that Coyote started to take offense. But as he looked at Yoder he realized the question was not judgmental but quite sincere, and it changed his mind.

"I'm a Hopi and I come from our reservation in Arizona, north of Flagstaff. Have you ever been to Arizona?"

"No. My people don't travel much."

"Yes, I see that with your buggies, your clothes, your farms."

Schrock asked him, "Why in the world would a Hopi be involved with something like this? Or even be in Washington, D.C.?"

"I came to Washington because our chief and one of the senators from Arizona were friends. The senator wanted a page who was a First American, as he called it, and I was selected. It came with a benefit: it paid for my college. I have always been interested in shamanism, in consciousness, and for me the Institute I work for is like a tribe, and Michael, Professor Gillespie, is our shaman. Does that make sense to you?"

"Yes, it does. We call the others, those who do not choose to follow the Amish way, the English. I understand your sense of tribe. For the rest I guess I will see."

Schrock next turned to Weldon. "You have the look of a soldier but something else."

"Special Forces, two tours Afghanistan," Weldon answered. "I come from Tidewater Maryland, and I paint houses. What about you?"

"I have been lucky; I farm a holding that was my father's," Schrock answered.

"I was able to buy my property," Yoder added.

"Is it hard to buy a farm?" Michael asked.

"Yes, very. Property values have gone way up. There are fewer farms available. It is a big problem for us," Yoder explained.

Gradually conversation ran out, and they rode the last twenty minutes each in his own silence. When the bus pulled in behind the abandoned roadhouse, like an engine revving they got up and stepped off the bus with the video team, leaving the bus crew still on board. As soon as they were outside, Michael looked over at the roadhouse and immediately recognized the accuracy of the descriptions he had gotten from the viewers. Michael and Coyote walked off by themselves for a moment, then came back to Weldon.

"This is the place, we both agree?" Weldon asked, looking at Coyote.

"Yes," Coyote agreed.

The three of them began to walk around the gravel parking area, while the others were talking and getting ready.

"You're going to do this Coyote," Weldon said. "I'm going to wait in the bus, just as you waited on the ship. I brought a book Barbara gave me," he said, holding it up. Then he put it in back in his pocket, and the three men held hands, eyes closed, sinking into meditation.

"We are of one intention, one mind, in this. Coyote is our guide," Michael said. Then they opened their eyes, turned back to the others, and found them ready to go. Michael went over to the video team and got two radio mics, hooked one up on his shirt and took the other one back to Coyote, who pinned it on his shirt, hooking the power pack on his belt. When they were linked, Coyote and Michael walked over to Yoder, Schrock, Baskerville and Johnson.

"Are you all going?" Michael asked, and when they said yes, he looked at them, saying, "Here's how this works. Coyote and I are going to walk ahead. We are both wired for audio so that there is a complete record of what is said. If there is a way for you to get wired to listen that's okay. But you all walk behind us; you can spread out as you like. You can talk quietly amongst yourselves. But don't talk to us. Does everyone understand?"

They said they did, and so they walked across the old parking lot and entered the woods. Michael cued in the audio record, saw the video crew were shooting, and the others had been given ear phones. He said to Coyote, "You are with the girl. Is she alive?"

"No. I stand by what I said earlier. He killed her in the motel. He put her over his shoulder. She wasn't very heavy, and he was in good shape," Coyote said as they walked through the trees. They had walked for about an hour, then Coyote stopped.

"He was tired. He put her down here. He was hungry again. He thought about leaving her body here, but decided he needed to go deeper in the forest. So he picked her up again. Her bowels and her bladder emptied as he did that, and he was bothered by the smell. Her body was stiffening in, what do you call it?"

"Rigor mortis."

"That's it. It was bent from being on his shoulder but becoming awkward to carry."

They walked another hour and were at the foot of a hill when Coyote stopped again, as did Michael. The others gathered nearby. "He was tired, and he hated the smell. He had a folding shovel. I described it in the first session." Coyote was now acting what he perceived. "It was raining. He didn't dig a very deep grave," he said, and walked over to where a rock face stood out. He reached down and pulled back come branches. It made other branches move, revealing a naked foot.

"That's just what the hunter said he saw," Johnson said.

Coyote knelt and began to dig with his hands and very quickly exposed the body of Rachel Swayze, now badly decomposed.

"Stop, Coyote, don't dig anymore. This is a crime scene," Baskerville said. Johnson took out a GPS and noted the location.

Yoder and Schrock walked up to the body and looked down at the girl.

Schrock knelt down and brushed away some leaves covering her face. "She has something in her mouth. It looks like a sock," he said.

Baskerville and Johnson traded a look, then Baskerville looked at Michael and Coyote.

"That exactly what you predicted," he said.

"Yes, and I think you will find she was struck on the right side of her head and it cracked the zygomatic arch."

"What is that?" Schrock asked.

"It's the point where the jaw bone connects to the skull," Michael answered.

"We will come and get her body," Yoder said.

"No," Baskerville replied. "I'm sorry, but we have to bring a forensics crew up here. They will get whatever evidence is to be found and bring the body back for an autopsy, so we can know how she died."

The two Amish men looked at one another, and accepted what Baskerville said. "We understand."

"Coyote, we do not know how to thank you. This was definitely godly. It has brought Rachel back to us."

"Listen, we have to go," Baskerville said. "There is no cell service up here. We need to get back to the bus so I can get a forensic team up here."

"Please. Forensics I don't know about, but I do know about wild animals. We should cover her again so that no animals find her," Yoder said.

Coyote responded, "He's right."

And so they reburied Rachel as Johnson laid out an arrow of rocks pointing to the grave. Then they all hiked back to the bus.

"I thought this area had been searched several times," Yoder said to Baskerville as they walked back through the woods.

"It was, elbow to elbow. I don't know how it was missed, but it was. I think we have to acknowledge that had it not been for the Hill Institute, Michael, and Coyote, she might never have been found."

When they got back to the parking lot behind the abandoned road house, Weldon jumped off the bus and went over to Michel and Coyote.

"It worked," Michael said. "Just as you found... you know..." he said, looking around to see who might be able to hear them, "so Coyote found this girl's body," and they hugged in a huddle.

As soon as they all loaded into the bus, Baskerville called the county coroner, explained what they had found, and asked him to send up a forensic team to the coordinates he gave, explaining about the arrow of stones.

"I want you to do a full workup, and then bring the body back for an autopsy. This is a murder case, possibly first degree," he told whomever he was speaking with. He hung up and turned to the others on the bus. "They'll leave immediately. It will be close, but I think they will be able to get the body out today, so we will do the autopsy tomorrow as soon as the coroner can do it. Probably right after church.

Then you can claim the body and take her back to your community. I am so sorry for your loss," Baskerville said to Yoder and Schrock.

"At least we have her now," Yoder answered, "and we will be able to bury her in her family's plot."

"Now what happens?" Schrock asked.

"Now we have to catch whoever did this. I will contact you about that Monday, after we have the autopsy results. That will tell us things we don't know yet."

They rode in silence for a while, then Yoder asked Coyote, "Did you talk to her spirit? Is that how you found her?"

"No, it's not like that," Coyote answered. "It's like a memory. You're married. Are you married?"

"Yes, of course. I have four grown children."

"Can you remember your wedding?"

"Yes. Certainly," Schrock replied, surprised at the turn of the conversation.

"Picture it in your mind. Do you have it?"

"Yes."

"Can you remember what the room looked like? What your wife's dress looked like? Can you remember what the meal after the wedding was like?"

"Yes, I could describe all that to you."

"That's what remote viewing is like. You can smell things, not really of course, but you recognize the smell. You can visualize things. When Michael asks me a question, what he is doing is like steering my memories, only they're not my memories. They are the impressions his questions evoke."

"I see. I think I understand. When we went into the forest you were with Rachel and her killer. Is that right?"

"Yes, exactly. Michael has taught us how to do this. He calls it a protocol. I think of it as a ritual. Like a vision quest I did when I was a boy."

"Is God involved?"

"Isn't God involved with everything?" Coyote asked. "That's what my people believe."

"Is it the same for you?" Schrock asked Weldon.

"Yes. Michael's questions focus your consciousness; you become linked. He calls it a bio-circuit of intention; he is the rational side. You just stop thinking and let sense impressions and a kind of knowingness flood into you. It's a skill Michael teaches. And after you do it for a while you get to be more confident. Just like any other human skill. All the stuff you see in the movies and on television" he said, then realized the Amish didn't have or see either. "Excuse me, I understand... your people aren't in that world."

"You see us as a tribe?" Yoder asked.

"Yes, I do. As you see me as an Indian belonging to a tribe with some kind of Indian religion, I see you as a tribe of Christian Caucasians who have taken themselves out of the world. You are living a path. So am I."

Yoder and Schrock looked at Coyote as if he had suddenly appeared before their eyes. They "saw" him for the first time, and Michael could see the respect in their faces.

"This is not about the supernatural or occult or any of that," Michael said. "We do research into the nature of consciousness. My only interest in religion of any kind is anthropological."

"You don't believe in God?" Schrock asked, appalled.

"I believe in the great unity of consciousness, and that consciousness is fundamental and causal; and I don't mean just human consciousness. Humans culturally have a tendency to package consciousness in religion. I understand that, respect it and why it happens, but I am not religious in that sense," Michael explained.

Schrock and Yoder clearly had not expected any of this; nor had Baskerville and Johnson, who had silently witnessed the exchange. Michael could see their trouble reconciling what they had just witnessed in the forest with what they were hearing now.

As if by common agreement, they all got up to do various things and moved around the command bus. When they sat down again, they talked at a superficial level. On the drive back to Lancaster, they dropped each of the Amish off at the head of the driveway to their farms, which were about five miles apart on the same road.

When they got to the Brattlestone Inn, Baskerville asked, "How would you like to go back?"

Michael looked at the other two, and said, "We'll drive. It's only about three hours. Including driving in from the airport it would take that long by plane and be a lot more hassle. Can you rent us a mid-size car, one way, to be picked up at the Institute?"

"Yes, I'll see that it's taken care of. Do you want to stay for the autopsy? It's scheduled for ten tomorrow morning."

"I'd like to witness it, yes," Michael answered. "What about you two?"

"I pass," Weldon said. "I've seen enough dead children."

"I've seen this girl in my mind, that's more than enough," Coyote said.

"Okay. Michael, I will pick you up at the inn at ten a.m.," Baskerville told them.

"Thank you again," Johnson added. "It's going to take me a while to process all this, I have to confess. But, just personally, I thank each of you very much. This has been eating at our community for weeks."

Baskerville and Johnson shook hands with them, got back on the command bus, and drove off.

CHAPTER FIFTEEN

With a welcoming fire in the hearth, beamed ceilings and paneled wainscoting, Michael could imagine George Washington coming around the corner into the inn's lobby. As soon as they were inside, Weldon said, "I want to get out of these clothes. Too many memories."

'Me too," Coyote replied. They arranged to meet in half an hour for dinner, and by ten were in their four-poster beds, asleep.

True to the minute, just as they were finishing breakfast, Baskerville appeared, and Michael went off with him to the hospital.

When they got there, Michael followed Baskerville to the basement and down a corridor to the morgue. On their way a pathologist in his late thirties in hospital greens stepped out of the operating room. He was about five foot three, with thin hair and rimless glasses. He looked at his watch, saying, "Thank you, Gordon; you are right on time." Turning back, he said, "Gowns are on the right, as are gloves." As he entered, Michael could see the young girl's partly decomposed body, partially covered by a sheet, lying on a stainless-steel autopsy table. A moveable light and a microphone hung from the ceiling over her; two gowned assistants stood on the other side of the table.

"Michael," Baskerville said, "I want you to meet Bob Straus. Bob, this is Professor Michael Gillespie, who is helping us on this case."

"Yes, I heard that very strange things happened to recover the body. You'll have to tell me about them sometime," Straus replied, taking off his glasses, pulling a cloth out of his pants pocket, and polishing the lenses. "My wife has an interest in such things."

"What have you learned, Bob?" Baskerville interjected.

"This is a late fourteen-year-old pubescent girl who was in robust health. But you know that. She was captured and tied up using duct tape." As he spoke, Straus pulled the sheet back and showed whatever had led him to that conclusion. "But she was probably untied later, because she scratched someone's face pretty severely," Straus continued. "It's just possible after all this time that we might still be able to get a DNA match if you catch someone. But it is not guaranteed."

"Was she raped?"

"Oh yes, and she was a virgin. There was tearing. She fought back, and the killer stuffed a sock, probably one of hers, into her mouth. I would hypothesize this was to stop her screaming, so possibly this happened indoors in a place where other people might overhear. I think she suffocated as a result of the sock. At some point after that, before rigor mortis set in, she was put on a metal floor that had some rust and was not new, probably a pickup truck bed."

"We have second degree, for sure," said Baskerville in response. "Was she struck on the right zygomatic arch?"

Straus looked nonplussed, then admitted, "I didn't think to look for that."

"Well, please do so," Baskerville told Straus.

"Tomorrow, Gordon. It will wait until tomorrow. I have a T-time at noon. You know how long it takes to drive to the country club."

"I'm sorry, Bob, I really must insist," Baskerville replied.

"Alright," Straus replied with irritation. "Step out please while I do it."

Michael and Baskerville went out of the operating room and sat across the hall in a small lounge area decorated with tired green Naugahyde chairs.

When they were seated, Baskerville turned to Michael, saying, "I have to tell you, hanging around with you is one of the weirdest things I have ever done. Everything you sent in your report has checked out, and I still don't understand how you got that information."

Twenty minutes later Straus came out looking rather chastened.

"Gordon, I don't know how I missed it; probably because I don't think I have ever seen it before in a situation like this. The killer is right-handed. While she was alive he struck her with a blunt instrument, about two inches wide and probably slightly curved. The first thing that came to mind was the handset of a wired phone. Where do you still see a lot of those? She bled internally from the fracture, and it ran into her throat. Because of the sock she couldn't spit the blood out, and that's the cause of the suffocation."

"That's first-degree murder, Bob. I know it was an imposition, but this makes a big difference."

"I understand. Sorry I got testy earlier. I should have caught this. Give me twenty-four hours, and I will have a report on your desk. This is a bad guy, Gordon; you need to catch him."

"We will," Baskerville said, shaking Straus' hand, then he and Michael left. On the way back to the inn, Michael asked, "So what now?"

"Now, Michael, we take the rest of your stuff very seriously. Based on what your viewers said, and your analysis, we will figure out who this guy is."

When they got to the inn Coyote and Weldon were waiting in the lobby and ready to go.

Baskerville thanked them all with real passion, and they drove away feeling they had done good work. They stopped in York at the Public Fish House for a very tasty lunch of Maryland oysters and two pounds of wild caught steamed Gulf shrimp with the restaurant's special spicing and cocktail sauce, and quarters of iceberg lettuce with blue cheese dressing. All washed down with Dogfish Head ale. Michael explained everything he had seen and heard at the morgue as they ate. It was a celebratory lunch, given extra passion because for weeks they thought they had failed.

"So now what, Boss?" Weldon asked.

"I guess we're finished," Michael answered.

"I don't think so," Coyote said.

"You don't think so?" Michael responded.

"Yeah. I don't think they're going to find him."

"I don't either," Weldon said in support. "I don't think this guy is anywhere near here, and I think he could do it again."

"I agree," Coyote added. "This ain't over yet. That's my feeling."

"You both could be right; I guess we'll see. But now we need to get back. I'm going to have to go talk to Kassimir, I am sure."

"God, these things are so intense that it seems like a year ago we did the missile project," Weldon commented, and they all agreed. They got back to the Institute just as it was getting dark, parked the rental car in the little brick pad in front, and went their separate ways.

Michael walked back to his house, glad to be home. He caught up on some news and went to bed, wondering how Tracy was doing in the Amazon and when he would next hear from her. She should be coming home soon, he thought with happiness as he fell asleep.

He was at the institute the next day, taking a break for a second cup of coffee, when Karen paged him to say Jake Garth was on the phone. When he picked up, Garth asked him if he could come out to Langley. Fifteen minutes later he was on the road to the CIA.

After passing through security and being given a visitor badge, he was met in the agency's famous lobby and taken up to the executive floor. Denise Mailman, Kassimir's secretary, was sitting behind her desk. She got up when he came in and put out her hand. "Professor Gillespie, how nice to see you again," she said with a smile. "Dr. Kassimir is waiting for you. Won't you go in."

When he did, he immediately saw Kassimir sitting in one of the leather chairs that were grouped around a glass-topped coffee table and a couch.

Seated in other chairs around him were his deputies, Herbert Waterman and Stanley Potter, also Jake Garth. Michael had never been sure what Garth's status was.

As soon as Michael took a seat, a Filipino steward came in carrying a silver tray on which were a modern Norwegian style silver coffee pot, sugar, and creamer, along with four cups and saucers. Michael remembered the man's name was Manuel. As they went through the ritual, one by one, of Manuel pouring their coffee, they made small talk catching up; but Michael felt a change from when he had been with them last.

When Manuel left, Kassimir said, "Michael, this is the second time; your country thanks you. We owe you," and it was clear he meant it.

"It was fascinating. You've seen the videos?"

"We have," Kassimir answered.

"They are amazing," Waterman declared. "It seems so 'ordinary' as it's happening that you forget how it ought to be impossible."

"Paradigms are cultural, not scientific, Herb," Michael responded, sipping his coffee. "Remote viewing is only strange if you are blind to the matrix of consciousness and think that consciousness is only physiological, trapped within your skull."

"Would you consider going directly on the federal payroll? We could move your entire operation and place it under..." Kassimir said.

"I don't want to do that," Michael interrupted. "I want to stay just as we are. The university, the house, Georgetown; the entire setting is just right. When you do this kind of work, Sam, you have to think differently. Things that are normally big influences like time and space are hardly factors. Psychological conditioning, familiarity, anything that facilitates attaining and sustaining intentioned focused awareness; those things matter. You have to become aware of the nuances."

"Okay. I can see that," Kassimir replied. "There is a secret sauce, I get that. So, what do you need?"

Michael hadn't expected the question, but he had an answer. "I need about five hundred thousand dollars spaced over about two years so that Gilbert and I, and his post-doc elves, can take our biometric monitoring systems up to a new level. We have a growing body of data that suggests the anterior cingulate area of the brain plays some role in accessing nonlocal consciousness, but we don't really understand it. We need to up our game."

"Alright. We'll do that. Coordinate with Jake," Kassimir said, looking at Garth.

"My case officer," Michael said with a laugh.

Kassimir and the others just smiled.

"Yes, in a sense that has become part of his job," Kassimir said. "What else do you need?"

"Steady funding and uninterrupted good health," Michael answered with a laugh. "I am ahead of the game on one point because you have taken care of the funding; I know Barbara played a role in that..."

"She helped us see how to structure it," Potter suddenly spoke. "I worked with her on it; she is very persuasive about your research. You're going to be stable for at least five years, and I see no reason why it would stop after that."

"That's good to know."

"There will be no media this time," Kassimir said, changing the subject.

"Not a problem for anybody on my side. We have presumed we all say nothing about any of this," Michael said.

"Correct. Consider this top secret, need to know, and please make sure all your people understand."

"You can be comfortable about that," Michael responded.

"You are going to be given awards. That's how the government says, 'thanks'. There will be a ceremony. It will be here. Everyone involved will be getting a decoration. Of course, that's going to be secret too," Kassimir said, making a wry facial gesture. They sat without speaking for a moment, then Kassimir began once more, "Thank you again, Michael." He stood up, and Michael knew the meeting was over.

They all stood and shook hands, and Michael left knowing he would probably never be able to talk about anything he and the others thought of as the Missile Probe. It would be as if one of the most exciting weeks of their lives had never happened. It was very different from the Vision Probe, the Institute's only other interaction with the government which had put them in the media spotlight for months. This was the secret world. Driving back, he found that editing out those powerful experiences from public knowledge left him feeling very weird, and he wondered how spies lived their lives as if they were two people. He decided he didn't care for it.

CHAPTER SIXTEEN

Noah Ebersole was on his way home, thinking about what he was planning, imagining what he would do, when memories of raping Rachel Swayze flooded back into his mind. He hadn't thought about her in days, and as he did so he remembered her body, feeling her young breasts, and realized that for the first time he could do it without fear and panic flooding his emotions about being arrested. He felt that was now behind him and, as he drove, he gave himself over to a blend of what he planned and what he had done, seeing each moment, focusing on different visuals, different sensations.

When he got home he made himself some hot chocolate with milk and extra sugar. He sat down looking into the fire as he thought about how he could get a girl. He could bring her up to the single-wide and keep her tied up and naked for weeks. What could she do? There was no phone. No mobile service. No electricity, no lights to flash off and on. No one ever came up here. He decided to put a gate across the entry to his lane. Then no one could get in, and you couldn't really see the trailer from the lane. If he had to kill her, well, the forest was right there. He knew how to do it, and it would be much simpler where he now lived. Fantasizing about a naked girl and her capture aroused him again, but he suddenly realized that while all his plans were good, the girl he had been watching at the church was not the way to go.

Looked at in a certain way, he thought, capturing Rachel had cost him his home. Even if it wasn't a very happy home, he knew the people. Knew the rhythms of life. Now he had found a new home. If he was going to take another girl, he didn't want it to cost him his comfortable home in the woods and the best pay he had ever made. A corporal in the Army made about twenty-six thousand a year. At twenty-one dollars an hour he was making twice that. A mistake could force him to leave another community, and he might get caught this time. You have to keep that in mind, he told himself, imagining life in a prison cell.

No, this wasn't the right girl. But that made him think of Hollins. It was less than an hour and half up the road. If he did it right, he could get a girl and bring her back with no one knowing about it. Hollins was far enough away that no one would connect her disappearance with a mechanic down in Rural Retreat who was part of the Evangelical Christian community. No one down here, he told himself, knows anything about Rachel and the Amish. How could they, why should they?

As he had done with Rachel, he began planning his campaign, just as he had watched his captain instruct his lieutenant, who told him and the others in the squad what the plan was. People's lives depended on good planning; his life now depended on it. It was all in the prep.

The next day after work he went to the church thrift store again and bought clothes and a pair of shoes like those he had seen men his age wearing when he was in Hollins. As he paid for his purchases, he felt proud that he could buy them without having to worry about money. Beneath that he felt he had built a new life. He didn't feel afraid. There was no reason Rachel should intrude on this new life, he told himself. I've gotten away with it, and I liked it, and I want to do it again, he thought.

Over the next two weeks he went to Hollins three times, each time to a different place. Eventually he decided that Hollins was not the right community. The girls came from families that had money. He had seen boarding school girls and private college girls when his family or friends went into Lancaster in their buggies. Those kinds of people, he thought, would pay people in addition to the police to search for their daughters. Why raise the risk, he told himself? As he sat in a pub looking at two freshman girls, the decision point came when he also realized college girls were too old. What he liked was fourteen to fifteen. It wasn't colleges he needed to focus on, it was ninth graders.

He went to the library. He had never used a computer, but one of the librarians showed him how to use Google, and he quickly located the public high school in Wytheville, the next town north of Rural Retreat on Interstate 81. Much closer than Hollins. He had considered the high school in Rural Retreat, but as he thought about it that seemed too close to where he lived and worked.

The more he thought about how he could abduct a girl, going through the steps one by one, he realized that he needed a way to stop the girl from screaming or fighting, and it reminded him of something he had been taught by the older brother of a friend when he was ten and collected butterflies. The next day he went to the Southern States Co-op and bought a bottle of John Deere Ether Starting Fluid and a roll of duct tape, then he went to the supermarket and bought a box of Kotex Super Overnight sanitary pads.

The next weekend he drove up to Wytheville. It was a town about four times larger than Rural Retreat, with eight thousand people. It was also slightly more upscale. As he drove down the road that ran in front of the high school, he happened to notice a girl's field hockey game and pulled over and watched from his truck. He saw girls the right age, but they didn't do it for him. Then he went downtown to a place where teens hung out, and it looked much more promising. He realized the problem to solve was how to capture the girl so that no one noticed. He had never paid any attention to cameras before, but once he noticed them, he saw them everywhere. That meant he had to capture the girl somewhere where there were no cameras, like on a residential street, he thought. He spent the next hour driving up and down such streets in Wytheville, getting a granular sense of the territory. As he was doing this, memories came back of reconnoitering villages in Afghanistan. It was all in the prep, just as his captain kept saying.

It took another two weeks before he found the girl. She often walked to school. Like Rachel she had a lithe, well-shaped body with small but evident breasts. She was blonde. He couldn't see her eyes. He got the school's game schedule from the library computer; he had come to love Google but had no interest in email or anything else. He saw her at two more games and got close enough to listen to her and her friends. He learned her name was Jessica.

His time became a pattern. He was at work by eight o'clock and stayed at it until four thirty, with thirty minutes for lunch. He often ate with Seabuckle or Henry Jones, a man in his forties with wiry salt and pepper hair and the kind of stringy musculature Noah associated with this region of Virginia. Jones said very little, and that almost always about work. They all respected one another's skills, so although very different, the three men got on.

Twice a week after work and one afternoon over the weekend, he went up to Jessica's school and home; he had now worked out where she lived. Otherwise he went home where, before it got too cold, he worked on a deer and rabbit fence for the garden he planned on starting in the spring. He cut down a pine tree and two hardwoods and laid in four cords of wood and built a cover over them. He got a larger propane tank for the refrigerator, stove, and water pump, and a fifty-gallon kerosene tank for his lamps. He built a larder for the simple foods he liked to eat and equipped his kitchen from the thrift store. By November he was ready for winter.

He rarely thought now about the police or anyone else trying find him. He had made his footprint as small as possible. The only time he had felt vulnerable was when he went in to get a Virginia driver's license. But he got the woman clerk to make his middle name, Daniel, his first name. He told her a story about how he went by his middle name, but the Pennsylvania bureau had messed it up.

After several weeks of reconnaissance, he had Jessica's schedule. The coming Thanksgiving break was when he planned to make his move.

CHAPTER SEVENTEEN

A week after they got back from the Pacific, the award ceremony arranged by Kassimir took place. Michael received the National Intelligence Cross, Weldon and Coyote the National Intelligence Distinguished Service Medal, and the other viewers the National Intelligence Exceptional Achievement Medal; but it was all in secret. No one would ever know but they themselves and whatever secret archives the government maintained.

After that the Institute returned to its normal routines. Kassimir, true to his word, arranged a National Institutes of Health grant for the new biometric system that Michael and Gilbert, with help from Barbara, had designed. With the influx of funding they were soon consumed by that work.

Tracy called to say she hoped to be home by Thanksgiving if she could get down the river, out of the jungle, and catch a flight. She had arranged for her daughter, Sarah, who had started second grade at the Charlottesville Waldorf School with her brother's two children, to be picked up as soon as she returned. In their satellite phone calls Michael could sense Tracy's excitement to get back and start work on the papers and book she had planned on nonlocal consciousness and the rituals of the Amazonian tribe with whom she had been living.

The weather had turned cold, and on Sunday Michael was in his garden preparing his flowers and bushes for winter when he heard the phone ring. He went into the kitchen and picked it up to hear Gordon Baskerville's voice.

"What's up Gordon? Have you found him? It's been weeks; I wondered when I would hear from you."

"Hello, Michael. No, we haven't found him, that's why I'm calling. We have followed one line of inquiry after another, to no effect. The only person who resembles the description you gave us was a janitor named Noah Ebersole, but he left the community days before Rachel Swayze was abducted and hasn't been seen since."

"Have you searched for him?"

"Of course. He was a member of the Amish community who left during his Rumspringa period and surprisingly went into the army."

"I thought you told me the Amish were COs?"

"They are; no one seems to know why he did it. When he returned, they gave him a job in the community but would not accept him back as a full member, so after working for a while as the janitor at the school he left. Tracking him has been very difficult because, as you know, the Amish live in their own reality; they don't have much of a footprint in the modern world. No Twitter, Facebook, or even simple things like electric bills. More than that, his contact with Rachel seems to have been very limited."

"What was it?"

"That's what made us look at him. Remember the 'teacher but not a teacher' comment?"

"Yes."

"Well, he apparently taught some of the girls defensive martial arts so they could ward off non-Amish men who bothered them when they came into town. There doesn't seem to be much to it, but he is the closest person to your description; although honestly, I don't see it. Still, based on, well, you know..."

"What can we do to help?" Michael asked.

"Locate him; can you do that?"

"Maybe. Do you have a picture of him?"

"I have his driver's license photo, that's all. He bought a black Toyota truck; that was the other thing that caught Tim Johnson's attention. Your viewers saw a black truck."

"Okay, Noah Ebersole. Send me the picture. But the more I think about it, I don't believe that is the way to do it."

"What do you mean?"

"Let's not limit the search by starting with presumptions about a particular person. If he is not the person, we would hamstring the probe. If he is, it will all get confirmed again."

"Well, I leave it to you. When can you start? I'm getting a lot of heat up here," Baskerville said, then added, "I'm sending the picture to your email address as we are talking."

"Then when I go in on Monday, we'll start."

"Where will you search?"

"Based on what you are telling me, I guess we will have to start with the whole of America."

"You're going to try and find one person out of three hundred and eighteen million?"

"Yes, exactly."

After he had hung up, Michael went back out to his garden and began to think about how to design the protocol for this new probe, and by the time he walked down to the Institute on Monday, he had a plan.

The next morning, as soon as he got into the office, he had Karen begin to schedule the sessions. Seven viewers. He would have to do all the interviews, which wasn't optimal, but Gilbert was consumed by the biometric system they were building. He had decided not to use the picture of Ebersole. He was wary of starting on a false premise.

Karen came into his office after lunch with the schedule. Since all of the viewers had jobs or owned businesses, getting everyone scheduled was not easy; but they all wanted to help and she had worked it out. John Sacks was the first session, and he was scheduled for the next afternoon at three.

Michael downloaded a map of the United States, got his questions in order, and was prepped to go when Sacks came in. He was a very fashionable and trim man in his thirties. Along with his husband, Jerry, he owned the most prestigious and sought-after designer decorator business in greater Washington. Their studios were in old Chevy Chase, Maryland, where Jerry did the business side and John the designing and decorating. They specialized in embassies, mansions, Watergate condominiums, and tiny homes for the homeless, a re-housing project they supported.

Michael had first met John when he came to him because he regularly experienced precognitive dreams. He and John had liked one another immediately, and after two meetings Michael had asked John if he would like to try remote viewing. They had become close, and John had helped him acquire his Biedermeier dining room table and had helped him buy, at a big discount, the Brancaster leather and airplane metal chairs in his office at the Institute.

"It's been a while," John said as he walked into Michael's office.

"It has. How are you?" Michael asked, getting up to give him a hug.

For the next half hour they drank some coffee and caught up with each other as friends do. Then Michael said, "You ready?"

Sacks put down his cup, "Of course."

They went down to the egg, and once settled in it, put on the biometric helmets and sat for twenty minutes in meditation. Then Michael logged in the session and gave Sacks the task instruction.

"John," Michael said, handing Sacks a sealed envelope containing Rachel's picture, "I would like you to look again at Rachel Swayze."

"I've already told you everything I got."

"Yes, and very successful you were. This time we are looking for the person who did this heinous act."

"Oh, I'm on board for that," Sacks said with enthusiasm.

"Okay. I am going to say the word, 'target', and when I do you will be with the person who killed this girl." He paused as John moved his body slightly to get more comfortable. "Tell me when you are linked."

Sacks sat with his eyes closed for a moment as Michael watched his brain patterns change.

"I'm with him."

"It's a him?"

"Yes. Definitely."

"Give me your impressions."

"Oily. Greasy."

"Okay."

"Machinery around me. Not like a factory. More like they fix things."

"Are you inside or outside?"

"Inside but I can see out. There are big doors like a barn. Here, let me draw it," Sacks said, and took his tablet and drew a sketch. He worked on it for a few moments; it began to look like something he would sketch for a client.

"There is one big open space but several doors. It's on a street. Not a lot of traffic though."

"Are there any trees?"

"Yes, although only a few."

"John, I'd like you to go up into the air to the tops of the trees and rooftops."

"Okay. I'm there."

"Look to your left, what do you see?"

"It's a town. I sense a lot of red brick. This is not a big town, Michael... nothing like a city, more like a village really... Maybe a few thousand people. Maybe less."

"There is something you see that stands out from other things, something that will tell me I am in the right place. What is it?"

"Railroad. There's an old-fashioned depot. I'll draw it," and he did.

"Anything else?"

"Not really. This guy is happy, or content might even be a better word."

"Tell me about him."

"He's in his twenties, early, I think. Physically strong. Smarter than people think he is. Anonymous farm boy face. Odd, he's quite religious, but isn't really. Wait a minute," Sacks said. "He's planning to do this again. He got away with it. He's planning now to do it again. He likes it. There is something twisted about this guy."

"Alright, John. I'd like you to go to where this man lives. When I say 'target' you will be there. Target."

"Woods. Lots of trees. Green. I have a strong sense of green. It's very quiet. Strong sense of nature."

"Okay."

"A shape. Metal. Like a shipping container. That's about it."

"Alright, John, please look at your tablet. You will see a map of the United States. Please go over it and ask yourself, is this man located within the area portrayed by the map?"

"Pretty gross scale," Sacks observed as he looked.

"We have to start someplace. I'm sure there will be at least one more session to fine tune it. For now, just make the smallest circle you can."

Sacks moved his hand over the tablet palm down. "It's somewhere here," he said, taking the stylus and drawing a small circle. "I think that's it for now."

Michael logged out of the session and brought the light back up.

"I want you to catch this guy, Michael. He's going to do this again," Sacks said, looking at his watch. "I have to go. That new billionaire senator who bought himself a seat has purchased a very nice property up in the embassy area on Massachusetts. I'm decorating it and redesigning the gardens with Fumio. I just love blank checks," he said with a laugh.

"Please tell Fumio I appreciated his suggestions for my terrace."

"I will. Gotta run," Sacks said, and they both left the egg.

Michael was just sitting down at his desk when Karen came in.

"Tracy called while you were in the egg. She'll be back middle of next week."

"Really? I didn't expect her for another ten days," Michael answered.

"She said she was just a short way down the Rio Negro and came to a village where there were two entomologists from the Smithsonian. She told me they had a pontoon plane, and there was a seat open. They are going to fly her to where she can catch some kind of internal short hop to a larger airport, then to Miami and home."

"Wonderful. I hope I can include her in this new phase of the Amish girl probe, but the session I just finished has left me very uneasy. We may have a short fuse on this. John thinks he's about to do it again. Who's next?"

"You have Jefferson Yu at three thirty, and Weldon at five when he gets off his painting job. Then Coyote and Constance tomorrow."

Yu showed up as scheduled, and his session went much like Sack's had. Yu identified some of the tools that were in the place where the killer worked. He sold them in his hardware store, and once again, Michael noted that skills from a viewer's normal life carried over into his remote viewing. Yu also thought the killer was planning to strike again, and it left Michael with an even greater sense of urgency. His location mark slightly overlapped that of Sacks.

Weldon came in at five, and after a half hour catching up they went down to the egg. Weldon also saw the killer as a man in his twenties, just as he had the first time. He expanded on the fact that the girl and her killer had a relationship in which he was a teacher, saying what the man taught was a physical activity.

After Weldon left, Michael sat in his office going through the session data, noting all the places where there seemed to be overlap, and saw Weldon's circle overlapped Sack's and Yu's. Most alarming though, every viewer had stressed a sense of urgency because the killer was planning to abduct another girl.

The next morning Coyote and then Constance reiterated much the same story, adding details of their own and providing consensus to imagery and sense impressions already advanced in the earlier sessions, as well as the same sense of urgency.

By the time he had finished with Constance, Michael had decided not to do any more sessions but to complete the analysis and contact Baskerville. After everyone else had left, he walked down to Martin's Tavern on Wisconsin, glad to get out even though it was cold. He had a fish dinner and listened again to the audio of the sessions with his earpods as he ate. When he was finished, he walked back and called up the maps from each session, then merged them. It produced a kind of splatter shaped circle about twenty miles across, centered on a town he had never heard of, Rural Retreat, Virginia. He looked it up on Google Earth; it had a population of about fifteen hundred, which accorded with what the viewers had described.

Next, he ran the audio through the robo-transcribing program and broke down the transcribed concepts into patterns, correlating them with the biometric data. He factored in past success for these same kinds of concepts. By three o'clock that morning he had produced the hypothesis document to guide fieldwork. By the time he walked back to his house, it was after four.

As soon as he got up the next morning, he called Baskerville.

"Gordon, I have done five sessions, and I think it's enough. Every viewer thinks this guy is planning to do this again, and soon, very soon. I stayed up most of last night doing the analysis, and we have actionable field hypotheses."

"Do you know where he is?"

"Within a roughly circular shape about twenty miles across. Also, there is a high probability he lives in what I think is a trailer or single-wide. He works in some kind of motor repair shop."

"Is it Noah Ebersole?"

"You rarely get names with remote viewing, and I can't be sure because all I have is that head shot on his driver's license, although I didn't use it for the reasons I told you. That said, height and weight seem to match. The viewers agree the killer is in his twenties, over six feet, physically strong, anonymous kind of farm boy face. I even have some drawings, as well as drawings of the building front of the shop where he works, and the single-wide where he lives."

"Where is this man?"

"The consensus zone is centered on Rural Retreat, Virginia."

"Never heard of it; where is that?"

"Me neither. It's down in Virginia in the Blue Ridge Mountains."

"Then we have extradition issues."

"Gordon," Michael said to Baskerville's Zoom image. "I did five interviews, and all five of the viewers felt he is about abduct another young girl. We have to act."

"It's not that simple," Baskerville responded. "You can't arrest him yourself. And how do you think the local sheriff will respond? This isn't a movie. We don't actually have any evidence on Rachel's murder, and you can't have evidence of a crime that hasn't happened yet that only exists in the man's mind."

"I take your point, but I have to balance that against another young girl's life. The killer seems to have a sexual fixation on girls that are fourteen or fifteen. I think we have to act."

"Could you pinpoint it better than the twenty-mile circle?"

"Yes, that is precisely what I plan to do. I'm going to ask Weldon and Coyote to drive down with me. It's about a five- or six-hour drive from the Institute to Rural Retreat. You know the drill. One by one I will take them to the edge of the circle and ask them to locate both the workshop and the single-wide. But as you say, we have no authority to act."

"No, you don't. This is going to take some time, if it can be done at all. As I said, there is no real evidence against this guy. It is just the accuracy of your remote viewing work in locating the body that justifies any of this. The Uniform Criminal Extradition Act and the Uniform Extradition and Rendition Act require that I have to get a judge to issue a warrant, then go to the governor's office to get the governor to request extradition from the governor of Virginia. Do you have a sense of how much time we've got?"

"Time measurement is not easy to do with remote viewing, as I have told you, because in the nonlocal domain time is an information point not a defining limitation. I will say this. All the viewers have a sense of real urgency, and based on some other recent research, I would say a week, maybe ten days."

"I don't know if I can get things to move that fast. Let me get on it and I will get back to you, maybe later today, or it might take a day or two."

After they hung up Michael was left with a sense of foreboding so strong it was physical. He got up from his desk and went for a walk to let his thoughts and his stomach settle.

The next day when he was in Gilbert's lab working with him on the new biometric set-up, Weldon and Coyote came into the room.

"Boss," Weldon said, "we've got to talk."

Michael was taken aback by the urgency of Weldon's comment, and looking at Coyote, he could see that he too seemed to have the same sense of urgency.

"Okay, guys, let's go up to my office. Gilbert, keep on it, and I will come back when we're through."

They walked up to Michael's office, and as soon as they were seated, Coyote said, "Both Weldon and I, and we talked with John Sacks, Jefferson, and Constance, and they agree, feel we have to act... immediately. This dude is going to kill another young girl, and he is going to do it soon."

"We feel sure," Weldon added, "that he has already found his target and is just waiting for the opportunity."

Michael explained his telephone call with Baskerville and what the extradition process was, then told them he completely agreed with them.

"As they say, the wheels of justice..."

"...Are too slow to save this child," Weldon said.

"Yes, exactly," Michael answered. "I thought about this all last night and was going to call a meeting, but you have anticipated me. Suppose the three of us went down there? I'll cover both your salaries. Coyote, can you get another DJ to stand in for you?"

"I think so. I'll make some calls as soon as we are through here," Coyote responded.

"I'll have someone else fill in for me. The contractor I am working for is kind of fascinated by the remote viewing work. I sometimes think he hires me just to hear the stories," Weldon said, and they all laughed.

"Okay, then it's settled. We'll leave tomorrow if we can work everything out."

"But what are we going to do?" Coyote asked.

"We'll start by locating where he works and lives. After that I guess we'll decide the next move."

"I don't know why, but I think we should take a four-wheel drive. Can we take your Cherokee, Michael?"

"Of course. Alright, let's get it sorted out. I think we should allow a week; it will take most of a day to drive down there, and the same coming back. If Weldon thinks we may need four-wheel drive, and given the forest in the consensus zone, I think the gear we got from the Navy is the call."

"We have to get this guy," Weldon said, and the pain in his voice made Michael remember how strongly his large friend felt about protecting children. Images of Weldon taking Tracy's daughter's class out for what he called a woods walk came into his mind. He saw their happy faces as they clustered around Weldon.

"I agree," both Michael and Coyote said, speaking together.

The three men shook hands and got up to do what was needed to get ready.

CHAPTER EIGHTEEN

By ten o'clock the next morning they were packed into Michael's jeep and heading down Interstate 81 to the consensus zone around Rural Retreat. As they drove, they talked about the foreboding that all three of them felt. Although Michael usually played the role of researcher, he was, in fact, an excellent remote viewer. It was his own experiences of nonlocal perception that had originally drawn him into consciousness research instead of taking the much easier path of conventional materialist neuroscience.

Weldon basically expressed what they all were thinking. "I believe at best seventy-two hours to stop this guy from raping and murdering another girl."

"You got it," Coyote concurred. "Every time I focus on this dude, I get this hot erotic rush of anticipation. There is something wrong with him. I think..."

"Wait a minute," Michael said, tapping his iPhone which was in its holder on the dash. "I want a record of this. So, let's start again." He got the phone set up, and said, "We are in my car driving down Interstate 81, outside of Roanoke. Present are Michael Gillespie, Weldon Shelcraft, and Istaqa Chester."

After logging the date and time, he said, "Okay, let's start again," and Weldon repeated what he had said earlier, that he felt they only had about seventy hours before another girl was abducted. Coyote, after repeating his first statement, went on, "This guy has, I don't know... When he is thwarted, he can burst into uncontrollable rages. I don't think he meant to kill the first girl, but after initially accepting his attention she resisted him, and he acted out of impulse and anger; but he discovered he liked it."

Weldon sat silently for a moment with his eyes closed. Then he said, "I think this guy is a vet, and that is important for some reason. There is some benefit he got from that."

They decided not to stay in Rural Retreat or go into it until the following morning, when they would be fresh, so they took the exit to Wytheville and checked into the Wytheville Inn. Then they went to dinner at the Log House 1776 Restaurant. It had caught their eye, a three-storey log house surrounded by a garden. A survivor from an earlier age.

They had an excellent dinner with traditional southern side dishes and later went for a walk through the town. As they were walking, Coyote suddenly stopped and said, "This is where he plans to capture the girl. She lives somewhere around here." He ran his hand through his black hair, which he wore in a traditional pony-tail. "He's going to snatch her off the road somewhere. It isn't like the first time where the girl went willingly. This is a different deal."

"Do you know where this happens?" Michael asked.

"No. It's dark though... lonely... she's walking. This is so awful, Michael. We have to catch this guy."

They went back to the inn, went to bed, and were up and eating the motel's breakfast by seven thirty. As they ate, Michael said, "I think we should wait to go into Rural Retreat until about nine. We don't want to draw any more attention to ourselves than necessary. You all think this guy works in some kind of mechanic shop; let's wait until it opens."

After breakfast they drove down Main Street in Wytheville, then turned right on US-11, which took them into Rural Retreat, a town much smaller than Wytheville. They saw the green and white railroad depot immediately, and stopped and got out.

"He's here," Weldon said as soon as they were out of the car.

"In this building?" Michael asked as they walked toward the depot.

"No, but close," Weldon answered as they went into the building, where they got some brochures about the town. When they got back to the car they looked up at the sky and saw rain clouds gathering, and Michael said, "I have an idea." He raised the hood of his car and unscrewed a small nut, pulling off the wire and disconnecting his windshield wipers.

"You both think he works in a mechanic shop. There can't be that many in a town this small. See if you can pick the right one. Maybe we can get a look at this guy." They turned off Railroad Avenue onto Rural Retreat's version of Main Street, past the NAPA auto parts store and Subway sandwich shop. A short distance further along they saw the sign for Seabuckle's Motor Repair and were slowly going past it, when Coyote said, "Go back."

Michael went on a little further, so it wouldn't be obvious from Seabuckle's, then turned around. Just as he did, drops began to fall. He pulled into the parking area, and they all got out and went into the little waiting area on one side of the shop. Seabuckle came over to them, looking with some alarm at Weldon and Coyote, asking, "Can I help you?"

"Yes, my windshield wipers don't work, and as you can see, I need them. Could you take a look?"

"Both my guys are tied up right now, but if you can wait twenty minutes, I think we can get to it. Noah's almost finished," Seabuckle responded.

The name immediately registered, but they said nothing and sat down, took out their phones, and started looking at them. Weldon leaned over to both of them, saying softly, "He's here. I'm sure of it."

A few minutes later Noah Ebersole came over to them, asking, "How can I help you?"

Michael looked at him and knew this was their man, and he could see that Coyote and Weldon felt the same. Ebersole seemed to feel their attention, and his manner changed subtly.

"Do I know you? Are you here for me?"

"No. We've never met. We're from D.C. heading south, why do you ask?" Michael replied.

"The way you looked at me."

"Oh, sorry. You just got our sense of urgency. Not sure what we did, but we're here because my windshield wipers aren't working, and it's raining and looks like it is going to continue for a while, and we need to keep going."

"My mistake. Could you pull your car into the last bay? I'll take a look. Shouldn't be much of a fix," Ebersole said, and walked back to the workshop area.

Michael went out to the car and did as he was asked. Ebersole raised the hood, saying, "Could you wait where you were? Insurance doesn't allow customers to stay where the work is done."

"Of course," Michael answered, and went back to the waiting area. As soon as he got there, both Weldon and Coyote said, "That's the guy. That's our killer; what do we do?"

"We don't do anything. From what you and the others said I think he is going to take the girl to where he lives, so I think we should find that while we know he's working here. We know what he looks like now, and it is very much like John's drawing, by the way."

"I wish we could just take him now."

"But we can't. He hasn't done anything wrong yet, and there isn't any real evidence but our remote viewing that he killed that first girl. That's why Baskerville thinks he is going to have a hard time getting an extradition warrant."

"It's maddening," Weldon replied.

A few minutes later Ebersole came back out and said to Michael, "It was just a loose wire. A little nut had come loose. Odd, I don't know why. But I put a new nut on and everything is fine."

As he was speaking Seabuckle came over with an invoice. Michael decided not to reveal his identity and paid him in cash. Just as two cars pulled into the shop's parking area, they thanked both Seabuckle and Ebersole and left. As they were pulling out of the lot, Coyote shouted, "Stop."

He got out and walked back to the parking area and around the back. When he came back a few seconds later he got in the car, saying, "His truck, the truck I saw in my first session, is parked in the back. No question in my mind now; this is our man."

They drove back down Main Street, stopping at the Subway to get foot-long subways for lunch, then turned on Railroad back to the depot where Michael pulled into its parking lot.

"What's the plan, Boss?" Weldon asked as soon as Michael turned the motor off.

"The plan is to find the house. I assume he will work the rest of the day and stay there, so we have until, say, four thirty to find his place. Normally I would leave one of you here, drive off with the other one, see where the first one of you leads, then come back and have you change and see if the second viewer went to the same place. But this is too rural; the area is too large and our time too short, so I'm just going to ask you to speak up as you feel moved to do so. But first I am going to call Gordon."

Michael got out of the car, took out his phone and called Baskerville, walking around the lot as he did so. Baskerville's secretary picked up on the third ring and asked him to hold.

"How is it going with the extradition?" he asked as soon as Baskerville came on the line.

"I don't think it's going to work. There is no evidence that Noah Ebersole played any part in the death of Rachel Swayze. We don't even know where he really is."

"I do."

"Where are you?"

"Rural Retreat, Virginia, and I've just seen Ebersole, even talked with him. I saw his truck as well. It all matches, Gordon. Remember, we didn't search on Ebersole, we searched on the location of the killer. When we got down here to the consensus zone, we found Ebersole."

"What are you doing down there? Why are you there?" Baskerville asked.

"Because Weldon and Coyote came to me and said that Ebersole was planning to abduct another girl, and he was going to do it in the next seventy-two hours."

"Whoa. Michael, the law does not look kindly on vigilantes."

"We're not vigilantes. We're just concerned citizens who are going to stop something illegal we see happening," Michael responded.

"And when you do, what then?"

"Then we are going to take him to the local sheriff and tell him to call you. That's why I'm calling. To give you a head's up."

"Michael, I'm not sure how to answer that. You could put yourself in considerable legal jeopardy."

"A young girl's life is at stake; we'll take the risk," Michael answered. "I just wanted to let you know what is happening. Goodbye, Gordon; we'll be in touch," he said, disconnecting.

He walked back to the car and got in, powered on his laptop, and looked at the Google Earth map with the consensus zone marked on it.

"Okay guys, where are we going?"

Coyote and Weldon looked at the map and sat silently for a moment. Then Coyote looked at Weldon and pointed to a place within the consensus zone. Michael expanded the map until street and road names appeared, looked at it, started up the car, turned on the GPS, and drove out of the depot parking lot. Main Street turned into State Route 90, which became 680. They crossed over Interstate 81 and continued on what became both Blacklick Road and County 680. They saw a sign for a junction with County 681.

Coyote said, "Turn left," and looked at Weldon, who nodded in agreement. There was nothing but open farm land around them now, and Michael wondered where they were headed since all the sessions had described Ebersole's home as deep in a forest. They came to another junction with an unpaved gravel school bus road. Michael stopped, and then felt strongly they should turn onto it.

As he began the turn, Coyote said, "Yes, that's right." He and Weldon looked at each other and then at Michael. "Are you going to be a viewer too?" Weldon asked, and they all laughed.

"It seems so," Michael said, as they drove along the gravel road. Two miles later they were on the edge of a forest, and the road began to peter out. Just as Michael thought they were at a dead end, a small private dirt road appeared.

"Take it," Coyote said, pointing at the lane.

They were now on a path so narrow the trees on both sides almost brushed the car. As they continued, the road began to go up a hill. When they got to the ridge, on the right, they saw what looked like a cattle gate.

"That's it. That's what I saw, remember?" Weldon asked.

Michael slowed to little more than the speed of a walk, and they slowly went past the metal gate Noah had installed. Michael kept on for a few hundred yards more, then the road did come to an end. He pulled off into the woods so the car could not be seen.

They got their sandwiches out of the cooler, ate them, and worked out a plan. By then it was about three thirty in the afternoon and clouds were gathering; it looked like rain again. They walked back down the road to the cattle gate and climbed over the fence. They had only gone about a hundred feet when to the right, on the ridge, they could see a run-down single-wide mobile home, painted green.

Michael pulled out his phone and brought up the three drawings of the killer's home from the Amish Girl sessions. He held the phone at arm's length so they could all see them.

"Bingo," Weldon said.

"Yes," Coyote added. "This is what I saw. If you wanted to kidnap a girl and hold her some out-of-the-way place, you could hardly find a better one."

"I agree," Michael said as he began to walk over to the single-wide. "We know Ebersole is at work, so let's get a close-up look."

The three of them walked around the structure, then Michael went up to the door. It wasn't locked.

"I'm sure no one ever comes up here; what's the point?" Weldon said as Michael opened the door.

"Wipe your feet," Michael told them, doing just that on the mat in front of the door, then took his shoes off altogether. The others followed suit, and they went in and looked around the sparsely furnished room. Coyote flipped the light switch on the wall. Nothing happened. Weldon went over to the old-fashioned dial phone on kitchen wall and picked up the handset.

"The line's dead," as he gestured to the kerosene lamps in the room.

"No wonder the police couldn't find Ebersole," Michael said. "No electric bill, a wood stove, no phone."

"Propane stove and refrigerator," Coyote added. "Like you see on parts of the res."

"I'll bet he doesn't have a bank account or credit cards," Michael added.

"Off the grid, below the radar," Weldon replied. "This guy is a ghost."

"None of this would be a problem for him," Michael observed. "He grew up in an Amish community where this is normal, not a hardship."

They went into the bedroom and immediately saw that eye bolts had been screwed in the wall at the head of the bed, and ropes were tied to it. At the foot of the bed eye bolts were screwed into the floor and more lengths of rope were threaded through the eyes.

"This is where he plans to keep her," Michael said, as Weldon picked up one of the rope ends and tugged it.

"Yep, Boss, we've got the right guy; no doubt about it now."

The rain started, and they could hear it pattering on the metal roof.

"So now what?" Weldon asked.

"That depends on whether you all think tonight's the night."

Weldon sat down, and so did Michael and Coyote. They sat in silence for several minutes.

"No. I don't think so, I think it's tomorrow. I get the sense this guy has scouted a particular girl; he has a plan," Coyote said.

"I agree," Weldon answered. "I get a very strong image of him capturing her on a dark street or road. Somehow he knows she will be there. There's a church nearby."

"Alright, good. We're not equipped anyway," Michael said, looking at his watch. "It's four fifteen. I think we need to get out of here and prep for tomorrow."

They checked to make sure there was no evidence of their having been there, then left the single-wide, closing the door and walking back to the car. They started back down the way they had come, and once out of the woods and on paved roads in the farm land, they were just passing a barn when Weldon shouted, "Go behind that barn so we can't be seen."

Michael did as Weldon asked, and they got out and peered around the barn. Thirty seconds later they could see Ebersole's truck coming up the road, and they watched as it turned onto the dirt lane and vanished into the woods.

CHAPTER NINETEEN

Tonight was the night, and Noah could hardly concentrate on his work. He was thankful the workload was light that day, and after lunch he asked Seabuckle if he could take the afternoon off to run some errands. Seabuckle agreed to let him go, and he punched out.

Growing up, musical instruments had not been a part of his Amish life. In that world playing a musical instrument was considered a way of inappropriately attracting attention to oneself. It stimulated pride and showed a sense of superiority. Even in church this was true. Amish church songs all came from something known as the Ausbund, a centuries old High German songbook which had no musical notes.

But when he had gone on Rumspringa and gotten a job at the motorcycle repair shop, the Highway Men had introduced him to their music. People like Victor Olsson, Copperhead, and Rory Gallagher, and he loved riding and listening to that music. When he pictured himself with the girl there was a musical score in the background. There was no place in Rural Retreat or even in Wytheville to get what he wanted; he had looked. The closest larger city was Christiansburg, about an hour away, and that's where he went.

When he got there he found a Best Buy, and after looking at several options and talking to the sales guys on the floor, he decided the best choice was a Klantop MP3 player and radio he could strap on his arm. He bought it and some upgraded earpods that one of the salesmen recommended, then stopped at a Burger King to eat dinner. He knew he was probably under video surveillance and had planned for it. He went over to a cineplex, looked at the movies, and bought a ticket for the next show and a second one for the ten o'clock movie, as always paying cash. He didn't think any of this would matter, but as his lieutenant had told them over and over, little details made a difference. He found a seat, watched a very violent movie which had the effect of getting him even more excited, left the theater, tore the ten o'clock movie ticket in half, put that half in his pocket, and drove back to Wytheville.

By then it was about six thirty, which was perfect. It was already dark. He drove into the neighborhood where the girl lived. He knew that Friday nights she went to her church for a youth gathering and then walked home. He cruised the area, checking for the third time that there were no cameras, then went to a run-down discount gas station he knew had no cameras and filled up his tank. He emptied his bladder as he had been told to do before battles so that would be handled, went back into the station and bought some snacks. Back in his truck he checked his bottle of ether and unwrapped one of the sanitary pads. He'd never actually seen one before except in a woman's magazine ad someone had left at the shop, which is what gave him the idea.

He had previously tested how quickly the ether evaporated, gauged how much time he would have, and put the pad on the seat. It was now eight thirty.

By nine Noah was in place. He parked on the shoulder of the road, got out a map, and appeared to be searching for directions while looking down the road where he could just see the church. A few minutes before nine thirty he picked up the sanitary pad and saturated it with the ether, being careful to open the windows so he wouldn't put himself to sleep. Then he stuffed the soaked pad into a double plastic sandwich bag and tucked it into his jacket pocket. Holding a flashlight, he got out of his truck and opened its hood and peered in as if something were wrong. No cars went by, and he knew from his earlier reconnaissance that parents who came to pick up their children all tended to go in the other direction.

It was very dark by then, with only the smallest sliver of moon in the night sky. After about five minutes he saw her. She was walking by herself down the dark road to her house on the other side of the street. When she was abreast of him, he called out to her.

"Oh my God, I am so glad to see someone. Do you have a phone? My battery is dead and I have to call a tow service or I'll end up spending the whole night here."

As he expected, the girl crossed the street. He gave her his best smile, saying, "Something has gone wrong, I am not sure what. What a hassle."

The girl came closer and peered into the engine compartment. As she did so he pulled out the sandwich bag, extracted the ether-soaked pad, and clamped it over her mouth. She struggled, which excited him, but then she quickly went limp. He laid her on the seat in the cab of the truck, quickly bound her hands and feet with duct tape, and put a strip of tape over her mouth. He slammed down the hood and was away. The whole business had taken only three minutes.

Feeling he had everything under control, he headed back to his single-wide, figuring he had about an hour before anyone became concerned, more than enough to get home. As he drove he became more and more excited, and when he turned onto Blacklick Road, where in the course of a day only a couple of cars might go, he could not resist. He pulled over and quickly unzipped the sleeping girl's jacket, unbuttoned her shirt and pulled up her starter bra. In the light of the cab he could see her small breasts, the size of teacups, and her small pink nipples. He leaned over and sucked on them, and when they became erect, he almost climaxed in his pants.

He drove up the dirt lane to his house, opened the gate, and pulled the truck in near the door. He got the unconscious girl out, slung her body over his shoulder, triggering memories of Rachel, and carried her into the single-wide. He didn't even bother to light the kerosene lamps in the living room but went straight back to his bedroom and threw her on the bed, tearing her clothes off as fast as he could. As he was tying her hands and feet with the pre-rigged ropes, she began to come back to consciousness and struggled against what he was doing, which only aroused him further. She could not cry out because of the tape over her mouth, but incoherent agitated sounds came through.

He lit all the lamps, went and got the ones in the living room and lit them as well, and went over to his dresser and got the MP3 player he had just bought. He put in the earpods and turned on the music; the night he had fantasized about for weeks was ready to begin. He turned, and in the light of the soft light of kerosene lamps that lined the room, he looked down at the girl who looked back at him with terror in her eyes. For the first time he could really contemplate her body, and he slowly looked at her from head to foot.

While Noah was abducting the girl, Michael, Weldon, and Coyote were putting on the camo gear the Navy had given them, getting out their rain ponchos because it looked like it might rain again. Then they drove back out to Noah's house. As they came up his dirt lane they saw his truck. They pulled back up into the woods and quietly got out, with Weldon leading walked up to the clearing around the mobile home. They waited a moment, watching the door, but nothing happened. Michael gestured and they went quickly across the clearing to the door. Michael pulled it open and they quietly entered the living room and started down the hall towards the light.

Her legs were spread by the ropes, and he could see the small cleft of her sex. It was perfect, just as he imagined, and he could keep her as long as he wanted and kill her whenever he wanted. The stimulation of these thoughts and what he saw almost drove him mad, as the music pounded in his ears. He hurriedly unbuttoned his shirt, pulled it off, dropped it on the floor, and unbuckled his belt.

As he did so he thought he heard something, but it was only a small sound, hardly noticeable, and he was too aroused to give it any thought. He leaned over to untie his work shoes, and when he began to straighten up, he was suddenly grabbed from behind by Weldon, lifted off the floor, and slammed so hard into the wall face first that the wood panel sheets splintered. He slumped unconscious to the floor, with his pants around his legs.

Michael, who had begun videoing with his iPhone as they came down the hall, gestured for them to stand back and go into the hallway. He took picture after picture, and then a video to add to the one he had made from the hallway with Ebersole standing over Jessica's body on the bed. There would be no question of proof this time. No issues over what had taken place. It only took a few seconds, and when he was done, as Weldon and Coyote came back into the room, he went over to the girl, removed the tape over her mouth as gently as he could and pulled a blanket over her naked body. He began to untie the ropes which bound her arms, while Coyote and Weldon untied her legs. He threw them the ropes and they took them and used them to tie Ebersole's arms behind his back and to bind his legs.

"It's okay. No one is going hurt you. We're here to help," Michael said, as they were doing this, "What is your name?" he asked.

"Jessica" she answered. "Jessica Littlefield." Then she began to sob uncontrollably. Michael took her into his arms and held her to his chest as a father would. He felt her tears soaking through his shirt. After a moment he said, "Jessica, can you stand up? Are you able to get dressed?" The girl nodded and got out of bed, holding the blanket around her body. Coyote gathered up her clothes from the floor and handed them to her.

"Take one of the lamps," Michael told her, "and go down the hall to the bathroom and get dressed. Can you do that?"

"Yes," she answered.

While she was gone Michael went out to the kitchen where he had seen some rubber gloves, put them on, came back and went through Ebersole's clothes, found the plastic bag with the ether-soaked sanitary pad, opened it and smelled it.

"He knocked her unconscious with this," he said, showing them the bag and the pad. Then took a picture of it.

Coyote smelled it. "Ether, is that what this is?"

"Yes. I think we should search the truck. No, better, I think one of us should drive the truck back to the Sheriff's office," Michael told them.

At that point Ebersole began to come around, "Who are you, what are you doing? You can't just..."

"Noah, you're going to jail for this, and for killing Rachel Swayze."

"How do you know about Rachel?" he said with alarm. "I want a lawyer."

"Oh, you're going to get an attorney, but it isn't going to matter," Michael answered, and pulled out his phone and showed Noah the pictures he had taken of Rachel's body and the woods where it was found. Then the pictures he had just taken.

"You're finished Ebersole. You're going to go to jail for the rest of your life, or they are going to kill you."

They wrapped Noah in a blanket, wound tape around it, and Weldon and Coyote carried him out to his truck and threw him into the truck bed.

Michael drove the car, Jessica next to him; Weldon and Coyote followed in the truck with Ebersole. They made their way down the dirt lane to the gravel road, and then to 680 following the GPS to the nearest police, which turned out to be Rural Retreat sheriff's station. As they drove, Michael talked with Jessica, who was slowly recovering.

"Did you know him?"

"No. I loaned him my phone," Jessica said. With tears running down her cheeks she told him how Ebersole had captured her. As she spoke her fear was replaced with outrage, and Michael sensed her feeling of violation. They got to the Sherriff just before midnight, by which time Jessica was in control of herself. A couple of sheriff's cars were parked in the lot, and the bright lights made the station stand out from the quiet darkness all around it. They parked and walked into the station while Weldon and Coyote wrestled Ebersole out of the back of the truck.

Michael put his arm around Jessica, who leaned into him and said as they went through the door, "I am glad you brought me here instead of taking me home. I want to tell the police about this, and I don't want to do it in front of my brothers."

"I understand completely," Michael answered.

Inside there was a counter and behind it a female deputy.

"Can I help you?" she asked.

Michael identified himself and Jessica, but was only a few seconds into it when the deputy said, "If you will sit over there, I will get the appropriate person to talk to you..." In mid-sentence she was interrupted by Weldon and Coyote half-dragging, half carrying Noah Ebersole, hands bound, mouth taped, bloodied hair plastered to the side of his head, and a massive bruise forming on the entire left side of his face.

The deputy stopped talking, picked up the phone and asked for help. Seconds later two other officers came out from the back of the station. They stopped as they came into the station lobby, taking everything in, not sure what to do.

"My name is Michael Gillespie. I am a professor and director of the Hill Institute in Washington, D.C.. We are working with Gordon Baskerville, District Attorney of Lancaster County, Pennsylvania, and Colonel Tim Johnson, CO of the state police." He reached in his pocket and pulled out his card, and Baskerville's and Johnson's cards, which he handed to the woman officer.

"This man, Noah Ebersole, is a suspect in a murder in Lancaster, and we caught him just after he abducted and was preparing to rape and possibly kill this young woman, Jessica Littlefield. She wants to make a statement here at the station before she is taken home. I will show you video and pictures we took, proof of what she says."

The two male officers took Ebersole from Weldon and Coyote and steered him through a door to the back of the station, giving him his Miranda rights as they walked.

Fifteen minutes later a middle-aged man with balding brown hair and a gut came into the station. He saw them and walked over very purposefully. "I am Richard Dixon, the sheriff. Which of you is Professor Gillespie?"

"I am," Michael answered.

"I just got off the line with the Lancaster DA and Colonel Johnson, so I know a little bit about this." Then he looked at Jessica, and said, "Aren't you in Miss Barton's homeroom with my son?"

"Yes. And we're lab partners in science class. "

"I am so sorry you have had to go through this, Jessica," the sheriff said with real feeling. "Can you give us a statement of what happened?"

"I want to," Jessica responded. "I want you to put this man in jail for a long time, so he never does this to another girl. " The memories brought tears back to her eyes.

"Have you talked with your mother?"

"I want to do this before I talk to her."

"Professor, my deputy tells me that you have pictures or a video of this. Perhaps you and I could go into my office. Jessica doesn't have to see this, and Jessica," he said turning to her, "no one else is going see this either, except maybe at the trial."

Jessica nodded, giving him a sad smile, and the Sheriff and Michael went into his office.

"Let me see it," he said as he sat behind his desk, and Michael took out his phone and showed Dixon the video and the still shots he had taken. Dixon listened and made him play it twice, paying particular attention to what Ebersole said as he was tying Jessica up. Michael reached into his jacket got his handkerchief and used it to take out the bag with the ether soaked sanitary pad.

"Jessica will tell you why this matters, and it's evidence," he said, handing it to Dixon.

"That's about as cut and dried as a case could be."

"I hope so."

"I need to get a copy of that right away," Dixon said, pointing to Michael's phone.

"Let's download everything onto your computer," Michael replied. "Do you have a USB cable? I don't want to transmit this over the net."

"Good point," the sheriff replied, as he pulled open a desk drawer and took out a cable. They linked the phone with the computer, and Michael transmitted all the files.

"Now, do you want to tell me why you were there to take this? Indeed, why you are here at all, and how you could possibly have known from Pennsylvania that a not yet fifteen-year-old girl was going to be captured and where she would be taken? I don't understand any of this."

"Take Jessica's statement first. She's exhausted and we can't possibly understand what is going through her mind, her emotions. She wants to make this statement. We'll wait outside in your waiting room as long as it takes, and I'll tell you everything I know about this."

Michael went out to the waiting room where Coyote and Weldon were waiting.

"Personally, we would have been happy to work him over a little more before we brought him in," Weldon said.

"You don't need to worry. This guy is going to prison for a long time, no matter what. And how do you think he'll be treated in prison for trying to rape a fourteen-year-old girl?"

"Kill him?"

"Probably."

"What about Rachel?" Coyote asked.

"My guess would be that Baskerville will file for extradition, although I don't know that it will work."

"You said they don't really have any evidence except our remote viewing," Coyote continued.

"That's true," Michael answered. "But they certainly do with Jessica. Still, I don't think the Amish will let Gordon give up on this."

"I agree," Weldon said. "Those Amish men who were with us when we found Rachel's body had righteous hearts, and they're not going to walk away."

It took almost ninety minutes to do Jessica's interview, and it was going on three o'clock when her parents came into the station just as she and the Sheriff walked out of the interview room.

She ran into her mother's arms, then both her parents hugged her as everyone looked on. When they broke their embrace Jessica's father came over to them. "I'm Bryan Littlefield," he said, putting out his hand, shaking each of theirs. "Doris and I don't really understand what happened here, except you saved our daughter's life. We do understand that..."

"... And we will be eternally grateful," his wife continued.

"It's after three o'clock; we need to take Jessica home. But can we talk, say, after noon, maybe one o'clock tomorrow? Here's my number," he said, handing Michael a folded piece of paper. "This has been very difficult, and we all need to get to bed."

He turned to walk out but stopped when Jessica ran back and hugged all three of them one at a time. "Thank you, thank you. I will never forget you or what you did for me."

"And we will never forget one of the bravest girls we have ever known," Weldon said, and both Michael and Coyote nodded and smiled at her. Jessica gave them a smile back, then ran over to her parents, and they left.

"Professor, you're staying at the Wytheville Inn, is that correct?"

"Yes, and I haven't told you yet, but we brought in Ebersole's truck. The one he put her in. I am sure there is evidence in there; we haven't even looked. And here are the coordinates for his house. It is a green single-wide, tucked way back in the woods. I know you will want to go over both the truck and the house in the morning," Michael said, and Coyote handed over the truck's keys.

"It's outside in the lot. I locked it up."

"Why don't you all come in as soon as you are up. We'll need to take a statement from each of you."

"We will," Michael said, and the three of them gathered up their coats and left.

Having been up almost twenty-four hours, they all slept late, so late that the motel had put away their breakfast offerings. Rather than go to a restaurant they decided to skip the meal and go directly to the Sheriff's station. As they drove they discussed what to say.

"Okay, Boss, what do we tell this guy?" Weldon asked.

"The truth as clearly as you can tell it," Michael answered.

"That an ex-special forces housepainter and a club DJ had a vision telling them Jessica was going to be captured and raped, maybe killed. Are you serious? Did you look at that guy? He won't believe a word of that," Coyote said.

"It doesn't matter what he thinks. What matters for Jessica and us is that the record be as accurate as possible."

"What do we say if he asks us about Rachel... or the missile?" Weldon responded.

"Tell him anything he wants to know about Rachel. If he asks about the missile, which I don't think he will, tell him you cannot answer because of national security and classification. And that's the truth. Don't say a word about the missile," Michael instructed them.

When they got to the sheriff's station the officer behind the desk directed them down the hall to the sheriff's office, and he came out to meet them.

"Thank you, gentlemen. Are you ready to begin?"

"I think I should go first," Michael answered. "I am the best person to tell you what we did, how we did it, and why." Looking at Weldon and Coyote, he said, "Why don't you all go get something to eat." He looked at Dixon and added, "We'd been up almost twenty-four hours, and we skipped breakfast in order to get here as early as possible."

"I appreciate that, and yes, you men can go get something to eat. I would guess this is going to take a couple of hours." Turning back to Michael, he continued, "If you will follow me we'll go down to the interview room." When they got there two other people, a man and a woman, were already in the room.

"Professor Gillespie, this is Elizabeth Bullock and Roger Schmidt; both are in the Wythe County District Attorney's office." Then, turning to the attorneys, he said, "This is Professor Michael Gillespie, director of the Hill Institute in Washington, D.C., and a professor of neuroscience at Georgetown University."

Bullock, a rather stout stern looking woman in her forties, who obviously cared nothing about style, asked as soon as Michael was seated, "Do you require counsel?"

"No. I have nothing to hide about this. I will do my best to tell you everything I know," Michael said in response to her question.

Schmidt, a man also in his forties who looked like a former jock going soft, keyed the recorder and logged in the session.

Their questioning began, as he had expected, with how he came to be involved. To answer them he began at the beginning with Baskerville and Johnson coming to him when he spoke at the Army War College. They spent almost an hour going over that, and Michael could see they found the whole story very hard to take aboard, and that the room was becoming hostile and the questions not so much questions as accusations.

The questioning next turned to remote viewing. Michael explained to them the research he did at the Hill Institute and how he did it. Part way through that explanation, Schmidt interrupted him.

"I'm sorry, Gillespie," Schmidt said, deliberately leaving off Michael's academic titles. "I don't buy any of this psychic crap."

"I'm not selling anything to you, Schmidt," Michael said, by now quite irritated. "Believe it, don't believe it, I couldn't care less what you think."

"How do we know you aren't into this with Ebersole? You had some kind of falling out, and now you're trying to lay it all off on this hick, Ebersole."

"You really are stupider than you look," Michael responded.

"Let's try to take everything down a notch, shall we?" Dixon said. "I propose we take a break and get a cup of coffee, go to the bathroom, and reconvene in five minutes." Before anyone could move, Bullock, who had been quiet for some time and had been looking at her phone, suddenly spoke up.

"You're the guy who stopped the nuclear bomb from going off and destroying Washington about two years ago, aren't you?"

"Yes," Michael replied, adding, "and Coyote and Weldon were a big part of that team."

This answer changed the gestalt of the room in an instant, and Schmidt, now deeply embarrassed, quickly got up before anyone else and left the interview room. Michael got up and went to the bathroom. When he came out Schmidt, Bullock, and Dixon were standing outside the interview room in a huddle, talking. When they saw him coming, they went back into the room. When they were all seated the interview began again, only this time in a very different atmosphere. As they watched them, Michael explained how the video and pictures had been made. They watched Ebersole as he moved around Jessica, who lay nude tied on the bed, and both attorneys grimaced. A few still pictures, and that was all they could take. The interview went on another twenty minutes and finally wrapped up with Bullock thanking him for contributing to their understanding of what had happened to Jessica. Michael left feeling emotionally exhausted and with a real dislike for Schmidt.

He went out to the waiting room and saw Weldon and Coyote playing Go on a little portable set they had brought. They stopped as they saw him coming.

"How was it?" Coyote asked.

"I think I have spared you the struggle to get them to accept nonlocal consciousness and remote viewing. Not pleasant, but I think settled. Tell them whatever you want. We did our job. Ebersole will not be getting out for a long time. That's my takeaway."

"What about Rachel?" Weldon asked.

"That will be up to Baskerville; I don't think they have any sense yet what he plans to do. Who has the keys? I want to get something to eat. Where did you go?"

"Flourz is the call. It's on Tazewell," Weldon said, throwing Michael the keys.

"Flip you for who goes first?" Weldon asked.

"No, you go. I want to catch up on my email," Coyote answered.

Weldon walked down the hall and into the room. He was introduced, sat down, and it began.

"What do you do for a living, Mr. Shelcraft?" Schmidt began.

"I'm a house painter."

"Were you in the service?"

"Two tours in Afghanistan. Special Forces," Weldon said, looking Schmidt in the eyes.

"You married?"

"No."

"In a relationship?"

"What has this got to do with Jessica?"

"How did you get into this... what do you call it... remote viewing?" Bullock asked.

"I met Professor Gillespie. Sought him out."

"Why?"

"I had had some experiences."

"What kind?"

"I'm not going to talk about them. What is it you want?"

"We're trying to figure out how a housepainter like yourself came to believe he should drive down to rural southwestern Virginia to catch a man whom he thought was thinking about abducting and raping a fourteen-year-old girl he didn't know, and had never seen, before he actually did it." Schmidt said.

"Didn't Michael, Professor Gillespie, explain remote viewing to you? He said he did."

"Yes."

"Did you understand him?"

"Why don't you tell us?'

"If you didn't understand Michael, you won't understand me."

For a moment they all sat in silence.

"Are you willing to voluntarily return to testify at the trial?"

"Yes. I'm sure Professor Gillespie told you that if you notify us when it will happen, we will be here. We'll answer any questions under oath. Noah Ebersole is a bad man; he's sick, and I think he is a murderer. I think he would have murdered Jessica, in fact I am sure of it."

"The same way you knew where he was?" Dixon spoke for the first time.

"Yes. We were on his trail. He had captured, raped, and murdered another young girl. That's how we knew about him. By the way, is he going to be tried for Rachel Swayze's murder?"

"That's not for a sheriff like me to decide, that's for the judges."

They asked Weldon to go through his imagery, and he did. They asked no other questions, and when he was through they thanked him. He got up and went back to the waiting room where he found Coyote staring at his phone.

"How'd it go?" he asked, looking up to see Weldon standing over him.

"A little snarky, I thought, but no big deal. No way they understand remote viewing. Most of the questions were like, how could you have known... how did you know to be there ... that sort of thing. That and describing what happened. That's what they seem to care about. Mostly I think they want to see if our stories fit together. I just told them the truth. I'm sure you're going to do that, and I am sure that's what Michael did. For my money what really clinches it are the video and the pictures," Weldon said.

"Yep, you've got it. What I'm focused on is how this gets us to Rachel."

"I agree. I know Michael has talked with them, but I think it's up to Baskerville," Coyote said as he got up. He put his phone in his jacket, walked down the hall, knocked on the door and went in. Dixon, Schmidt, and Bullock were finishing sandwiches someone had brought them, but they stopped when they saw him enter.

"Please sit down," Dixon said, and Coyote did so. The interview began with the usual logon, then Schmidt asked him, "Please state your name. It's not Coyote, I assume?"

"No. My name is Istaqa Chester," Coyote answered.

"You're an Indian?"

"You think? Yes, I am Hopi."

"What do you do for a living?" Bullock asked him.

"I'm a DJ at the Fifth Dimension, a club in the Georgetown district of Washington, D.C."

"Your tribe is out West, isn't it? Schmidt asked.

"Yes. The Hopi reservation is in Arizona north of Flagstaff, if you know where that is."

"What took a Hopi Indian from his reservation to Washington, D.C.? I can't imagine many Hopi have done that?"

"One of the senators from Arizona wanted an Indian to be a page, and I was selected. It got me a scholarship to George Washington University, and I just stayed after that. Then I met Professor Gillespie."

"What do you think of Professor Gillespie?" Schmidt asked him.

"I don't know enough about neuroscience to comment, but I know that people who do think a lot of him, and I can't imagine people like Barbara Strickland would work with him if he weren't first class."

"Barbara Strickland?" Schmidt asked; clearly the name was not familiar.

"Nobel Laureate in physics," Bullock told him. "One of the leading women scientists in the world. My daughter, the one who wants to be a chemist, has her picture on her mirror. How in the world is a person like that involved in this?"

"Barbara's one of Michael's viewers just like me."

"Barbara Strickland is a psychic?" Bullock asked, aghast.

Her response irritated Coyote, "Yes, we all are. Professor Gillespie has figured out as a scientist how to open to the spirit, as we would call it in my world. He is a White shaman.

"Let's not get off track," Schmidt said. "Why don't you just tell us your story of how all this got started and what happened?"

For the next forty-five minutes Coyote did just that with few interruptions. They had already heard the story three times, once from the sheriff recounting what Jessica had told him, once from Michael, and once from Weldon. By the time Coyote was finished it was nearly seven o'clock, and they all got up and finally left the room. Weldon and Michael were waiting for him.

Dixon said, "I'm not sure any of us are really much clearer about how this all went down than we were when we started. I certainly have never seen anything like this."

"But we thank you for what you did, and for your agreement to come down to testify. I'm not sure how much we want to get into the remote viewing part, but what you witnessed, what Jessica experienced, the video and photos, and evidence we found in the truck and his home, make it quite sure Noah Ebersole is going to spend many years in prison."

"What about Rachel Swayze? He murdered her," Weldon said.

"In Pennsylvania that is a capital crime, and they have the death penalty. We don't know enough about that case to comment. It's up to what Gordon Baskerville does," Schmidt said.

"We are going to arrange to send Ebersole up to him for an interview, and we will see what happens after that," Bullock added.

As they left the police station, Coyote asked Michael, "What about the Littlefields?"

"I was pretty sure this would take all day, so I called them and arranged for us to stop there on our way home tomorrow morning. I told them we couldn't stay long because we had hundreds of miles to drive."

"Well, then, how about going back to 1776; they had a Chicken Verde Pecan that looked interesting," Coyote said. They all agreed and went back to the log house for a final dinner.

The next morning they stopped at the Littlefield's house on a pleasant cul-de-sac in a neighborhood just a short distance from where Jessica had been abducted. Michael had called before they left the hotel, and Marge Littlefield had invited them to breakfast with the family. Jessica hugged each of them as they came in, and they were happy she did not seem too scarred by her experience. As they ate, they explained once again how they came to be involved, and like Dixon, Schmidt, and Bullock, it was obvious the family really had no way to integrate the story into their world.

Finally, Marge, an accountant in her early forties, as she had told them, said, "I don't understand very much of what you have just said, but I will forever be in your debt for being there to save our daughter."

"Amen to that," said her husband.

With a final hug from each of them for Jessica, they were on the road by ten o'clock and back to D.C. in time for a late dinner.

For the next two weeks Michael heard nothing, and both Tracy and Barbara returned, Tracy from her trip to the Amazon and Barbara from China and a semester at California Institute of Technology working with postdocs doing fellowships. Tracy's daughter, Sarah, came back at the break so happy with Waldorf School that Tracy transferred her to the Washington Waldorf School, and life returned to its familiar rhythms.

CHAPTER TWENTY

For Gordon Baskerville the apprehension of Noah Ebersole placed him in a difficult position. He felt ethically bound to tell the Amish community what was going on, and he drove out to Samuel Yoder's farm, where John Schrock joined them. As they sat around the Yoder family's kitchen table drinking coffee and eating a pastry Yoder's wife had made, he explained what had happened and the current status of Ebersole. Both men listened to him without interruption.

When he was finished, John Schrock asked, "What about Rachel? The English girl Jessica was captured, yes, but not raped or, thanks to the Lord's mercy, killed. Rachel was murdered and her body dumped in the woods."

"My thinking exactly, John," Baskerville responded. "I have filed an extradition for interview with the court, and I think it is going to be granted. But here is the problem. We don't really have any evidence that he abducted Rachel or anything else."

"But you know he did it," Yoder said.

"Yes, yes I do. I am making the best case I can, and I think the D.A.s in Wythe County also think it is true. But it is going to be hard to prove in court. It would help a lot if he would confess. What you can be comforted by is that he was caught in the act with the girl down there and is going to do decades of time for that no matter what happens up here. But we'll see. I've arranged for a transportation service to bring him up to Lancaster."

"We thank you, Gordon, and I hope you have thanked the Hill Institute people," Yoder said. "Please keep us informed about what happens, and we will tell the community. I know they will be grateful as well. If there is anything at all we can do to help, please let us know."

A week later on Monday morning, Baskerville was sitting in his office about to leave for court, when the state police contacted him to say that Noah Ebersole had been brought in the previous night and was being held at the county jail. He explained that the trial he was doing would run that day and the next, so he arranged to do the interview after lunch on Wednesday. It was agreed, and they told him that Ebersole had asked for a public defender. One had been assigned to him and was meeting with him later that day.

On Wednesday Baskerville had lunch by himself at his favorite farm-to-table restaurant. All through the meal he thought about how to handle the interview, and the more he thought the more he realized how very weak his case was. Slowly, though, a strategy emerged in his mind. He went back to his office and picked up the report Michael had written. With the interview transcripts, the analysis and drawings, it was over a hundred pages thick, and the cover said, "The Amish Girl Evidentiary Probe," with the Hill Institute seal under that. It all looked very official. He had already marked it up, and little plastic tabs stuck out all through it. He put it in his briefcase, told his assistant where he was going, and left for the jail.

He got there just on time at two o'clock, and found the public defender was already with Ebersole. He entered the interrogation room and found them sitting and talking, which stopped as soon as he came in. Ebersole looked both surly and frightened. The public defender, Abe Goldstein, an orthodox Jew in his late thirties wearing a yarmulke, whom Baskerville knew to be a competent and fair attorney, acknowledged him with a gesture, which he returned, and sat down.

"Noah, my name is Gordon Baskerville. I am the District Attorney for Lancaster County, and I am aware of what happened in Virginia. You are here for an interview about Rachel Swayze."

"What about Rachel Swayze? What's happened to her?"

"You raped and murdered her."

"That's crazy. I don't know what you're talking about. When I left the community, as far as I knew she was fine."

"What was your relationship with Rachel?"

"I didn't have a relationship with her. I was a janitor at the school she attended, and I taught her and a bunch of other girls how to defend themselves after they were molested by English boys in town. That's it."

"Would you say you were a teacher, but not a teacher."

"I suppose you could say that, but so what?" Ebersole said defiantly.

"So, you deny that you had any contact with Rachel other than what you have just outlined?"

"Yes, and you won't find a bit of evidence to the contrary because none exists. So why are we doing this?"

Baskerville reached into his briefcase and pulled out the report Michael had sent him. When Goldstein and Ebersole saw the title on the cover page they shared a look but said nothing.

"Okay, let's start at the beginning," Baskerville told them, opening Michael's report. He said nothing about how the data had been collected or about remote viewing. He went through several pages which they couldn't read, coming to his first tab.

"You left the community several days before you abducted Rachel, but you had arranged to meet her." •

"I don't know what you are talking about," Ebersole replied.

"You bought her some, I guess you would call them, English clothes at a thrift store, and the two of you left the area."

Ebersole said nothing.

"You stayed at a non-chain inexpensive motel, sharing a room, and it was there that you raped her. When she resisted you, to keep her quiet you stuffed one of her white socks in her mouth, and raped her. She fought back and kicked you in the balls. The pain was terrific and made you crazy angry, and you took the handset from the phone by the bed and struck her. It fractured her right zygomatic arch, where the jaw fits into the skull," Baskerville continued, paging through the report, reading an extract then looking at Ebersole.

"What are you talking about? You've been watching too much television. I never did any of those things."

"Gordon, my client denies all of this. Why do you keep going? What evidence do you have for any of this?"

"In a minute, Abe. Let's continue for a moment more. I'm not sure she was dead when you left the motel or merely unconscious, but the fracture caused internal bleeding that clogged her throat and she couldn't spit it out, and she died. That deliberate blow that caused the fracture is the difference between first- and second-degree murder. I want you to think about that distinction."

Ebersole fidgeted in his seat but said nothing.

"You put her body in the back of your truck and drove around the area trying to figure out what to do with it."

"You can't prove that."

"You got hungry. You hadn't eaten breakfast. You passed a White Castle and stopped and had something to eat."

"You're crazy, man. You're making this up," Ebersole said belligerently.

As Goldstein listened he took notes, and from his expression seemed both confused and alarmed. Ebersole seemed to be made increasingly uncomfortable by the detail.

"While you ate you decided to take her body up into the State Game Lands. You drove up there and...," Baskerville stopped and dramatically paged through the report, seemed to read something, then continued, "you drove into State Game Lands 159 where you saw an abandoned roadhouse." He selected an unlabeled copy of a drawing from a remote viewing session, as well as a photo of the roadhouse, and slid them across the table to Goldstein, who examined them, then looked at Ebersole.

"You draped her body over your shoulder, took an entrenching tool out of your truck, and walked into the forest for about two hours, then found a place to bury her you thought no one would ever find. It was raining. You were tired, and you dug a shallow grave and covered her body with the dirt you had dug out, adding branches and leaves so it would look like nothing was there."

Goldstein and Ebersole both sat silently as Baskerville spoke.

"Look, Noah. I know you raped and killed this girl; you know you raped and killed her, and you did it just as I have described. I get that. I really only have one question."

"What's that," Ebersole asked in a shaky voice.

"I understand rape, and I understand murder. I have seen them before. What I haven't seen and what I don't get, is how you could rape and murder this fourteen-year-old girl, throw her body into your truck and drive around with it, and casually stop at a White Castle and eat not one, not two, but three hamburgers? How could you be that cold, that uncaring? I try to picture you sitting in the White Castle eating those hamburgers with her body lying in your truck bed. I just don't get it."

Baskerville closed the report, and the three of them sat silently for a moment. Then he added, "I want to be clear with you here, Noah. Just as they have you dead to rights in Virginia, my question is not whether you are innocent or guilty, but whether I make this a capital case. If I do that, after a lot of toing-and-froing through appeals by Mr. Goldstein, who is an excellent attorney and will do his best, you are very lucky in that regard, you will ultimately lose. You will spend those years in solitary confinement locked in a windowless space about the size of a closet for twenty-three hours a day. After all the appeals, which I am quite sure will fail, given what we have, the state will then put you to death by lethal injection."

Ebersole sat wordlessly, looking between Baskerville and Goldstein.

"So, this is the moment of truth, Noah," Baskerville continued. "Either you plead guilty and I will be willing to make it life in prison without parole. Or death. Your choice."

"Gordon, can we have the room? I'd like to talk with my client," Goldstein said.

"Of course," Baskerville responded, put the report back in his briefcase, got up, and left the interrogation room carrying his briefcase.

As soon as the door closed Goldstein turned to Ebersole, saying, "He's right, Noah. This is the last stop that will determine whether you live or die. There is no way he could have that kind of detail, down to the three hamburgers, unless they have witnesses, surveillance video or something. I assume what he was reading was from witness testimony. Let me ask you this. I'll do the best I can for you, but I would be lying if I didn't tell you that the decision you make in the next few minutes may determine whether you live or die. Is Baskerville telling the truth?"

Ebersole sat silently for several minutes, a range of emotions reflected in his changing expressions. Finally he said, "How could he know those things?"

"I don't know, but that isn't the issue. Are they true?"

Ebersole began to weep, "I didn't mean to kill her."

"Not the issue. Did you?"

"Yes, it's all true. I don't understand how they could know any of this, but yes, it is true."

"Are you prepared to take District Attorney Baskerville's offer and plead guilty to avoid capital punishment?"

"I'll never get out, will I?"

"No, you won't. I am afraid your life, that life you have known, is over. I'm sorry. But when you add Virginia's charges to these charges, you're going to spend the rest of your life in prison. At least, though, you'll be in the general population. You won't be on death row in solitary confinement, so you'll have at least some kind of life," Goldstein said, folding up his yellow pad and putting it in his briefcase.

"Do you authorize me to state that you will plead guilty? I ask you this formally."

"Yes," Ebersole responded with a bitter persecuted expression on his face.

"Alright, thank you, Noah. Would you sign this please," he said, taking a form from his briefcase and sliding it over to Noah, who signed with the pen he was offered.

"For what it is worth, in my opinion you have made the right choice," Goldstein said. He got up, went over to the door, and told the deputy outside, "Mr. Ebersole needs to be taken back to his cell. Thank you." Then he kept on going and went out to the waiting room where he found Baskerville.

"He will take your offer and plead guilty," he said, handing Baskerville the form Ebersole had signed. "Someday you are going to have to tell me how you got all that granular information."

"Was it accurate?" Baskerville asked.

"Yes, apparently it was ... down to even the little details. The hamburgers, for instance; not one, not two, but three. I don't understand any of it."

"Someday, after this is over, Abe, we'll have lunch and I will tell you about this case and the Virginia one. For now, all I can say is, thank you. I think we have reached a just outcome, and I believe the Amish community will think that as well."

"Given his confirmation of the details and what you have from Virginia, I agree justice has been done," Goldstein said, and the two men shook hands. As soon as he had left, Baskerville took out his phone and punched in Michael's telephone number.

ACKNOWLEDGEMENTS

Once again, I thank my wife Ronlyn for her encouragement, support, and copy-editing, and my dear friend Holly Thomas who did it all again, just to be sure. I also want to thank Beth Alexander who supports my work in so many ways, and the friends who read for me, and gave me feedback.

AUTHOR'S BIO

Scientist, futurist, and award-winning author Stephan A. Schwartz is the columnist for the journal Explore, and editor of the daily Schwartzreport.net. For more than 40 years he has done consciousness research, and is one of the founders of Remote Viewing and the anthropology of consciousness. He is the recipient of the 2017 Parapsychological Association Outstanding Contribution Award, on the 2018 OOOM Magazine (Germany) list of the 100 most Inspiring People in the World, and a 2018 recipient of the Albert Nelson Marquis Award for Outstanding Contributions.

Current academic and research appointments: Distinguished Consulting Faculty of Saybrook University, Fellow of the William James Center for Consciousness Studies, Sofia University.

Prior academic appointments: Senior Fellow for Brain, Mind and Healing of the Samueli Institute; BIAL Fellow; founder and Research Director of the Mobius laboratory; Executive Director of the Rhine Research Center; and Senior Fellow of The Philosophical Research Society. Government appointments: Special Assistant for Research and Analysis to the Chief of Naval Operations, consultant to the Oceanographer of the Navy.

He is the author of more than 150 technical reports and papers, 22 academic book chapters, four non-fiction books: *The Secret Vaults of Time, The Alexandria Project, Mind Rover, Opening to the Infinite,* and *The 8 Laws of Change,* winner of the

2016 Nautilus Book Award for Social Change, and two novels before this one, *Awakening – A Novel of Aliens and Consciousness*, winner of the 2018 Book Excellence Award for Literary Excellence and, *The Vision – A Novel of Time and Consciousness*.

Made in the USA
Monee, IL
07 March 2022